Penguin Books
The Blinder

Barry Hines was born in 1939 at the mining village of Hyland Common, near Barnsley, where his father worked down the pit. Educated at Ecclesfield Grammar School, he achieved the honour of being selected to play for the England Grammar Schools' soccer team. On leaving school it was perhaps a natural, though temporary, step to play football for Barnsley, mainly in their 'A' team, while also working variously as an apprentice mining surveyor, a labourer mending hydraulic pit props, and as an assistant in a blacksmith's shop. Following this interlude, he entered Loughborough Training College where he studied Physical Education for three years. On the completion of his course there, he came south to London where for two years he taught physical education in a comprehensive school. Barry Hines, who has now returned to the North, is married and has one child.

The Blinder (1966) was his first novel; it was followed by *Kes* (published in 1968 as *A Kestrel for a Knave*) which became an immediate best-seller and was made into a popular film. His latest books are *First Signs* (1972) and *The Gamekeeper* (1975).

Barry Hines

The Blinder

Penguin Books

Penguin Books Ltd, Harmondsworth,
Middlesex, England
Penguin Books, 625 Madison Avenue,
New York, New York 10022, U.S.A.
Penguin Books Australia Ltd, Ringwood,
Victoria, Australia
Penguin Books Canada Ltd,
2801 John Street,
Markham, Ontario, Canada, L3R 1B4
Penguin Books (N.Z.) Ltd,
182–190 Wairau Road,
Auckland 10, New Zealand

First published by Michael Joseph 1966
Published in Penguin Books 1969
Reprinted 1977, 1979

Copyright © Barry Hines, 1966
All rights reserved

Made and printed in Great Britain by
Hazell Watson & Viney Ltd,
Aylesbury, Bucks
Set in Linotype Pilgrim

For Margaret

'And finally, Upper Sixth : Hawk ! Those people will report for detention straight after school tonight.'

The school turned round to have a look at him, but Hawk wasn't there.

'I have news however of a much more pleasant nature concerning Hawk. It seems that he had another successful outing with the England youth eleven last night, and managed to score four times in their five nil victory over Wales. This, I am led to believe, is quite an achievement.'

Again the school turned round to have a look at him, but Hawk wasn't there. He was in the bushes at the side of the school field.

He popped out of the rhododendrons and looked down the slope to see if the classrooms were still empty.

'Come on, Jenny, they'll be out of assembly in a minute.'

'Hang on, I can't go in like this.'

They hurried through the bushes, trampled into muddy paths like the shrubberies of public parks, and halted as they neared the school.

'See you inside.'

Lennie ran out across the grass, the wet tufts swishing and wiping at his sludgy shoes. On to the asphalt, and past the empty rooms to the boys' entrance round the side. Jenny watched him go, then stepped out and walked down to the girls' entrance. Edmund Leary, the Head Boy, was on late duty, and when he saw Lennie opening the door he wrote in the book, Hawk U.VI.A. Lennie walked straight past him to a radiator and started to dry the two dark stains on the knees of his trousers. Leary watched him.

'This is the third time you've been late this week, Hawk. And you're supposed to be on late duty.'

'Bollocks! I've been here ages.'

'Everyone's complaining about you not doing your share of the duties.'

'Are they?'

'I'm going to see Doctor Bennet about it.'

'Tha can see Doctor Crippen if tha likes.'

When Assembly dismissed, Lennie still had his knees pressed to the radiator waiting for the natural shade to return to his trousers. He didn't look round at the passing crowds whispering and pointing behind his back. Harry Andrews joined him and looked down at the rising steam.

'Hey up, Len! Where you been?'

'Celebrating.'

'Where?'

'In t'bushes.

'Who with?'

'Jenny.'

'Again! You'll both get expelled if you're caught.'

'I know.'

'It's not worth the risk.'

'There is no risk at half past eight in the morning. What's first lesson?'

'Art appreciation.'

The long pews in the lecture theatre were full when they walked in.

'Here he comes, Mr Football himself!'

'This is your life, Lennie Hawk!'

Lennie stepped up behind the teacher's desk and gave them V signs all round, conducting the hecklers like an orchestra. The girls looked at each other and blushed. The boys tried to shout him down. He grinned and vaulted on to the desk, then leapt across the space to the front bench, and strode above parting heads from bench to bench until he reached the back where he stopped; and threatened to drop down on Leary. Leary moved over and started a chain reaction of shuffling which left the boy at the end without a seat. Harry Andrews walked up the steps and stood at the end of the row.

'Come on, Harry, there's bags of room.'

'There's no room on here!'

8

'Shut thi mouth, Leary. Come on, Harry.'

'I said there's no room!'

'There will be if I knock thi through that bloody window! Now get up bed.'

Lennie brought his legs up on to the seat and turned sideways in a tight bunch. He braced his feet against the boy at his other side and pushed his back into Leary. The girl at the end was struggling to retain her place when Mr Priddle, the senior English master, walked in.

'Find another seat, girl. It's quite obvious there's insufficient room at the end of there.'

The curtains were swished and the projector switched on. The picture skidded and tumbled around the blackboard while Mr Priddle adjusted the focus. Then it was still, all square.

'Today I would like to show you some pictures of Greek archaeological discoveries, from which we can depict certain aspects of the Greek way of life.'

He began to flick the pictures through, lecturing and questioning at each one.

'Here's one for you, Hawk. As you know, the Greeks were the founders of the Olympic Games, and a great deal of their pottery shows the various athletic events. What do you think of this example, Hawk?'

The picture showed a vase being lapped by running figures.

'Him who painted that had about as much idea of running as a bloke without legs.'

'Well! You astound me, Hawk. I thought you of all people would have appreciated good movement.'

'It's all wrong.'

'Many scholars consider it a masterpiece of its kind.'

'It's either a comic race or they're all motor morons.'

'Motor morons?'

'They've no co-ordination, their right legs and right arms are both going forward at the same time instead of right leg, left arm.'

There was silence in the dark while everyone looked.

'You're right, Hawk. I must say I've never noticed that before.'

Mr Priddle was on dinner duty. He filled the spare places, then banged the table top with a serving spoon.

'Heads bowed. For what we are about to receive.'

The chant was taken up by the children. Lennie slid a beaker off the table, bent at the knees and threw the water on to the legs of the boy standing opposite.

'May the Lord make us truly thankful.'

'Ooooooo!'

Charles Leary jumped back and knocked his chair over. All heads bobbed up and the prayer stopped. Mr Priddle prompted them.

'For Christ's sake. FOR CHRIST'S SAKE!'

'For Christ's sake. Amen.'

'Sit down.'

Mr Priddle walked round the tables to Leary who was holding his trouser creases between finger and thumb and shaking them as though a scorpion was creeping up his leg.

'You, boy. Was it you who caused that disturbance?'

'Yes, sir.'

'Why?'

'Somebody . . .'

'He was having a quick drink and he dropped his beaker.'

'No one's asking you, Hawk. Were you thirsty, boy?'

'No, sir.'

'Did you find the morning's work so dry that you were in urgent need of refreshment?'

'No, sir.'

'No doubt the Lord will punish you for your irreverence at a future date, but meanwhile report for detention to-night; detention, oh yes, Hawk. Where's that essay you owe me?'

'I gave it to you, sir.'

'When?'

'Can't you remember? I gave it you in the corridor yesterday, no, Wednesday afternoon.'

'I don't remember.'

'At break.'

'There's no sign of it.'

'I hope you haven't lost it, sir, it took me ages.'

'I'll have another look at home.'

Mr Priddle turned away. Harry Andrews shook his head.

'You lying hound, you'd get away with murder.'

'You rat, Hawk.'

'What's up, Leary?'

'I'm going to tell our Edmund about this.'

'Don't frighten me, I won't be able to eat my dinner.'

Lennie appointed Leary to clear the table and went to the gym with Harry. They removed the top section of the box and Lennie jumped inside for the football they had hidden there. Harry went in goal at one end. Lennie was both teams and the commentator.

'Greaves slips it inside to Hawk who feints, beats his man and shoves a beautiful ball to Law, he moves quickly into position for the return, receives it and shoots. Goal! No! Andrews brings off a miraculous save. What a keeper this boy is.'

The door opened and Mr Rowley, the History master, stepped inside.

'What are you two doing in here?'

Lennie flicked the ball up into his hands.

'Playing football.'

'Who's given you permission?'

'Mr Brook.'

'Mr Brook doesn't allow anyone in here at lunch time.'

'He allows us.'

'Just you two?'

'Any first teamers who want to practise.'

'I've never seen anyone practising.'

'They're not as keen as us.'

'If I were Mr Brook, I'd have these doors locked.'

'That's up to him, isn't it?'

'Don't be impertinent, Hawk.'

'I'm not being.'

'And don't argue.'

'I'm not doing.'

'Yes you are! Out! – Both of you.'

'Mr Brook says we can stop in.'

'I don't care a damn what Mr Brook says.'

Lennie and Harry looked at him. Mr Rowley went red and Lennie concentrated on balancing the ball rotating on the end of his finger.

'I'll see what Mr Brook has to say about this.'

He turned and banged the side of the door, rattling the wire-covered glass. Round the corner, his gown pulled tight across his back like the shiny shell of a black clock.

'Fat bastard.'

'You want to go steady, Len.'

'He's a rotten sod.'

'I know that, but you want to be careful.'

'He goes about looking for bother.'

'He's always like that.'

'Only because everybody's shit scared of him.'

'Think he'll see Brooky?'

'No, they're like cat and dog. Anyway, bugger him, let's get cracking. And they're lining up for the second half. I wonder what the managers have had to say during the interval.'

Lennie stood beside the centre forward waiting for the second half to begin. It was a still, grey morning with the sky pressing down on the clouds like the weight on pit props. Mr Rowley stood with a whistle in his mouth and a great belted raincoat over his belly. Mr Brook stood on the line and a few boys on bicycles toured the field, from pitch to pitch. The centre forward rolled the ball to Lennie who retreated into his own half and aimed his kick out to the wing. The ball rose and travelled diagonally across the pitch, curving down like a rainbow at the feet of the running wingman. The ball had beaten the full back for him. All he had to do was dribble it down the line and centre. The forwards moved up in anticipation. The centre half ran across to tackle. The centre was low and hard, travelling at knee height parallel to the ground. Lennie pivoted on his left leg and swung his right, pointing his foot like a ballet dancer. The ball would have gone a long way if the net hadn't stopped it. Lennie signalled the goal by raising his right arm. Mr Brook spun a full circle on one heel, and a man standing further along the touchline walked up to him.

'There's no wonder they're all breaking their necks to sign him on.'

'Who, Lennie?'

'I've heard that much about him I thought I'd come and have a look for myself.'

'Are you a scout, then?'

'Huddersfield.'

'You've no chance?'

'I can look for nowt, can't I?'

'We've had every manager in the First Division up here trying to persuade him.'

'He's a good un, there's no doubt about that.'

'The Town have still got their fingers crossed about him.'

'They could do with a good inside man.'

'He's played in the first team, you know.'

'I know. He scored twice against Chelsea.'

'He's going to be a world beater.'

The man turned and looked at Mr Brook. 'That doesn't take much doing in this class of football.'

'Top class, I mean.'

'You can't judge a player on one match.'

'That's what he says, anyway.'

'Who?'

'Lennie.'

Lennie had the ball near the corner flag with his back to the pitch. Two defenders were trying to take it from him, but he shielded it with his legs and shifted it along the line towards the goal. They tackled in turn, thrusting in, recovering, then thrusting in again. But Lennie retained possession, and looked over his shoulder for someone in a goal-scoring position. He stopped the ball, wedged his foot underneath and trapped it between his boot and his shin, then lifted and lofted it with an outward flick into the centre. The centre forward headed it into the net. Lennie grinned and turned away. Rowley ran from the centre circle blowing his whistle.

'No goal.'

'Why?'

'Foul.'

'What about the advantage rule?'

'The foul was against you, Hawk.'

'What for?'

'Obstruction.'

'You must be blind.'

'Less of that, Hawk.'

'How could you see anyway? You've never moved out of that centre circle all game.'

'Hawk, don't argue with the referee!'

'Referee! I don't know how you've the cheek to put that whistle in your mouth.'

'Come away, Hawk.'

'Shut thi face, Leary, before I fill it in for thi.'

'You'll be off if I hear any more of that.'

'Think I'm bothered?'

'Get off, Hawk. Off!'

Lennie walked off past Mr Brook and the Huddersfield scout.

'You overstepped the mark a bit there, lad.'

Lennie trotted down the field. Mr Brook turned to watch the game.

The Huddersfield scout left.

Lennie got dressed and walked down to the bus stop where an old woman was waiting.

'Has the sixty-five gone?'

'What time is it?'

'I don't know.'

'A young lad like you ought to be walking.'

'I've done enough walking this morning.'

'When I was your age we had to walk.'

'I know, that's what they invented buses for.'

'Don't be so cheeky.'

She turned away, and when the bus came Lennie was upstairs and had sat down before she had creaked and levered her way on to a side seat just inside the door. He looked out at the avenues of tidy semis branching off the main road. The lines of trees on the pavements were all in rags. His arm was squeezed against the window ledge by someone sitting down. It was Cyril, the Town Physiotherapist.

'Hey up, Cyril.'

'Hello Len. How you going on then?'

'Steady.'

'Been playing?'

'Yes.'

'At school?'

'Mmm.'

'It can't be doing your name any good, you know, playing up there.'

'I know.'

'I bet you never break sweat, do you?'

'No, I don't have to kill myself.'

'And we're crying out for a good inside man.'

'I know.'

'It's wide open.'

'They'll probably buy somebody.'

'Where they going to get fifty thousand pound to buy a good inside forward? Players they've got there now are as good as owt they'd get for less.'

'There's nowt I can do about it, is there?'

'Not while you're still at school, there isn't.'

'I'll be down in t'holidays.'

'Boss keeps talking about you.'

'He was down at our house again last week.'

'He's scared stiff of you signing for somebody else. He thinks you're waiting for a better offer.'

'I've had plenty of better offers.'

'Why didn't you take 'em then?'

'I don't know.'

'I can't see what's holding you back.'

'Hey up! This is my stop. Ta ra, Cyril.'

'Going to watch 'em this afternoon?'

Everyone looked at Cyril because he had turned round and was shouting down the bus to Lennie.

'Ye!'

'I might see you then!'

Lennie ran down the steps with a bumperty-bum, bumperty-bum. Cyril turned to the front and everyone lost interest.

'Hey you! Have you paid?'

'Course I have!'

And he was away through the crowd already on the platform. Through the market square and along the main road to the Anchor, where he turned off into a street of terraced houses. Sloame Street where he lived. Down the entry into the yard and along the flagstones to the kitchen. He added his blazer to the hump behind the door and walked through into the living-room which faced out, on to the street. His mother was on her knees wiping the hearth. Steam was rising from the damp cloth and the drying tiles. She looked up over her shoulder.

'Hello, love, you're early.'

'Where's my dad?'

'He's gone to t'club for an hour. He says he'll meet you outside t'brewery at half two.'

'Is that today's paper you're kneeling on? I haven't seen it yet.'

'What's a matter with you?'

'Nowt.'

'There is.'

'All right then, there is.'

'I can read you like a book.'

'You ought to have been on t'stage with your talent.'

'What's up, have you lost?'

'I don't know.'

'What do you mean.'

'I got sent off so I came away.'

She knelt up and placed her hands on her thighs.

'Oooo Len, will you get into trouble?'

'I suppose somebody'll have summat to say.'

'Was it one of your teachers?'

'Rowley.'

'That's him who's always on at you, isn't it?'

'He hates my guts.'

'What were you doing, making your mouth as usual?'

'He disallowed this goal and I started to argue.'

'I thought so.'

A car stopped outside. Mrs Hawk stood up and looked through the net curtains.

'Isn't this Mr Brook, Len?'

Mr Brook was looking up at the door. He stepped close to the house out of sight and there were two knocks.

'Wait a minute! Fetch him round, Len. Eee, look at t'house.'

Lennie walked out of the back door and past the two houses before the entry. Mr Brook was still standing at the door when he came out into the street.

'Hello, Len. Did I get the wrong house?'

'No, we don't use the front door.'

'I see. I've brought your towel, you must have forgotten it.'

'That's not mine.'

'The lads said it was.'

'It's not mine.'

'Hello, Mr Brook.'

Mrs Hawk shoved Lennie out of the entry end.

'Hello, Mrs Hawk, I was just returning this towel, but Len says it's not his.'

'No, that's not our Len's.'

'I was passing this way so I thought I'd drop it in.'

'Won't you come in?'

'No, I don't think so, Mrs Hawk.'

'Nay, you might as well have a cup of tea while you're here. I've just mashed.'

'Thank you.'

They trooped down the entry in single file, stepping out on to the flagstones like a team of three. The yard was black muck. Brick paths had been set across it to the row of lavatories and bin holes running parallel to the houses.

'How did you know where we lived?'

'I had a rough idea, and then I asked at the end of the street.'

'We don't use t'front door, it's draughty, so we hang a curtain and have rugs behind it.'

'Oh yes.'

'Come in.'

'Thank you.'

'Come and sit here by the fire.'

'No, I'm fine, thanks.'

He sat down on a dining chair, sideways on to the table. Lennie sat down in the big armchair by the fire.

'There's your tea here.'

'Thank you.'

'Would you like a biscuit?'

'No, thanks.'

'He's just been telling me about this morning.'

'Yes, it was unfortunate.'

'Was it his fault?'

'I suppose it was.'

'It was a ridiculous decision.'

'I dare say, but you know it's useless to argue with the referee.'

'He doesn't know anything about football.'

'It's the rules of the game, once the whistle goes, that's it.'

'Are you sure you won't have a biscuit?'

'Anyway I'm sick of it, lousy football and lousy reffing. It's ruining my game.'

'I've been telling him, Mr Brook, he's too much to say for himself, our Len.'

'I ought to have been playing for t'Town this afternoon instead of wasting my time up there.'

'I think you'll be better off going to University and getting a degree before you start thinking along those lines. There'll be plenty of time afterwards.'

'That's what I keep telling him; but his dad's as bad as he is; always edging him to sign on. Do you want another cup, Mr Brook?'

'No, thank you, I'll be off now.'

He stood up. Mrs Hawk stood up.

'Thank you for the tea.'

'You're welcome.'

'Are you going to the dance tonight, Len?'

'Might do.'

'Should be a good do.'

'So they say.'

'I may see you there, then.'

'I'm sorry about that towel.'

'It was no trouble, Mrs Hawk. I was passing this way. Cheerio, Len.'

'Ta ra.'

Mrs Hawk accompanied Mr Brook to the street and stood on the pavement rubbing her bare forearms with her hands until he turned into the main road out of sight. She ran in, excited.

'Fancy him calling, wasn't it good on him?'

Lennie was reading the paper and he didn't answer.

The crowd poured out of the gates like water from a sluice gate. Marching music blurted from the Tannoy and the flood-lights had been switched down to half power. Lennie and his dad concentrated on staying together. They didn't speak until the rush had been filtered by side streets, and they could walk without touching anybody.

'They were lucky today, Dad.'

'Ar, they didn't deserve a point.'

'They're not playing well, are they?'

'Terrible. They're going to have to get some new players from somewhere.'

'They can't afford any with t'crowds they're getting.'

'They'll get no bigger till they do summat about it.'

'They never looked like scoring, did they?'

'That forward line couldn't bust its way out of a paper bag.'

'They're scared to shoot in case they miss. I wish I'd have been playing.'

'Tha should have been instead of wasting thi time this morning.'

'I could make a world of difference to that side.'

'What tha waiting for, then?'

They turned down Sloame Street, and the warm windows cast light patches on to the pavement between the blobs of the street lamps. The same tune muffled through the walls as they passed from house to house, fading then swelling between the space of each lighted window.

'Hey up, Dad, that's sports report, I'll race you.'

'I should think so.'

'I'll give you to that lamp start.'

Lennie slowed down while his dad walked to his handicap. He started to run before he reached it. Lennie shouted out and sprinted after him. Down the street and round the entry and on one leg like Charlie Chaplin, Lennie laughing at his dad, Mr Hawk laughing and puffing in the lead. The narrow passage magnified and hollowed the sounds like the noise in a swimming bath. Mr Hawk reached the kitchen door and fumbled with the latch, excited and tense like a child in a chasing game. Lennie roared up behind and crashed into him. The door flew open on to the washer behind, and they fell over the trestle in a heap. There was a scream from the living-room and the middle door opened, lighting the scene. Mrs Hawk stood with her arms crossed on her chest. Two glass marbles stared from a lump of putty.

'Lord above! Who is it? Arthur, is it you?'

'Who the bloody hell do you think it is?'

Blood coloured her face and she stepped closer. Kitchen lights popped on at either side and doors were eased open.

'Is everything all right?'

Mr Hawk crawled to the door and looked out.

''Course it is, you nosy buggers.'

'Arthur, they'll hear you!'

'That's what I said it for.'

'For God's sake come in, both of you.'

She tried to close the door but Lennie was acting as a door stopper.

'And Arthur Hawk wins with a last desperate lunge through the tape.'

'Lennie, get up and stop acting so daft.'

He stood up and she slammed the door. The faces peering into the night withdrew one by one, closing the doors and blacking the lights: leaving the yard dark and silent behind them. It was bright inside, with the table laid and the radio on. The fire was so big that the tongue ends of the flames were licking the back of the chimney out of sight.

'Been doing a bit of smelting, Mam?'

'What do you mean?'

'Size o' t'fire.'

'No, just baking.'

'I'm buggered.'

'I should think you are an' all, carrying on like that at your age. It isn't good for you.'

'What about Stanley Matthews? He's nearly as old as my dad.'

'I know, but he's used to it.'

'Can you imagine my dad trotting out in t'First Division?'

'Your dad's a job to get round t'table in a snooker match.'

'He wouldn't be playing either if he'd worked thirty years in t'coal like I've done. Blokes like him don't know they're born.'

'You're only jealous, Dad.'

'I should think I am an' all when they're getting hundred pound a week for playing football. I'd have played for nowt if I'd been good enough.'

'Here, come and get your tea and stop talking about football.'

'And there's our Len here, he could be international class if he wanted.'

Lennie was sitting at the table cutting bread, and stacking the slices like a pack of cards.

'Look at that Billy Meakin across t'backs. Have you seen him when he comes home? Posh suits, big car. They tell me he's a life like a lord.'

'Do you mean him that went away straight from school?'

'He went to Birmingham.'

'And they say he'd a job to read and write when he left St Edwin's.'

'He's no need to read and write now, has he?'

Lennie was digging a crater in the sugar basin with a spoon, but he couldn't uncover the glass floor because the basin was too full and after each scoop the sugar trickled back down the sides into the hole.

'He wants to go to University so that he can get a good job afterwards.'

'I know what I do want.'

'What?'

They asked the question simultaneously, turning on him like two searchlights.

'Some tea.'

They relaxed, and Mrs Hawk fetched the frying-pan through and swilled two plates with tomatoes and sausages.

'I could eat a horse between two bread-vans.'

Lennie broke a slice of bread and wiped half of it round his plate. It turned red and limp like a soaked bandage.

'Going t'club, Dad?'

'Mmmm.'

'Are you going, Mam?'

'I suppose so. What's this dance in aid on up at school?'

'Famine relief.'

'What's up, are t'dinners bad?'

'Don't be so ignorant Arthur. Who you going with?'

'Frank and Bill.'

'That Frank James is nowt but a bother causer.'

'Only when he's had summat to drink.'

'I don't know why you still knock about with them two.'

'What do you mean?'

'Well, both of 'em working down t'pit and off boozing every night, I can't see what you've got in common.'

'Nay, Mary lass, don't condemn a lad just because he's a collier.'

'I'm not doing, but I think they're t'wrong sort o' mates for our Len when he reckons to be studying and all that.'

'You're nowt but a snob, Mam.'

'I'm nowt o' t'kind. I'm just thinking what's best for you, that's all.'

'Don't you think it's up to him who he knocks around with?'

'That's right, you encourage him.'

'Who's encouraging him? How many times have I warned him about smoking and drinking?'

'Only because you're frightened on his football being ruined.'

'And what you frightened on?'

'What you both getting worked up about? I only have a couple of pints on Saturday nights.'

'I know, love, it's your dad.'

'That's right, blame me.'

'He's not bothered what you do as long as you're playing football.'

'And you're not bothered what he does as long as he's working himself to death at school.'

'I want him to make summat of his life.'

'Don't I, then?'

'He's got chance of a lifetime, our Len, if only he'd realize it.'

'Do you think I don't know?'

Mrs Hawk started to clear the table. Mr Hawk checked his coupons.

'Are you washing up straight away, Mam?'

'I'm going to have a minute first. Why?'

'Let me get washed then, because it's murder getting your hands under t'tap when there's a sinkful of pots.'

He stripped off to the waist and walked into the kitchen. The column of running water was broken into splinters when he put his hands into it.

'Where's towel?'

'Here.'

He ran into the living-room with his neck stretched forward like a goose, to stop the drops dripping off his chin end on to his chest. Mr Hawk screwed his copy coupon into a ball and threw it on to the fire.

'Another week older and not a penny richer.'

Lennie got dressed and watched the television until it was time to go. He put his duffle coat on.

'Ta ra, then.'

'And don't be late.'

It was drizzling. As he walked past the front door he banged it twice with the side of his fist.

'L-E-E-N!'

'Get on, you silly young bugger!'

'Don't you know you can kill folks frightening them like that!'

He ran up the street to the main road. Couples passed hunched up against the rain, the girls walking tick-tock tick-tock, linked to the sides of their long-striding partners. Cars sizzled up and down the road like fried eggs between the lighted shop windows. He turned into the taproom of the Anchor. Frank and Bill were playing darts.

'Hey up, Len.'

'Frank, Bill.'

'Hey up, Len.'

He walked to the bar.

'Pint, Len?'

'Yes please, Stan.'

He drank the top inch, then carried his glass to the leather bench running round the walls.

'Want a game, Len?'

'No, I'm not bothered.'

'We'll just finish this off then.'

Frank stepped to the line and stood square on to the board. He gripped the darts tight and flicked them with a swift clipped action. They stuck horizontally and were hard to pull out. Bill eased up to the line and stood sideways looking at the board with one eye like a bird. He aimed before each throw, and flighted the darts high into the air, so that they bombed the board and stuck out like ticks.

'Good arrows.'

They packed their darts into plastic cases, and slipped them into their inside pockets before assembling their glasses and joining Lennie.

'Go to t'match, Len?'

'Yes.'

'Terrible, wasn't it?'

'Town were.'

'They'll be going down if they don't watch it.'

'Did thar go, Frank?'

'I was working.'

'On Saturday afternoon?'

'I've been telling him; he might as well pack his bags and go and live in t'pit baths.'

'I'm getting some cash in while I've a chance. There's talk of 'em laying men off.'

'Tha's nowt to worry about, it won't be t'face men who'll get t'bullet.'

'I don't care; anyway it's worth it, I brought twenty-eight quid home again this week.'

Bill stood up.

'Pint, Len?'

'No, I'm all right.'

'Drink up, Frank.'

Frank drank up and Bill went for two pints.

'How will you go on at your house, Len, if thi dad gets thrown off?'

'We'll manage, I suppose.'

'Don't tha ever bother? Tha knows, still being at school.'

'I've always enough, so I never think about it.'

'I couldn't wait to leave to get some money in my pocket.'

'Money's not everything though, Frank.'

'No, but it's nearly.'

Bill returned from the bar, concentrating across the floor like a tightrope walker. He hadn't spilled a drop when he lowered the two pints on to the beer mats.

'I've just been saying, Bill, I don't know how he goes on for money still being at school.'

'Me neither. And he could be earning twice as much as us if he wanted.'

'Does tha mean if he signed pro?'

'He could be making a mint.'

'Why don't tha, Len?'

'I don't know.'

'I wish I'd t'same chance, don't thar, Frank?'

'Still going to university then?'

'I reckon to be, but I don't know as I'm bothered.'

'Tha wants to make thi mind up.'

'He's too much bloody talent, that's his trouble. He don't know whether to make a living out of his head or out of his feet.'

'It'd be grand to have a choice, what's thar say, Frank?'

'Why don't tha know, Len?'

'I can't explain it right, I just don't want to be committed, that's all. That's why I fancy university sometimes, it'd get another three or four years over, but then there's always t'exams at end of that.'

'There wouldn't be if tha signed pro.'

'I don't like the idea of signing on, anyway I'd get fed up of training, day in, day out. I'd like a bit of both.'

'Tha wants jam on it.'

'He want's another pint an' all, his glass's got cobwebs on it.'

Lennie smiled and stood up, waiting for them to empty their glasses.

'I'll get these, Len.'

'Thar all right, Frank.'

'Nay, tha can't afford to be buying us beer on thy money.'

'Sit down, I'm not so hard up.'

Frank sat down and Lennie walked to the bar past two girls
at the next table.

'Mine's a Babycham.'

Lennie grinned and nodded to the other.

'What's yours, love, a whisky and orange?'

They laughed and watched him to the bar and all the way
back to his seat.

'Fixed up then, Len?'

'What time we going up?'

'Where?'

'School.'

'We're going to t'Mecca aren't we?'

'I thought we were going up to that dance at our place.'

'We've changed our minds, it'll be no good.'

'How do you know! Are you clairvoyant or summat?'

'Big word, isn't it?'

'Not as big as Indistinguishable.'

'Clever bugger, tha knows what I mean.'

'Why don't tha say it, then?'

'Cos we're not all as brainy as thee.'

'Steady on, Frank, it's Saturday night.'

'He's too bloody clever sometimes.'

'What's up with you both! It'll be a change, won't it?'

'There'll be nowt but a load of school kids there.'

'It's an open dance.'

'What about birds?'

'What about 'em?'

'They might be too classy for us.'

'They're not too classy for me, are they?'

'Thar different. Anyway, tha knows 'em.'

'I shan't know 'em all.'

'They won't be like t'birds at t'Mecca though, Len, they won't
be our sort.'

'Oh, bugger you, then! You two can please yourselves but I'm
going.'

They all had a drink of their beer.

'What we doing then, Bill?'

'It's up to thee, Frank.'

'It won't be all la-dee-da, will it?'

'I can tell you; you've as much chance of getting a shag up there as you have at t'Mecca.'

'I suppose thar should know.'

'What we doing then, Bill?'

'I'm easy.'

'Well, I am.'

'If you're both easy, we'll go then. Get 'em in, Frank.'

The room was filling up. The two girls at the next table stayed. They were drinking Babychams out of shallow glasses. The cherries stuck with plastic swords looked like the pickled balls of the deers leaping on the glass sides.

'Two certainties here.'

'Hey up, Frank, he's assessing form again.'

'I wonder where they're going?'

'Why don't tha ask 'em, Len?'

'Going to t'Mecca, then?'

The girls looked round. The nearest one turned sideways on her chair.

'What's it to you?'

'Not as much as it is to you.'

'What do you mean?'

'I can't discuss it publicly.'

'Hark at him!'

'Come outside and I'll let you know in private though.'

'No thank you!'

'Go on! Don't be a spoilsport all your life.'

'You're not my type.'

'They're all your type.'

She shrugged her chair round and the other girl had to have a drink to stop herself from laughing.

'Tha wa' made there an' all, Len.'

'I still am.'

'He's a modest bleeder, isn't he?'

'Are we off then?'

Lennie stood up and put his duffle coat on over the top of his sweater. Frank and Bill walked to the door in their suits, their hair shining like patent leather under the smoking light globes. Lennie followed them, and the two girls watched him all the way out. It had stopped raining.

'Are we walking, then?'

'We'll race thi. Us two on t'bus.'

'Look, there's one in.'

'I'll give you to that post box start.'

'What's tha always want to be racing for?'

'It's going! Run, Len!'

Lennie sprinted, leaving Frank and Bill shouting and whistling behind. The bus moved slowly, then accelerated smoothly as the traffic cleared. People on the pavements turned to watch as he veered out of the gutter and the passengers sitting sideways on the long back seat stared as he came closer. He ran yard after yard an armslength away, neither gaining nor losing, yet too far away to jump on. The engine slotted into top gear. Lennie dived for the pole and pulled himself on to the platform. He rang the bell, then sat on the steps with his head between his legs. The bus stopped and the conductor ran down the stairs until he was blocked by Lennie at the bottom.

'Did you ring t'bell?'

Lennie nodded without looking up.

'What for?'

'To stop t'bus.'

'You're on, aren't you?'

'My mates are not, though.'

Frank and Bill jumped on, and tumbled about the platform gasping and shouting.

'Made it!'

'I'm knackered!'

'It wasn't worth getting on, we must be nearly there now!'

'Let me sit down, Frank, before I tumble down!'

The conductor stood up behind Lennie, grinning down on them.

'Been running, lads?'

They looked up kinking for breath, waiting to follow him upstairs. Lennie stood up and rang the bell. He turned to the people on the side seat who had watched him chasing.

'You didn't want me to catch it, did you?'

The bus droned up the hill out of town, past the lamps stringing the roadside like topaz beads, and stopped at the top opposite the school gates. The school stood black against the sky like a castle in the dark. They crossed the road and walked up the drive to the front door.

'Hey up, Len, what about finding an open window?'

'Not tonight, Frank.'

'I thought tha reckoned to be against paying.'

'I am in most cases. It grieves me every time I go to t'Mecca and give four bob of dad's money to them greasy bastards.'

'Well then!'

'This is different though, Frank. Nobody's making owt out of it.'

'I'm sure my half dollar's not going to make much difference.'

'Would half a dollar make any difference to thee if tha wa' starving?'

'I suppose so.'

'Well, come on then, you stingy bugger, thar as tight as a camel's arse in a sandstorm.'

Frank and Bill followed Lennie up the steps to Leary who was standing at the door. They all looked past him across the foyer through the open doors of the Assembly Hall. A screen of people blocked the view. Their backs were turned as though facing a bonfire in the centre, and the hard beat of guitars banged through the flickering dusk above their heads.

'Haven't they provided thi with a uniform then, Edmundo? They do down at t'Mecca.'

Leary inspected the three of them individually.

'I would have thought the Mecca was more your style, Hawk. This is a respectable dance.'

'They're all my style, Leary, old love. How did you finish up this morning?'

'We won, eight two.'

'You managed to hold out then?'

Lennie turned to Frank and Bill who had stepped behind the one double door which was closed.

'This is my mate I'm always telling you about. He's a good bloke.'

'You're an ill-mannered swine, Hawk.'

'Hey up, Leary, who's that bird?'

He indicated a girl who had just stepped out of the Hall, and was wanting to approach, but did not want to interrupt.

'That bird happens to be my sister.'

'Bloody hell! Tha never told me tha'd got a sister.'

'It's not the sort of thing one does tell you, is it, Hawk?'

'Come along chaps let's hang our cloaks. See you later, Ted.'

'Yes, much later, I hope.'

The Hall was packed. A group was playing on the stage at the far end, three guitars and drums. The headmaster's table had been pushed to the back and was piled with instrument cases. The high oak panels corseting the walls had been laced with coloured streamers, and lengths of twisted crêpe paper looped from globe to globe, intertwining like wind-crossed telephone wires. The lights were off. Candles burned from bottle necks on the window ledges down both sides. Frank and Bill drifted, and left Lennie nodding and smiling just inside the door. The music stopped, and the solidity of the dancers cracked like crazy paving. Harry Andrews walked across the floor to Lennie.

'Hey up, Len. Been in the Anchor?'

'Just for a couple. Any talent about?'

'Jenny's been looking for you.'

'Has she?'

'Lot of staff here. There's Rowley there, look.'

'Fat bastard.'

'Brooky's here.'

'Wandering about like a lost sheep, I suppose.'

'He asked if you'd come.'

'They're going to have a ten rounder at t'interval.'

'Who?'

'Rowley and Brooky, both stripped off.'

'Can you imagine Rowley? It'd be a horrible sight.'

'He'd look just like that Michelin man.'

'Hey up, he's here.'

Rowley was progressing through the crowd like an elephant through trees. His wife followed directly behind, taking advantage of the cleavage. From the front she was completely hidden. Lennie made no move and Rowley stopped before him. Mrs Rowley stepped from behind and looked hard at Lennie.

'I'm surprised to see you here, Hawk.'

'Why?'

'I thought you'd have been too ashamed to show your face after this morning.'

'Why should I? This is nothing to do with this morning.'

'So this is the boy you're always telling me about, Alfred?'

'Yes this is him, this is the notorious Hawk.'

She looked him full in the face and did not look away until Lennie returned her gaze.

'I suppose it would be too much to expect an apology, Hawk?'

Lennie turned his eyes back to Rowley. Mrs Rowley immediately resumed her former vigilance.

'Yes, it would, because I don't regret what I did this morning.'

'Have you no manners, boy?'

'It isn't a question of manners, it's a matter of principle.'

'Really, Hawk!'

'Surely, Alfred, all this can wait until Monday.'

'I just wanted him to know that the matter hadn't been forgotten, that's all.'

'Why, what will you do?'

'I shall inform Doctor Bennet first thing.'

'Alfred! Is there any need to take it so far?'

'Claire, will you please keep out of this! You have no idea of the circumstances.'

'Won't an apology do?'

'You've heard what he has to say, he has no intention of apologizing.'

'Well, young man?'

'Look, I'm sorry, but I can't apologize for something I don't regret.'

'O come along, Claire! He's not worth appealing to.'

He swivelled round and blasted his way into the ruckuss. Mrs Rowley gave Lennie a shrug of her shoulders and showed him the palms of her hands, then she followed her husband.

'Exit the big bad wolf.'

'It'll take more than him to get me down.'

'I wouldn't mind getting his wife down, would you?'

'She's all right, isn't she?'

'She wasn't half giving you the glad eye.'

'There's no wonder, married to a twat like that, I feel sorry for her.'

'I bet he leads her a dog's life.'

'Can tha imagine him on t'job? They ought to pay her danger money like they do down t'pit.'

Harry laughed out, shaking his head, his eyes sweeping the crowd.

'Your mates look set up.'

'Where?'

Harry pointed to Frank and Bill spinning in the revolving crush. Lennie slipped two fingers into his mouth and blasted out a screaming whistle.

'Bloody hell, Len!'

A girl standing with her back to him hunched her shoulders as though the roof was falling in, then spun on him, snarling. 'You lunatic, Hawk.'

He gave Frank and Bill the thumbs up, and Jenny, round the other side, responded to the whistle like a dog. Harry drifted.

'Hello Len, on your own?'

'I've come with my mates, why?'

'O nothing, I just thought you were bringing me, that's all.'

'I never said that.'

'I just thought you were.'

'Do you want to dance?'

'Please.'

They stepped on to the floor and were immediately caught up in the current.

'You look nice tonight, Jenny.'

'Thank you.'

'Had your hair done?'

'This afternoon.'

'It suits you.'

Lennie was looking over her shoulder, winking and pulling faces at people he knew. A girl whispered to her partner, who turned to look. Lennie draped his tongue on to his chin and crossed both eyes. The couple danced on.

'What are you laughing at?'

'Nothing.'

'Len?'

'What?'

'Have we finished then, us two?'

He kept his face hidden over her shoulder.

'Len?'

'Well it's no good getting too involved, is it?'

'I think we've already been involved, don't you?'

'I mean with us both going away next year, and all that. We can't say what's going to happen, can we?'

'I suppose not.'

'We're all right as we are, aren't we?'

'You are, you mean. But I'm not going to be one of your harem girls.'

'Nay, Jenny!'

'Because that's what it amounts to, two dozen girls at your beck and call.'

'You're exaggerating. It might run to ten, but not two dozen.'

'It's not funny.'

'Don't be so serious. You know what Chesterton said, don't you?'

'What?'

'Life's too serious a thing to be taken seriously.'

'It's all right for him, he isn't going out with you.'

'Have you heard that joke about that girl who went to Italy for her holidays?'

'Yes, thank you.'

'Pity.'

He reached out and tapped the far shoulder of a boy dancing past. The boy turned in that direction. Jenny shook her head. 'Will you ever grow up?'

He tracked the couple like a private detective using Jenny as a shield, manoeuvring her close for another tap, this time with his knuckles. The boy spun round and picked on the nearest pair at his injured side.

'Is it you who keeps tapping?'

'What?'

'Keeps tapping me on the shoulder?'

'Me? What do I want to tap you for?'

'That's what I'd like to know.'

'No, it's not me.'

'Well it's somebody.'

'It's not me.'

'It's a good job.'

'Why, what would you do about it?'

Lennie held his breath to hold the laughter, but it burst out and poured over Jenny's shoulder like sick. The antagonists turned.

'Hawk! I should have known it was one of your childish tricks.'

'Why don't you threaten him then? Go on. Tell him what you're going to do to him.'

'Oh, be quiet.'

The couples parted and Lennie was still giggling when the dance ended.

'I'll have to go and see how my mates are going on now.'

'Ha ha.'

'What's that for?'

'Since when have you ever bothered about your mates at a dance?'

'Well, they didn't want to come, you see, and I feel responsible.'

'I know, Len, I know.'

'You never believe anything I say.'

'Is there any wonder?'

'Don't be like that, Jenny. Jesus. What's Brooky want?'

'Where?'

Mr Brook was standing on the edge of the floor staring at the centre like an angler watching his float.

'He doesn't look as if he wants you to me, he's not even looking this way.'

'He's just jerked his head at me. I'll see you in a minute.'

Lennie approached Mr Brook up his line of vision, making him start as though the float had jerked under.

'Hello, Len! I wondered if you'd come.'

'Did you?'

'Yes I . . . Enjoying yourself?'

'Not bad.'

'It makes a pleasant change for me, all this company.'

'Why, don't you go out much?'

'Yes I go out, but it's not the same on your own, is it?'

'Haven't you got any mates?'

'Most of the men I know are married.'

'Don't you fancy it, then?'

'What?'

'Marriage.'

'I wish I could.'

'What do you mean?'

He was staring past Lennie, down the centre of the floor
again.

'What? O nothing. I was just daydreaming.'

'Ladies and gentlemen! Could I have your attention, please!'

Leary was on stage talking to the microphone. Behind him
the guitarists were tuning their wires, listening with their heads
cocked, like a bomb disposal unit.

'We are now going to hold a dance competition!'

Leary waited for the cheers to fade.

'The dance is up to you, twist, shake, jive, you can even waltz
if you like.'

Some older members of the staff laughed and Leary smiled
into the mesh.

'Would any of the staff care to act as judges? Mr Rowley and
his wife perhaps? Thank you. And what about Mr Brook? He
should know something about movement, ha ha. Mr Brook?
Thank you. Right, ladies and gentlemen . . .'

Lennie ducked behind Mr Brook and yelled through his hands.
'GET DOWN LEARY!'

Mr Brook jumped and jerked round but Lennie was away,
weaving through the crowd like Groucho Marx. People near the
stage turned and pinpointed the call to Mr Brook who was
standing in a space blushing and shaking his head, pointing to
himself in a protesting dumb show.

'Thank you for those few kind words. Right, ladies and
gentlemen, off you go!'

The group let fly. Lennie circled the room for a partner, when he saw Jenny refusing to dance he backtracked, like a ballbearing falling down the silver U in a slot machine. He approached a girl in a grey pinafore dress from behind. Her calves shone like wet pebbles, and her swinging hips twitched the hem of her skirt like a well-oiled pendulum. It was Leary's sister. She was talking to her brother.

'Could I have this dance please?'

'I'm not very good.'

'I don't believe you.'

She looked at her brother. Lennie took her hand and led her on to the floor. She faced him and they caught the beat, timing it like the jump on to a moving train. Fast. Straight into the rhythm with no bodily contact. Most of the dancers were now round the edges watching and the three judges strolled in the spaces like kings in palace gardens. Lennie was bouncing like a rubber ball. His partner was more restrained, using her arms and body more than her legs. She was serious, averting her eyes, concentrating on her movements. Lennie was trying to will her attention, smiling and prancing round her like a cock bird, making the floor jump under him. They began to attract the attention of the spectators who were tapping in a unified thump, and the music developed a compulsion which in turn drove the beat, harder and faster. Lennie was sweating like a bull, and his partner loosened up, as though soaking up all the excess rhythm overflowing from his body.

'Go on, Len! Go on!'

'Make it go, Len! Make her have it!'

The crowd began to inch forward forcing the pairs on the outside to close inwards out of their path. The whole floor was jumping as though a monster under the boards was trying to push its way up with panicky insistence. When the other competitors saw that they were creating no impression they broke off and merged into the clapping stamping ranks of the advancing phalanx. Mr Rowley retreated.

'Let's get it over with, Brook.'

'Let them finish first, Alfred.'

'Well, Brook?'

'I agree with your wife, let them finish.'

36

The crowd closed in shouting encouragement. Boys bumped into girls from behind and rubbed up against them, jostling and shoving them to the centre. The two dancers were generating excitement like stabs of lightning.

'Good Lord, this is a debauchery!'

Mr Rowley stood firm and held his arms out like a policeman at a riot, but his wife and Mr Brook weren't listening, they were shouting and stamping with the rest. The circle closed like a clawing hand. The guitarists with their flexes straining behind them, ended the number with a twang and whine. Everyone stopped, then sagged. The air throbbed, then froze.

'There's no need to vote, is there?'

'What do you mean, Brook?'

'It was a one-horse race.'

'Meaning Jane Leary and Hawk, I suppose?'

'Of course.'

'Well, they're not getting my vote! That wasn't dancing, it was sheer obscenity.'

Mrs Rowley watched Lennie flick a folded handkerchief loose, and wipe his face. The handkerchief turned grey and soggy like a wet flannel.

'O come on, Alfred.'

'Don't tell me you're voting for them as well?'

'Of course I am, there may as well have been no one else on the floor.'

'That settles it, then.'

Mr Brook approached the platform. Leary stooped to receive the decision, then straightened and announced it to the microphone.

'Ladies and gentlemen! The winners, Miss Jane Leary and our own Leonard Hawk!'

He cut the applause by nodding to the group to begin the next number.

'You'll have to excuse me, I must cool off.'

'You're coming back, aren't you?'

'Yes, why?'

'When most girls say excuse me, it usually means Ta Ta.'

'I'll be back.'

He watched her disappear through the shifting throng.

'Hawk!'

He turned. Mrs Rowley was sitting by the wall. He walked across to her and sat down.

'Congratulations.'

'Thank you.'

'Where did you learn to dance like that?'

'O, up and down, nowhere in particular.'

'I wish I could.'

'It's easy, you just run wild.'

'My husband tells me it's your favourite pastime.'

'What, dancing?'

'No, running wild.'

'Don't believe him, it's all lies.'

'All?'

'A good two per cent, anyway.'

She laughed and stood up.

'Would you like to dance, Len? You don't mind me calling you Len, do you?'

'Why should I? That's my name.'

He took an orthodox stance with one arm round the waist.

'I'm surprised at your being able to waltz.'

'I'm not totally uncivilized, you know.'

'I meant I didn't think it would be in your line.'

'It's not, but it's useful for chatting birds up.'

'I see.'

Lennie was fidgety, and kept glancing round and looking over Mrs Rowley's shoulders.

'Looking for Jane?'

'Who?'

'She's a charming girl, she's been for tea a couple of times with her brother.'

'What does she do?'

'She works for her father.'

'Hey! Your husband's spotted us, he looks chuffed to death.'

'Are you worried?'

'He'll think I'm dancing with you to spite him. It's the sort of trick he expects of me.'

'Well, are you?'

'No.'

'Why are you dancing with me, then?'

'Because you asked me.'

'I see. Just passing time on until Jane comes back.'

'No, 'course not! I shouldn't have bothered if I hadn't wanted.'

'Thank you.'

'Anyway I'm grateful for the way you stuck up for me. You're a good sort.'

'You know why he dislikes you, don't you?'

'Because he's jealous.'

'You conceited young devil!'

'It's true. He's jealous because I'm young and I'm a good footballer, and he's . . .'

'And he's what? Go on.'

'Old and fat.'

'He's not all that old.'

'No, but he's fat.'

'He can't help that.'

'I can't help being a good footballer.'

'He thinks you're a fool.'

'I know that.'

'He thinks it's a crime that a boy with your brains should waste so much time playing football.'

'He's never played or he wouldn't talk like that.'

'Isn't it a waste then?'

'Of course it isn't!'

She stepped away as though he had spilled something between them.

'Don't get angry.'

'What do you expect? You've no idea what I feel like when I'm playing.'

'I don't suppose I have. What do you feel like?'

'I can't explain it right. You'd have to see me play to understand what I mean.'

'I think I know.'

'There's some things that your body can express a lot better than words.'

'I know, Len, I know.'

'When I'm on a field I sometimes think I could work wonders.'

'Do you always talk like this?'

'Look, I'm not bragging! I'm just telling you the truth!'

'All right, all right. Don't get so worked up about it.'

People were staring. Mrs Rowley smiled from side to side as though they were talking about the weather. The music stopped and they stepped apart.

'Thank you, Len. I'll come and watch you play some time, then perhaps I'll really be able to understand you.'

'I'll get you a complimentary ticket next match I play for the Town.'

He followed her back to her husband.

'I've just been dancing with the champion, Alfred.'

'So I see.'

'I'm not in his class though, I'm afraid.'

'I don't know about that, you're ever so light on your feet.'

Lennie looked down at Mr Rowley's black shoes, planted on the floor like two flat irons. Jane was standing at the door with her coat on. Lennie passed between Mr and Mrs Rowley and walked across the empty floor to her.

'You're not going, are you?'

'I've got to, Edmund's getting his coat.'

'You're a grand 'un.'

'There's nothing I can do about it.'

'Do you have to go with him?'

'He's got the car.'

'Just when I was beginning to enjoy myself.'

'I'm sorry.'

'I bet he's only going because you've been dancing with me.'

'We're calling at friends.'

'Can I see you in the week some time, then?'

'I don't know. Father doesn't like me using the cars much, and the bus service is hopeless.'

She tightened the belt of her raincoat, shortening it to show her smooth legs up to the knees.

'I shall be coming into town on Wednesday evening though. I'm going to the ballet at the civic.'

'On your own?'

'Yes.'

'What is it, *Swan Lake*?'

'No, it's modern. It'll be right up your street.'

'I bet it will.'

'You're not interested, then?'

'I'll see.'

'Please yourself.'

'What time does it start?'

'Seven thirty.'

'I'll see you outside about quarter past, then, if I go.'

'I shall go in if you're not there. Cheerio.'

'Ta ra.'

She turned and walked into the corridor. Her black hair swishing round the rim of her upturned collar.

'Hey!' She looked back.

'Have you got your gold medal?'

She laughed and walked out into the night. A car engine was running. Lennie listened until the door squeezed shut then turned back into the dance.

'Now then, Jenny, my old love.'

He searched round, but only found Frank on his own, standing smoking.

'Hey up Frank, where's Bill?'

'He's fixed up.'

'What about thee?'

'Does it look like it?'

'I wondered what tha was looking so happy about.'

'Ready for going yet?'

'I'm looking for Jenny.'

'That blonde tha wa' dancing wi' early on?'

'That's her.'

'She's gone.'

'How's tha know?'

'I've seen her.'

'On her own?'

'Wi' Bill.'

'You lying sod.'

'It's right.'

'The bugger.'

'What's up, didn't he ask thi permission?'

'O bloody hell! Let's bugger off then if tha's got 'em on.'

Frank followed Lennie to the cloakroom. Three youths in blazers and flannels were chasing each other through the avenues of overcoats, giggling and grabbing at each other's clothing. They ran past Frank and jostled him into the padding of coats.

'Hey watch it or I'll bang you!'

'Shut it, Frank, haven't you ever had a few too many?'

'Ar, but I don't act like a two-year-old when I have.'

'Tha usually too pissed to know what tha acts like.'

Lennie grabbed his coat and walked up the corridor, leaving Frank at the mirror combing his hair. The dance had ended, and the crowd leaving the hall forked right and left to the cloakrooms.

Mr Brook was standing in the foyer looking round with his hands in his pockets.

'Just off, Len?'

'Yes.'

'Had a good evening?'

'Not bad.'

Lennie stepped back into the line of the corridor.

'Where the bloody hell is he?'

'You wouldn't like to come for a coffee, would you?'

'They'll all be shut.'

'I mean round to my place.'

'I thought you meant a coffee bar.'

'I'll run you home afterwards.'

'I can't, I'm with my mate.'

'Tell him you're taking a girl home.'

'He knows I'm not.'

'Can't you tell him something?'

There was a commotion down the corridor. Boys were staring through the mesh partition into the cloakroom.

'I say, Len!'

But he was away through the crowd. Frank had backed up to the mirror and was being threatened and pushed by a half circle of boys. Another group was sympathizing with a boy balancing a bloody handkerchief on his face.

'What's up, Frank?'

'I banged him.'

'What for?'

'He was laughing at my suit.'

'Who is it?'

'One of them kids who was running about.'

'Come on, let's bugger off.'

'So I banged him.'

They were jostled and jeered, and had to use their shoulders to knock their way through. Lennie sorted them out for Monday as they forced their way up the corridor. Outside, car doors were banging and voices called Good night, Good night. As they walked down the hill under the orange light Lennie began to sing.

'When you come to the end of a perfect day.'

Frank looked at him and laughed.

'And finally the results of Saturday's soccer matches, which were played against teams from the Emily Brontë School. The under-fifteens lost by three goals to two, the second eleven won two nil, and the first eleven won eight two. I would like to see Hawk in my study at break this morning.'

Harry Andrews ran round the school looking for him. He found him in the Library reading the papers.

'Come in! – Sit down, Hawk.'

Lennie walked across the carpet to the chair set at an angle before the desk.

'No, there.'

Doctor Bennet pointed to one of the two leather armchairs sitting at either side of the fire like young elephants. Lennie sat down and looked up at the Yorkshire seven-a-side cup on the mantelpiece. Doctor Bennet poked the fire, then leaned back in the other chair.

'Mr Rowley's been in to see me, Hawk.'

'About Saturday?'

'Yes. I would like to hear your version of the incident.'

'It's the same as his, I suppose.'

They both waited.

'You've nothing more to say, then?'

'No.'

'I see. Mr Rowley said that you refused to apologize.'

'I did.'

'Even though you admit you were wrong?'

'Yes.'

'Isn't that being a trifle arrogant?'

'I suppose it is, but I'm not sorry.'

Doctor Bennet picked up the poker and pushed back a piece of coal which was spurting flame like a gas jet and blowing smoke into the room.

'Mr Rowley wants to take the captaincy away from you.'

'Does he?'

'He says a more stable person should be appointed. He's going to see Mr Brook about it.'

'Is he?'

Lennie squinted at a team photograph on the back wall, above a bookcase.

'You don't appear unduly worried at the prospect.'

'I'm not.'

'Doesn't the honour mean anything to you?'

'Not much, because I'm wasting my time playing for the school anyway.'

'Are you now?'

'If I left I'd be playing in the First Division inside a fortnight.'

'Hawk. I hope you're not over-estimating your ability.'

They were both leaning forward at the front of their chairs.

'I'm not. I know that I've got it in me to be a great footballer.'

'Well! I've heard of confidence, but . . .'

Doctor Bennet straightened his legs and let his body fall back, so that he curved to the carpet like a slide in a recreation ground.

'I'll tell you what it's like when I play for the school. It's like you doing the same lessons as 1C.'

Doctor Bennet scrambled back up his seat.

'Now don't start over-estimating my ability as well.'

'You can see what I mean though, can't you?'

44

'I've heard it rumoured many times that you were turning professional.'

'So have I.'

Doctor Bennet stood up chuckling. 'Beware false prophets, eh?'

Lennie stood up.

'Right, you may go.'

He walked to the door and opened it.

'By the way, Hawk.' He stood with the latch raised like a pecking beak. 'I hear you're working very well.'

'Thank you.'

'Even though your essays do tend to arrive a trifle late, and occasionally get lost in transit.'

Lennie hid his face behind the door and smiled out into the corridor.

'Is it English you intend to read at University?'

'That's what I told them, but I don't know yet.'

Doctor Bennet shook his head and looked into the fire.

'Right, Hawk, that's all.'

Lennie walked down the corridor through the gangs of boys talking and sucking milk up straws. He approached a boy standing with his back to the notice board, feeling the radiator behind him.

'Now then, Parsons. What about Saturday night?'

'What do you mean?'

'Tha knows what I mean.'

'I didn't say anything.'

'You lying hound!'

'It wasn't me.'

'I heard thi. If there's anybody wants banging it's him.'

'I never ...'

'What tha going to do about it, then?'

Lennie stepped in. Parsons leaned back, staring, with his chin tucked into his neck.

'I'll show thi who wants banging.'

Spectators gathered and dammed the corridor, until Leary appeared on the scene, shouting.

'Outside! Come on, everybody outside!'

They scattered, ferreting for the cloakroom and toilets, exposing Lennie threatening Parsons against the radiator. Parsons was sweating, rearing back like a striking snake with his head pressed on Saturday's team sheet.

'Stop it, Hawk, you're burning my arse.'

'What's going on?'

'Mind thi own business, Leary.'

'He's threatening me.'

'Let him go.'

Leary pulled Lennie's arm, and Parsons slipped out and tried to run down the corridor. Lennie snatched his sleeve and held it at the cuff.

'Get off! Get off! Tell him to get off, Leary!'

Lennie reeled him in like a big fish and gripped him round the body with both arms. Leary tried to separate them, and all three became locked like worms in a tin.

'I'll show thi, Parsons lad.'

'Let go.'

'Let him go, Hawk.'

'Thar next, Leary.'

They bounced from wall to wall, fighting to free their arms from the tangle. Lennie stuck his leg behind Parsons and tried to push him over, but he clung on and staggered back, dragging them all down in a revolving knot. Lennie tried to stop the fall by bracing his right leg against the weight, but it was out of control and his ankle turned and squeezed as the load settled. His leg crumpled and he yelped out from the bottom of the pile.

'My ankle! Get up! Quick, get up!'

He thumped at Leary and Parsons and they scrambled up and looked down at him.

'Bloody hell, I bet it's broken.'

He pushed himself off the floor with his hands and good leg. Leary reached down to help.

'Get away, you interfering bastard. Just thee wait, Parsons.'

He leaned back on the tiles with his leg hanging loose like a crippled bird. Leary set off down the corridor with Parsons behind him, looking back. They returned with Mr Brook.

Mrs Hawk looked up, and stood with her iron poised over a shirt. When she saw Mr Brook helping Lennie from the car she banged the iron on to the asbestos square, and ran round to the front.

'What's happened, Len?'

She reached out to help him but he shrugged her off.

'I've sprained my ankle.'

'Is it bad?'

'It'll be all right.'

'The doctor says he's to rest it for a few days.'

Lennie hobbled to the entry, stepping on the toes of his right foot as though the pavement was red hot.

'Are you coming in, Mr Brook?'

'No thank you, Mrs Hawk. I've had enough time off this morning.'

'Thank you for bringing him home.'

She caught Lennie up outside the back door and reached out to help him over the step.

'Gi'oer, Mam, I'm not a cripple.'

'I'm only trying to help you.'

He sat by the fire with his leg straight out on a stool like a man with gout.

'I feel like a bloke with gout.'

'Have you had your dinner?'

'No.'

'Eee, we haven't much money but we do see life.'

As she walked into the kitchen Mr Hawk passed the front window like someone crossing the screen.

'There's my dad here.'

'Where?' She came to look, as though he was pointing to a photograph in the paper. 'Are you sure? He's only just gone.'

' 'Course I'm not. I've never seen him before.'

Mr Hawk hung his jacket under his cap behind the kitchen door, and turned the lapel back to take his snap from the inside pocket. He walked into the living-room and placed the grease-proof packet on the corner of the table.

'What's a matter, Arthur?'

'We're on strike. What's up wi thee?'

'I've sprained my ankle.'

'What doing?'

'I went over in t'corridor.'

'Are they after more money again?'

'Is it bad?'

'Doctor says I've to have a month off.'

'Doctor says you've to have nothing of the kind. Who's to blame this time?'

'There's trouble over a new contract, and there's talk of 'em laying some men off.'

'What about you?'

'I don't know. If they throw me off this button job I'll be struggling. I can't do any heavy work now with this back.'

'Aren't we hampered? If it isn't one thing it's another.'

'There's a meeting on Wednesday morning in t'club.'

Mr Hawk stood with his back to the fire and watched Lennie walk across the rug.

'What's it like?'

'A lot better. I think I'll have a walk down to t'Dale.'

'Ar, get off, a bit of exercise'll do it good.'

Mrs Hawk took the tablecloth by its four corners, and lifted it up like a tramp's bundle.

'He'd be better off stopping in and getting some work done. He hasn't done a stroke since he came home on Monday.'

'What do you think I was doing all day yesterday?'

'You were reading.'

'Well, then.'

'I mean real work, studying and writing and that.'

'What do you think ...? O shut your mouth, Mam, you don't know what you're talking about.'

'Hey! who do you think you're talking to?'

'My dad, didn't you know I was cross-eyed?'

'And don't be so clever.'

'For crying out loud, get down to t'ground, Len, and let's have a bit a peace in t'house.'

'Ar! And you get off to that meeting.'

'Don't worry, I'm going. Get thi coat on, Len.'

'You'll do owt to keep him away from his books, won't you?'

'A lad his age doesn't want to be stuck inside all day. He can work tonight.'

48

'I can't, I'm going out.'

'What did I tell you? Where you going?'

'Ballet.'

'Ballet, what ballet?'

'Civic theatre.'

'Don't lie to me.'

'All right, then.'

'Who you going with?'

'Frank and Bill.'

'Now I do know you're lying.'

'Tha can do wi'out going boozing midweek.'

'I'm not going boozing.'

'Where are you going then?'

'I've told you.'

'Not wi' Frank and Bill, tha not.'

'I'm going with a girl.'

'Who is she?'

'I met her on Saturday.'

'What do they call her?'

'Jane.'

'Do we know her?'

'No, you'll have heard of her dad, though. D. S. Leary.'

'Leary. You don't mean that Leary who owns them paper mills up Bank Side?'

'Him who's on t'Board o' directors at t'Town?'

'That's him.'

'He's t'chairman, isn't he?'

'All satisfied now?'

'Bloody hell.'

Lennie got off the bus and walked across the car park behind the stand. The thwack of leather and voices calling, carried over the walls and out of the ground. He pushed the Players and Officials door open and stepped down the three steps into the foyer. It was empty so he crossed the corridor into the tunnel. Clifford Anderson, the manager, turned from the line side at the footsteps behind him.

'Hello, Len, holidays already?'

'No, I've had a few days off with a sprained ankle.'

'All right now?'

'It's still sore.'

Lennie toed the touchline with the manager and they watched the practice match, hands in pockets, side by side.

'Bobby injured?'

Lennie nodded across to Bobby Prince who was jogging down the back straight in his tracksuit.

'He got his thigh knocked in Saturday. He'll be all right though.'

'How long's Stan been a centre forward?'

'First time this morning.'

'He looks lost.'

'I shall be turning out myself if we don't find a goalscorer soon.'

'What you really need is a good class inside forward.'

'Got any more good news, son?'

Clifford Anderson glanced at him without turning his head, then stepped back into the tunnel and stamped his feet to clear the mud. Bobby Prince ran between them, and they both turned at the crunch, crunch of his boots on the red shale. He passed in front of the terrace and called to the groundsman sweeping up amongst the crush barriers. They both laughed, and the sound flew up like a bird into the girders of the empty stand.

'How's school, Len?'

'Fine, thanks.'

'I hear Duncan Kerslake was in town last week.'

'He came to our house.'

'I didn't know they were interested.'

'He was waiting for me when I got in from school.'

'Good offer?'

'Forty basic, plus umpteen bonuses.'

'Fwew! Why didn't you take it? There's no better club in England.'

'Don't know, seems a long way to London.'

'Well, if their money can't tempt you, it's no good me trying, is it?'

'Will you be able to fix me up in the holidays? We're finished this term.'

'I'll be glad to, son. What about Saturday?'

'I won't be fit.'

'The week after then. Come down next Thursday night and we'll give your ankle a try out.'

'Which team will I be in?'

'I'll have to give you a run in the reserves to start with.'

'That's all right.'

'Then, all being well . . .'

'Good. I'll be off then.'

'Drop into the physio room and see Cyril before you go.'

'I will. Ta ra.'

As he walked up the tunnel Clifford Anderson shouted out on to pitch.

'Shoot, Roy! For God's sake, man, shoot!'

'I hope you're putting a tie on.'

'You've hoped wrong.'

'I'm sick o' seeing you in them blasted casual shirts. You never look decent.'

'What difference does a tie make?'

'You look a lot smarter.'

'What's smart about a strip of cloth hanging down t'front of your shirt?'

'There's plenty thinks so, anyway.'

'Let them wear 'em then.'

'O get out, Len, you can't talk to you.'

'I never was in the habit of talking to myself.'

'And what's that supposed to mean?'

Mr Hawk looked up from the television.

'I hope he's going out before Gunshot comes on 'cos I can't hear a bloody thing.'

'You ought to be coming, Dad. Bit a culture'd do you good.'

'Bit a culture! I'd sooner watch a hen sitting.'

'It might be all right.'

'I hope it is, old lad, waken me up and tell me about it when tha gets in.'

'You are narrow-minded, Arthur.'

'You would be an all if you suddenly found out that he was taking that Sonia Sharpe from up street instead of Leary's daughter.'

'Arthur!'

Lennie's laugh filled all four rooms as he ran upstairs. His dad looked up at the ceiling and shouted after him.

'What's up wi' thee? I'll lay ten to one that thar comes straight home if she doesn't turn up.'

Lennie was bent forward looking at the stills in the glass case when Jane tapped him on the back.

'You're risking it, then?'

'Hello. I'll try anything once.'

'You make it sound like a medicine.'

They pushed through the glass doors into the warm light of the foyer.

'Where are we going, then?'

'I've booked.'

'For me as well?'

'Yes.'

'Confident, weren't you?'

'I wouldn't have lost anything, they'd have sold the ticket if you hadn't come.'

An usherette tore the tickets and they found their seats. Lennie bundled his duffle up and threw it underneath. He held Jane's coat still while she leaned forward out of it.

'Thank you. How's your ankle?'

'It'll be all right.'

'Edmund told me about it. Yet another episode in the Hawk saga.'

'Big mate of mine, your Eddie.'

'I know. He's got pictures of you on his bedroom walls.'

'With pins stuck all over them?'

'Father was furious about that detention of Charles. He says he's going to have a word with you if he sees you down at the Dale.'

'Good lad, your Charlie.'

Jane stood up for the National Anthem. Lennie remained in his seat and looked at the programme. The man standing by his side reached down and pulled it out of his hands.

'Hey up!'

'Have you no manners, young man?'

'Let's have that programme back.'

'Get to your feet then.'

'What for?'

'The Queen of course.'

'I can't see her.'

He sprang up and snatched the programme as everyone else sat down. The lights dimmed for the first piece.

'Buy your own programme next time, they're only a tanner.'

'It's disgusting.'

Jane tugged at Lennie's sleeve, and leaned across whispering, 'Take no notice of him, Len.'

'The silly old bugger.'

'What did you say?'

'I said you're a stupid old bugger.'

'I'm not standing for that. I'll fetch the manager to you in a minute.'

A woman sitting directly behind leaned forward and prodded Lennie in the back.

'Do you mind being quiet? I can't hear a thing.'

'It's not me, missus.'

'Of course it's you.'

Jane nudged him and he turned round.

'Shsh.'

Paper crackled. Lennie looked down at the next seat. The man beside him was eating chocolates and screwing the crisp cups into tight balls.

'Jesus!'

He emptied the box, then dropped it and back heeled it under the seat.

'What's up, mister, are you starving?'

'How dare you?'

The woman behind pushed Lennie in the back.

'If you don't be quiet I'll fetch the manager.'

The curtain fell and Jane applauded.

'Didn't you enjoy that?'

'Champion.'

The curtain rose and the audience settled for the second piece. Three men took turns to dance with a girl, then dawdled in the corners waiting for her to make her choice. Loud breathing; Lennie looked at his neighbour whose chin was bouncing on his chest. People shuffled in their seats and whispered to each other as the man keeled over. Lennie grinned and leaned away to the other side of his seat. The man came to rest at an angle of forty-five degrees with his head on Lennie's arm. Lennie lifted his elbow and shouted down the man's ear.

'Oy!'

'Eh! Wha!'

He shot up. Lennie laughed out and the centre of the theatre began to buzz. The woman behind hutched along the row and returned with the manager. She pointed to Lennie in the dark.

'That's him, he's done nothing but cause a disturbance since he came in.'

The manager side-stepped along the row, excusing himself.

'Now then what's going on, sir?'

'If this boy doesn't leave, then I most certainly shall. I have occupied this seat for ten years and in all that time I have never been subjected to such disgusting behaviour.'

'Would you mind leaving, please?'

'I haven't done anything.'

'You've nearly stopped the show, that's all.'

'He's only come to make a nuisance of himself, he's no intention of watching the performance.'

'Come on, Len, let's go.'

'Don't you worry, I'm going. But I want my money back because I haven't seen a thing thanks to this ignorant pig.'

'I say! Did you hear that, manager?'

'Are you coming, or do I have to fetch the police?'

'Will we get it back?'

'Come on, Len.'

'No money can be refunded.'

'Can't it? I will stop the bloody show then.'

He stood up and cupped his hands to his mouth.

'All right! All right! Now will you come along, PLEASE?'

Lennie pulled his coat through his legs and followed Jane and the manager off the row, and up the aisle. The manager paid Lennie out of his own pocket and escorted them through the swinging doors.

'Ta ra. See you again some time.'

'I've never been so embarrassed in all my life.'

'It wasn't my fault.'

He began to chuckle.

'Did you see that bloke jump?'

'It's not funny.'

'What you laughing for then?'

They walked down the pavement with their heads back, laughing out. People passing turned to look, then carried on shaking their heads.

'Where are we going now then?'

'Anywhere ...'

'Coming for a drink?'

'Lovely.'

She took his hand and ran him across the black puddly ash of the car park.

'Which is yours?'

'Where are we going?'

'Anchor.'

'I don't know it.'

'I'm not surprised.'

Jane stooped down to unlock the door of the mini, stretching her coat tight over the curve of her arse. Lennie reached out to touch it, but pulled back when she straightened up.

'I expected a Bentley at least.'

'Father won't let us touch it, that's why he bought this.'

Lennie walked round the bonnet and waited for Jane to get in and unlock the door.

'He says even if we do smash it up between us, it won't have cost him a fortune.'

He guided her through town to the Anchor.

'Left here.

'Now straight on.

'It's there, look!'

She steered alongside the kerb, stopped; and leaned back.

'I don't know this part of town very well.'

'You'll be able to tell them you've been slumming when they ask you.'

'Funny.'

He ran round the front and opened the door, Jane swivelled, keeping both legs together, and waited for Lennie to pull her up.

'Bad luck.'

'What do you mean?'

'About the leg show. You learn to perfect that movement in these cars.'

'You can't blame me for looking though, can you? Especially at legs like yours.'

'Flatterer.'

'There's only one thing beats a bit of leg.'

'And what's that?'

'A lot.'

Lennie pushed the taproom door open and stood back for Jane to step past him. Frank froze with his dart pointed at the board and rounded his lips at Bill. When Lennie appeared behind her, he completed the throw, and the point stuck in up to the shaft. The door rushed back, then braked; and squeezed shut with a bump bump.

'Hey up, Len! Where you been?'

'Ballet.'

'Have you? We've just been to t'opera.'

He turned back to the board and threw his third dart. It hit at the wire and bounced out.

'What do you want to drink?'

'I'll have a glass of beer, please.'

'Are you sure? I'm rolling, you know.'

'Positive.'

'You can come with me regular.'

Frank and Bill suspended their game to watch Jane walk across the room and sit down, she looked around while Lennie ordered the drinks.

'This is a funny place.'

'It's all right, beer's good and it's clean.'

'It's not very comfortable though, is it?'

She pressed her knuckles into the leather bench.

'Everything's so hard and plain.'

'How do you like it, up to your eyes in carpets?'

'It's so bare; it makes me shiver.'

'Where do you go then? Don't tell me. That place out on the Fleece ... Queen's Head.'

'Mother and Father do. I've been a few times.'

'I'd sooner get two tons of coal in than go to that place.'

'You've never been!'

'Who hasn't? I've seen 'em, sitting about eyeing each other up, thinking they're marvellous.'

'Don't be silly.'

'It's right.'

'Well, it's a lot more comfortable than in here anyway.'

'It's not comfort they're after, it's effect. They'd sit on a bed of nails if they thought they were in the right company.'

'And what's so marvellous about the people in here, then?'

'Nothing.'

'They only come here because they can't afford anything better.'

'I know.'

'They're just as bad, then.'

'I know they are, they'll all be in the best room when they've been paid at the week-end. They'll get a bit of plush under their arse on Saturday night and they'll think they're t'king of bloody England.'

'Nobody's right for you, are they? Why don't you run away and find yourself an island somewhere?'

'I've found one. It measures a hundred by sixty and they've goals at each end.'

'And what about the other twenty-one players?'

'They don't count. It's just me, and the ball, and the goal.'

'You make it sound terribly selfish.'

'Do you want another drink?'

'No thank you, I'll have to go now.'

'Giving me a lift home?'

'Come on, then.'

Lennie returned the glasses to the bar and they walked out.

'Where do you live?'

'I'll show you.'

They got in and Jane started the engine.

'First left down here.'

'Where to now?'

'Whoa! we're here.'

'You lazy devil! It's only a hundred yards.'

'I just thought I'd show you; you might need it for future reference.'

'What number is it?'

'Ninety-six. Think you'll remember?'

'I'll never find it if I don't, they're all so alike, aren't they?'

Lennie hooked his arm round her shoulder, but she stayed stiff. He removed it and got out.

'What about Saturday night, then?'

'Yes, all right, where do you want to go?'

'Let's go to the ballet.'

She laughed and leaned across the seat.

'Where then?'

'Anywhere, I'll meet you outside the Town Hall about half seven and we'll decide then.'

'That's fine. Good night.'

Lennie dipped back inside the car and kissed her upturned face full on the mouth. He stood up and banged the door.

The sneck clicked. Mr Hawk looked at the middle door and waited. Lennie switched the kitchen light on and took his duffle coat off. He picked up a pile of books from the washer top, then walked through and placed them on the table. His face was still flushed from training. Mrs Hawk switched the light off behind him.

'Are tha fit then?'

Lennie nodded.

'It didn't give me any trouble at all.'

He stood on his left leg and twirled his right foot.

'And I didn't half give it some hammer.'

'Are tha playing on Saturday?'

'Reserves at Burnley.'

'I think I'll come.'

'You can do without gallivanting off there spending two or three pounds on train fares.'

'He said Burnley not Burma.'

'I wouldn't bother, Dad. If I play well and go down full-time next week I should be in t'first team next Saturday.'

'I thought you reckoned to be going on t'post these holidays.'

'I can't do both.'

'It'd be a big help, what wi' Christmas coming on and no sign of your dad going back to work.'

'Stop bothering about money, he's enough on his plate.'

Lennie moved to the table and sat down.

'Shut up now, Arthur.'

Mr Hawk stood up and turned the television on.

'I can't work with that on, Dad.'

'Bloody hell! It's like a deaf and dumb school in here all along. Why don't tha go upstairs?'

'Why don't you? I'll carry t'tele up for you.'

'You dad's no consideration for nobody. Lift your books up a minute.'

He lolled back holding his books while she removed the cloth.

'Right, you can start now.'

He remained against the chair back staring across the table at the wall.

'What's a matter, too tired to start?'

'Just thinking.'

'You know your trouble, don't you?'

He straightened up and pulled his history book closer.

'Shut up now and let me get this done. It's to be in tomorrow morning.'

He placed the essay on Rowley's desk and walked away. Rowley was discussing some previous work with Leary.

'Just a moment, Hawk.'

Leary straightened his papers and walked past him. Rowley picked up Lennie's sheets and looked at the first and last sides, then scanned through the middle like someone examining the filling in a sandwich.

'What's this, a Christmas present? This essay is exactly two weeks late. I can't possibly mark it now.'

'Please yourself.'

'If I did, I wouldn't give you higher than D for being so blasted lazy!'

'It'd be worth more than that in an exam.'

'You hope!'

'I know. It might be late but there's nothing lazy about the content.'

'That damned arrogance will be the downfall of you, Hawk!'

'Can I have it back then? I'll use it for revision.'

He reached for the spread of papers on the desk. Rowley placed a fanned hand across them.

'No leave it. I'll have a look at it. That is, if I may be allowed to view your precious manuscript.'

Lennie smiled down at his shoes.

'I could willingly murder you, Hawk.'

He dropped back and the chair cracked.

'You're a fool; a fool to yourself. A first-class brain, and you're just not interested!'

'Who says I'm not?'

'You! You say it with every action you make. You say it every time you produce work weeks late!'

He snatched the papers from the desk and waved them before Lennie's face like an angry husband shaking bills at his wife.

'Do you know why I'm even bothering to read this, Hawk? Do you?'

'Because it's good.'

'Exactly! Because it makes such a pleasant change to read work that is not merely a rehash of the textbook!'

He slapped the papers back on to the desk and covered them with his forearms, wheezing like a fat man who has just run for a bus.

'Now, get out, before you drive me mad.'

Lennie turned and walked to the door.

'I've got a Christmas present for you too, Hawk. Leary has been appointed skipper of the first eleven for next term.'

Lennie closed the door quietly and walked up the corridor along the side of the classroom. Rowley watched him out of sight then picked up the essay.

L. Hawk. U.VI.A. European History.

How far can the adjective 'Benevolent' be applied to Catherine the Great of Russia?

If the stories are true that she lined up her officers and inspected them for the purpose of choosing a lover : then as far as the selected man was concerned the adjective is very apt indeed.

The crowd was streaming away like sand through an egg-timer, and the ground was already half empty. The referee blew his whistle and the teams ran off the field. Spectators hung over the tunnel walls and booed the Town as they ducked past. Mr Hawk leaned on the barrier waiting for the second team result to be announced over the tannoy. 'Here is the second team result from Burnley. Burnley one, Town three.' Somebody cheered. Mr Hawk nodded and moved away along the deserted terrace and out through the gate on his own. Through the darkening streets, to the corner shop opposite the Anchor. The doorbell tinkled. The man behind the counter looked round from dusting the shelves of sweets.

'Classified results in yet?'

'They're due any minute.'

Mr Hawk propped his elbow on the counter, and scanned the magazines, displayed in rows like tumbled dominoes.

'Waiting to see how your Len's gone on?'

'They've won.'

'Wonders never cease.'

'There's not many teams come away from Burnley wi' two points.'

'I hear t'first team's lost again.'

'They were murder.'

'Think they'll go down then?'

'They will unless they buck up.'

There was a thump on the pavement. Mr Hawk ran out and carried the square stringed parcel back on to the counter. He cut the string and pointed down the stop press at the scorers. Hawk (4 mins) Hawk (23 mins) Schofield (62 mins).

'Good old Len.'

'Did he score?'

'Two.'

'That's a good start.'

'It bloody well is. Just you watch t'difference when he gets in that first team.'

He plonked four pennies on the counter and ran all the way home smacking his thigh with the paper like a jockey using a whip.

'They've won, love!'

'That makes a change anyway.'

'I mean our Len's team. He scored two.'

'He must have played well then.'

'Played well! I'll bet he blinded 'em.'

'Here, come and get your tea and stop getting so excited.'

'He's forced to be in t'first team next week.'

Training had ended. The players were wallowing in the adjacent baths, splashing and shouting. The noise bounced round the tiled walls like a ball in a squash court.

'Give my back a rub, Len.'

Lennie circled Bobby Prince's back with soap, working up a spongy lather before splashing it off. George Armstrong stood facing the wall, singing his heart out, his head lathered up like a bob of candy floss. Bobby vaulted the bath wall and connected the cleaning hose to the tap, warning the other bathers by pointing his finger over his lips. He pushed the nozzle flush to the crack of George's arse, then nodded to Lennie to turn the tap. The pipe stiffened as the water snaked through.

'I believe for every drop of rain that falls.

Someone gets W A A A O O O O O E!'

They scattered as George spun round and lashed out, squinting through soapy chinks, 'You lousy bastards! You stupid-looking bleeders!'

They peered round the door over each other's shoulders, like a vocal group. George drove them back with the hose, and water began to run under their bunched feet into the changing-room. Eddie, the first team coach, stopped it by threatening him with a bucket of cold water. He dropped the hose and belly-flopped into the bath like a hippopotamus. The others trooped back in and rinsed off the scummy water under the showers.

Lennie was changing in the 'big ring' with the first team players. He picked up a beaker of orange juice and carried it back to his clothes. The room was steamy and warm, and dirty kit was strewn around as though the place had been ransacked for secret documents. Lennie dried and dressed and was combing his hair in the mirror when Eddie popped round the door.

'Boss wants to see you, Len.'

Lennie looked at him through the mirror and spoke into the glass.

'Right.'

Pete Fowler went white, and the room quietened as Lennie put his comb away and walked out.

He knocked twice on the 'G' of MANAGER'S OFFICE and waited.

'Come in.

'Sit down, son.'

He sat down on the leather cushioned chair angled before the desk.

'I thought I'd break the news to you myself before the teams went up.'

'First team?'

Clifford Anderson nodded and smiled.

'Inside left?'

'Yes. Are you pleased?'

'I'm chuffed to death.'

'Good. Now listen, Len. I know you're young and you're inexperienced, but we both know you've got it, and I'm expecting a lot from you.'

'Don't you worry, Mr Anderson, they'll think a donkey's kicked 'em when I get cracking on Saturday.'

'I hope you're right, son.'

'Oh, there's something I wanted to ask you about.'

'What's that?'

'Expenses. You see my dad's on strike and there's not much money coming in. My mam wanted me to get a job on the post, but he said no. He said I'd be better off coming full time.'

'Right, son. I'll give you ten pounds a match.'

'Ten pounds! Jesus!'

'It's cheap at the price. But don't forget that all this is illegal.'

'Ten pounds. I didn't mean anything like that.'

Clifford Anderson tilted back on two legs and balanced with

the help of his foot pushed against the bottom drawer of his desk.

'Do you know, if I didn't know you better, son, I'd think you were taking the mickey out of me.'

'What do you mean?'

'Ten pounds a lot of money. You know very well you could be earning six or seven times as much.'

'Lot of money ten pounds.'

'Get away with you!'

He walked Lennie to the door with his arm across his shoulders.

'All the best, son. I've a feeling that things are looking up a bit.'

'I think you're right, Mr Anderson.'

He walked away from the manager's arm; back along the corridor to the dressing-room. The players were crowded round the board studying Saturday's team. Pete Fowler stepped away with his back to Lennie.

'Talk about being well in! Straight from school, one reserve game and that's it, he's back. What is he, some kind of superman?'

Lennie walked across to his peg and unhooked his coat.

'I play where I'm picked, Pete.'

Fowler spun round, flushed. The other players spread out to their places. Chris Hanson, the club captain, patted Lennie's back.

'Welcome back, lad.'

'Welcome back! He must be stuck two foot up t'boss's arse.'

'Less of that, Pete. He's been picked on merit and you know it.'

Lennie looped the pegs on his coat and walked up to Fowler.

'It's like I've said, the teams have nothing to do with me, but I'll tell you something. Now that I'm in it'll take a lot more than you to shift me.'

Fowler breathed in as though air had suddenly become scarce. Chris led Lennie to the door by the arm.

'Take no notice of him, Len. He's had t'hump on ever since he felt up that blonde's skirt and got hold of her balls.'

The players laughed, shattering the air like stones on ice.

'Come on, I'll treat you, I'll give you a lift home.'

He walked down the entry into the yard. His dad was standing outside the kitchen door, scraping clay from his boots on the edge of the flagstones. He looked at Lennie, then sat on the step and untied the laces.

'Well?'

Lennie took the spade from against the wall and tried to balance on it like a pogo stick. Mr Hawk pulled his boots off and placed them together between his feet. He looked up.

'Who tha playing for then?'

Lennie leaned the spade against the wall.

'First team.'

'Are tha? That's champion!'

He dropped back and shouted over the top of his head into the kitchen.

'Hear that, love? First team on Saturday!'

Mrs Hawk popped round the door.

'I'm not in China, you know. I heard him first time.'

'Aren't you glad?'

'I suppose you are.'

'Well, aren't you?'

'You could have cleaned them boots in t'yard. I'll have all that to sweep up again now.'

Mr Hawk carried his boots into the house and Lennie followed him.

'Are you coming to watch him then?'

'I'm not!'

'I can get you a complimentary ticket, Mam; centre stand with all t'nobs.'

'Do you think I've nowt else to do but watch twenty-two grown men run about after a bag of wind?'

'That's what I like about my mam, she's such an expert.'

'She'll be getting voted t'sportswoman a t'year if she's not careful.'

'I've better things to do wi' my time. Here, come and get your dinners now!'

They sat down and ate in silence. Lennie finished and laid his knife and fork parallel down the centre of the plate.

'I might as well tell you now. I saw Clifford Anderson about expenses, he's giving me ten pounds a game.'

'Ten pounds! Hear that, Arthur?'

'It's all unofficial, so you'll have to keep it quiet.'

'I say, Len.'

'I told him you were on strike and what with Christmas coming on I said we were struggling a bit.'

'Tha could have done wi'art spinning bad luck stories. We're not that hard up.'

'It'll come in handy, won't it?'

'Ar, we shan't burn it. But I don't like begging.'

'I didn't beg! He was glad to give it me.'

'Ten pounds a game. It's as much as you earn when you're working, Arthur.'

'Ten pounds, I was earning three times as much as that on t'face.'

'You're not on t'face now though.'

'No, but I wa' when I nearly got my bloody back broke, wasn't I?'

'Stop shouting then. I was only remarking.'

'I wish I'd never bothered now.'

'Never mind what your dad says. If they're willing to pay you, you might as well take it.'

'I just thought it'd help out, that's all.'

Mr Hawk finished his dinner and went straight upstairs.

He came down at five o'clock, puff-eyed and flushed from bed. Lennie was working at the table. Mrs Hawk was out. He walked into the kitchen and reached down for the *Evening Star*, which was folded like a fan on the mat. The headline on the back page read:

HAWK SWOOPS IN!

After only one reserve match, and a league game back in August, Lennie Hawk, the eighteen-year-old Town schoolboy, is pitched straight back into the Town side for Saturday's vital match at the Dale. When I spoke to Clifford Anderson this morning about this 'shock' decision he beamed at me and looked happier than I've seen him for months! 'I have the utmost confidence in the boy,' he told me. 'In fact I've got the feeling that he's going to take the whole team, and lift it up the league table by the scruff of the neck!'

Mr Hawk grinned and his sleep-swollen eyes closed to slits.

'Seen this, Len?'

He threw the paper on to Lennie's books. Lennie picked it up and read it.

'Big build up for thi.'

'They're trying to draw t'crowd with a new face. It's a key advertising word you know, "new".'

Mr Hawk stood and looked over Lennie's shoulder.

'What tha doing?'

'English – Marvell's poems.'

'I didn't know he wrote poems.'

'Who?'

'Captain Marvel.'

They both laughed and Mr Hawk sat down in the armchair by the fire.

'I hope tha didn't take no notice on me at dinner time. I shouldn't have said that to thi.'

'It doesn't matter now.'

'I know tha did it for us and I'm grateful, only . . .'

'You don't have to explain, Dad, I know what you were thinking.'

'Does tha? Well, that's all right then.'

Lennie bent over the table, with his hand to his brow like a gambler's eye shade. His dad lolled back in the chair, staring at the fire which glowed solid in orange and black patches, quietly, without flame.

'Tha knows, Len, it's a funny feeling when thi lad comes home, an' he's had to ask for money, because his father can't earn enough to keep t'house going.'

'It's not your fault that you're off work.'

'I know, but money's nowt even when I'm working.'

'It's only like paying board.'

'It's not, Len.'

'Why isn't it?'

'Because tha not working, tha still studying. And if that's what tha wants to do I reckon I should be able to give it to thi.'

'You've given me enough already.'

'Just another few years in t'big money, that's all I needed.'

'You never know, your back might get stronger.'

'No, not now; but it's a pity it couldn't have happened when we'd got thi all set up.'

'I'm set up now.'

'That lump a muck wouldn't have mattered half as much then.'

The back door banged, then there was a scuffle and a pause before Mrs Hawk pushed the middle door open with her foot, and struggled in, weighed down by two packed shopping bags.

'Don't open t'door, will you? It's bitter outside. Shift your things now, love, and let's have a bit a tea.'

Lennie removed his books and turned the radio on. Mrs Hawk spread the cloth. Mr Hawk sat up and split the fire to flames.

Jane smiled and lowered the window when she saw Lennie approaching.

'Hey, star!'

Lennie dropped into a gorilla run, trailing his hands over his shoes. She jerked her head in and slammed the window up. Lennie squashed his nose to it snarling and howling. A passing couple detoured up the Town Hall steps and hurried past, looking down on him. He returned to normal and Jane let him into the car, pulling him down and hugging him tight.

'Isn't it wonderful?'

'Who told you?'

'Father, after the Board meeting. He said he's never heard Clifford Anderson so enthusiastic before.'

'What did your dad have to say about it?'

'Well, he wondered if you were ready or not. But he said Mr Anderson almost jumped down his throat. "Ready!" he said, "this boy will be ready for England in a year." '

Lennie stared out of the window.

'Are you ready, Len?'

'I'm as ready as I'll ever be.'

'Nervous?'

'No, not yet. Are you going?'

'Of course I am! We're all going. Even mother's going to see you.'

'I thought she wasn't interested in football.'

'She's not usually but Claire, Mrs Rowley, rang her up and asked her to go along. Anyway she says she wants to see this wonder boy everyone's raving about.'

'You'll be making me big-headed if you're not careful.'

'A lot of people say you are already.'

'A lot of people are liars.'

'I suppose you'll be wanting an early night?'

'I'd better not be too late else my dad'll have a nervous breakdown. He's got a stop watch on me.'

'What do you want to do then?'

'Nothing, just drive around. Pre-match relaxation as they call it in the papers.'

Then she took him home.

'We'll celebrate tomorrow night, when we've won.'

'Mr Confidence himself.'

She leaned over and kissed his cheek.

'Best of luck. I'll be shouting for you.'

'Ta. I'll see you tomorrow then.'

When he walked in his dad looked at the clock. It was quarter to ten.

'Tha wants to get some supper now and get to bed.'

'I'm going to.'

When he awoke it was bright in the bedroom. He turned on to his back and looked at the curtains. Galloping feet passed under the window, followed by more galloping feet and an accompanying call, Ya! Ya! Ya! A lavatory flushed, and increased in volume as the door snecked open. B A N G. Back to a smothered refilling and crunch, crunch, crunch across the cinders up to the houses.

'Morning.'

Milk bottles clinked. A dog barked. Lennie got up and whooshed the curtains open. The sun was low in a brittle blue sky. He looked over to the lavatories and across the scabby allotments down to the pit pond, which shone solid like a blob of black ink, beneath the hump of the muck stack and the scramble of the pit. He looked down through the net curtains at his mother talking to Mrs Jackson on the flags. The murmur,

murmur of their voices filled the room like the buzz of blue-bottles in summer. He knocked on the window and stepped back against the wall like a man on the run. The voices stopped. He poked his fist round and knocked again.

'Len!'

He giggled and waited for the murmur to start again, then he knocked the nets so hard that the window rattled in the frame. He swished the curtains together and ran to the bed. He shoved the bolster under the blankets and dived down the bed side as his mother thudded up the stairs. The door flew open.

'Have you gone crazy?'

The dim quiet stopped her.

'And it's no good hiding under there.'

She swirled the blankets off in a great white wing. They parachuted over the bed side and Lennie rose with them over his head like a ghost. She screamed and chewed her knuckles. Lennie dragged the blankets off and skimmed them at her like a gladiator's net. She caught them and he ran round her downstairs. Mr Hawk was at the bottom of the stairs shouting up.

'What the bloody hell's going off?'

He stepped back as Lennie belted down on him like an avalanche.

'What's going off?'

Lennie stood with his back to the fire in sagging pyjama bottoms. The fire was still new and chunky, and yellow flames sprouted from the holes and cracks between the coal. Children's Favourites was on the radio and the street outside was busy.

'How's tha feel?'

'Champion.'

His dad looked at the slim, well-etched body.

'That could do wi' a bit more meat on thi chest. Tha'r a right tin ribs.'

Lennie looked down at his chest and puckered his lips.

'What you talking about? You can't be carrying weight around with you at inside forward.'

'I know, but you need a bit a summat behind you when t'clog starts flying.'

'They never get near enough for me to bother about that.'

Mrs Hawk opened the stairs door.

'Next time you get that bed in such a state, you'll make it yourself.'

'I never touched it.'

'I bet Mrs Jackson thinks you've a slate off.'

'I have.'

'You reckon to go t'Grammar school and you're as soft as a brush.'

'Every genius is possessed with a streak of insanity.'

'I bet they think you're not right round here.'

'You'll be able to tell 'em why now, won't you?'

'And get dressed! There'll be t'insurance man here in a minute.'

Lennie got dressed and had his breakfast. The insurance man came in time for the prayer at five to ten.

'Morning! Morning! Bit better sort today. Now then, young 'un, going to make a name for yourself this afternoon?'

'Don't know yet, do I?'

'How long's tha been interested in football? I bet tha's never been to a match in thi life.'

'No time in my job.'

'No time!'

'They've mentioned it in every house I've been in this morning. They're talking about nothing else.'

'Make a change from t'weather then.'

Mrs Hawk paid him and he marked the book.

'Well, I'll be on my way then. No rest for the wicked as they say. Best of luck this afternoon. Good morning!'

'Oo, Arthur, you are rude to that man!'

'Bloody insurance men. They've neither t'strength to work with their backs or t'gumption to work with their heads.'

'You shouldn't say things like that about people.'

'So they carry little books about and natter to women all day.'

'And our Len's getting as bad as you.'

'I never said a word.'

'That's just as bad. I bet he dreads coming when you two's in.'

'Bloody insurance men. What time's tha to be at t'ground?'

'Two fifteen.'

'Tha wants to go a little walk, get some fresh air down thi lungs.'

Lennie sat down and read the paper. A transfer headline straddled the back page. The centre column told the story, then funnelled off to forecasts and team changes. Lennie's name was included, printed in short stout capitals.

'I see I've got a mention.'

'I've seen it. I bet tha never sees it as little as that again.'

'What do you want for dinner, Len?'

Mrs Hawk wrestled into her coat and assembled her shopping bags.

'I'm not bothered, a sandwich'll do.'

'Tha'll want more than a sandwich inside thi.'

Mrs Hawk went out. Lennie mooched about; from the house, to the yard, to the street. He stood at the entry end with his hands in his pockets and said howdo to people passing. Then back to the fire. There was a knock and a whistle at the window and Frank walked past. Lennie stood before the fire and waited for him to come round.

'Hey up, Len! Hello, Mr Hawk.'

'Howdo, Frank.'

Frank pulled a chair from under the table and sat down.

'What's it like to be a star then?'

'I'll tell thi after.'

'What do you think to him, Mr Hawk?'

'He's not doing so bad.'

'I don't suppose you'll be going this afternoon.'

'No, I don't think I'll bother.'

'I didn't think you would be.'

'He's had his coat on four times and their team haven't set off yet.'

They put their heads back and laughed out. When they stopped the music on the radio began to play again.

'Nervous?'

'Not yet.'

'Tha'll be all right.'

'Bill going?'

'I'm meeting him from work. Where you standing, Mr Hawk?'

'Usual place, near t'tunnel.'

'We shan't see you then.'

'Why, where do you go?'

'Kop. How's courting going, Len?' He winked at Mr Hawk. 'What do you think to him, going out wi't'chairman's daughter?'

'He can pick winners better than me.'

'Got thi feet under t'table yet?'

'I'm hoping he hasn't.'

'He was better off wi' me and Bill looking after him.'

'What, a couple a ale carts like you?'

'Courting'll do his football no good, you know.'

'No, and beer won't either.'

'Not as tiring though, Mr Hawk.'

They laughed again and Frank stood up.

'I'll be off then. Coming in t'Anchor tonight, Len?'

'Might do.'

'All the best this aft, let's see thi blind 'em.'

'He will.'

He opened the kitchen door and stepped back to let Mrs Hawk come in.

'Hello, Mrs Hawk, I'm just off.'

She nodded and Frank left. The fire was big in the grate and the heat seemed to stretch the air like a drumskin. Music on the radio gave way to Sports Special and the match previews. The Northern reporter talked about the Town match:

'I shall be viewing at the Dale this afternoon, where the Town have brought in young Lennie Hawk, a local grammar school boy and England Youth International, at inside left. This is his second league game and he is still an amateur. It's rumoured that he has been approached by every club in the First Division and Clifford Anderson, the Town manager, says that he has turned down offers which would make most professionals boggle. He also says that Hawk is the greatest prospect he has E V E R seen, and he will be ready for England in a year. I shall be reporting from the Dale later on in the afternoon for our

Saturday Roundup and I will give you my decision then on this latest wonder boy.'

'Fancy our Len being on t'wireless.'

'Don't let it get thi worked up.'

'I'm not doing.'

They had their dinners. Lennie had a bacon sandwich and a pot of tea. Then they watched the clock tick round and waited until it was time to go.

'I'm off then.'

He put his coat on and scraped some change off the mantel-piece.

'All the best, lad, and don't worry, tha'll be as good as anybody else who's playing.'

'Best a luck, love, and be careful.'

'I'll wait for thi after t'match.'

'Right. Ta-ra.'

He walked to the ground. The wind was bitter in the shade of the houses, but the sun was warm when he crossed the streets. Knots of people stood around the ground, but it was still early for the crowds, and the turnstiles only clicked spasmodically. A man was displaying rosettes, stuck to a board like painted lettuce leaves.

'Favours! Favours! Don't forget your favours.'

A gang of boys raced past him, waving their scarves and mocking his call. They wore woollen hats with bobbles stuck on top like rosy apples. They stopped and gathered round a programme seller, who at the same time took their money and gave them programmes one-handed. Lennie pushed the door open into the foyer and walked along the corridor. The dressing-room was warm and clean and smelled of disinfectant. The kit was in order round the walls. The big, white shirt numbers read from two to eleven with the goalkeeper's jersey like a green full stop at the end. The massage table down the centre was draped with a clean towel, and bottles of oil were stacked at its head like bottles behind a bar. Lennie walked to number 10 and sat down above his boots. Eddie was cutting bandage into tie-up lengths.

'All right, son?'

'Fine, thanks.'

Geordie Paling and Wilson O'Niell were studying a racing paper. The other players arrived in ones and twos. They took their coats off straight away and stood talking, hands in pockets. Lennie looked at the clock. It was half past two. He took his shirt off the hook and hung his coat in its place. They were all starting to strip now, slowly and easily.

'Anybody want a rub?'

Chris climbed on to the table and lay with his face on his hands. Eddie began to pummel and rub him with oily palms. Chris moaned.

'Oo, stop it I like it, Eddie.'

Lennie sat in his white shorts and stockings and pulled his boots from under the bench. He squeezed the soft, black leather and turned them over. Long studs had been screwed in to grip the soft ground. Clifford Anderson opened the door and banged Pete Fowler standing behind it.

'All right, lads?'

He sat with the players in turn, speaking softly into their ears. Sometimes they laughed together, then he passed on to the next one. Lennie looped the new laces under his boots and tied them on top, on the tongue.

'All right, son?'

'I'm all right.'

'How many times have you been to the lav?'

Lennie looked up and they both smiled.

'Don't worry, son, they all feel the same, it's only the reaction that's different. Listen at Laurie, you'd think he was going to a party. And Chris there, he looks so relaxed you'd think he was getting ready for bed. But it's there inside just the same, they all feel the same.'

He slapped Lennie on the thigh and stood up.

'You'll be all right, son.'

Max was dispensing lotions like a chemist. Eddie was sweating. Clifford Anderson looked at his watch, then up at the clock and walked out. Lennie stood up and banged his feet. He pulled the red shirt over his head and tucked it in.

'Any tie-ups, Eddie?'

'Here, son.'

Lennie tied the strips of bandage high under the knee, then

slipped the bows round to the back and turned the stocking tops into slim neat bands. They were nearly all ready now, stretching and bending, and breathing deeply with hands on hips. The toilets were in constant use and could only be flushed every two or three players. Clifford Anderson returned and closed the door. He spoke to Pete Fowler who moved over and stood with his shoulder to it.

'All ready, lads?'

Lennie hooked two fingers into the drum of vaseline and smeared a thick streak across his eyebrows. He flattened his hair with his hand and sat down. They were all ready now. 'Right, lads. Two points this afternoon will be a good start to the Christmas programme, and I reckon if you all buckle down and give your best, then we can leave this bad spell behind today. But there's only one way you'll do it, and that's by playing yourselves out. You've got to play as a team, all calling, all helping, all the time. I want one hundred per cent effort for ninety minutes. Now is that clear, lads?'

They nodded and murmured, leaning forward with their heads down looking at the floor.

'Right then. You don't need reminding that these are a hard side. They'll go mad for the first ten minutes, so mark tight and play safe till you're panned in. Laurie, stick close and get that arm up when you're jumping, he's a bugger for back heading. Stan, you know who you're playing against?' Stan nodded. 'Hit him early, well out and he'll not want to know. Plenty of calling, and don't swamp Lennie early on. Right, off you go then and enjoy yourselves.'

They shot up like jack-in-the-boxes and fell into line behind Chris. Clifford Anderson handed him a ball. Eddie gave balls to the next three in line. Fowler opened the door and Chris turned before walking into the corridor.

'All the best, Len.'

Eddie, and Max, and Clifford Anderson all touched him as he passed. The other players called to him from the line.

'All the best, Len.'

The corridor shook from the stamping of feet in the stands. The foyer was full of men in overcoats, standing in groups, smoking cigars and leaning on sticks. An inspector in a peaked cap called their attention to the team, and they turned and parted to let them pass.

'Best of luck, boys.'

Mr Learie nodded to Lennie. 'Best of luck, Hawk.'

Then they were in the tunnel running out to the pitch. The crowd directly opposite saw them first, and started the roar which spread round the ground like a forest fire.

Chris crossed the red ash and threw the ball down. The line broke up and the players spurted off at tangents. Lennie sprinted and jogged, sprinted and jogged into the penalty area. Les Adams rolled him a ball. He swung first time and kicked it high over the bar into the kop. Les Adams watched it and the crowd went Woooo! He belted the next one into the top corner. The other team ran out followed by the three officials. The referee carried a shiny orange ball like a Belisha beacon. He placed it on the centre spot and whistled for the captains. Chris lost the toss and the teams changed ends. Lennie looked round the ground and up into the stands. It was a big crowd with no empty spaces at the terrace ends.

The Town inside forwards stood brooding over the ball like three witches. The referee looked at his watch, looked at his officials and blew his whistle. Bobby Prince rolled the ball to Lennie and ran off down the centre. Lennie waited for the rush of the opposing inside men, then back-heeled the ball and slipped between them like stepping through a swinging door. The ball was kicked down the field and the centre half jumped and headed it clear. The crowd roared and settled.

Play was too fast, and both teams tackled too swiftly and often for any pattern or rhythm to be established. Lennie clapped his hands and Chris pushed the ball. He was flat on his face when it reached him. The referee whistled and the opposing right half appealed against the decision with his arms out like an angler. The referee shooed him away and Chris placed the ball for the free kick.

'Push it short, Chris.'

'Get up t'field, Len.'

'Go on, push it short.'

Chris tapped the ball forward, and Lennie dribbled it straight at the right half who had only retreated the necessary ten yards. He kicked it too far in front and the crowd groaned as the right half gained possession. Lennie spurted into the tackle. His foot went over the ball and his fist swung on the blind side of the referee. The right half toppled backwards, holding his stomach as though he had been shot. Lennie retrieved the ball, swerved past a defender and cracked a long, high pass diagonally across the field into the corner. Geordie ran after it, and the full back was back-pedalling so fast that he over-balanced flat on his arse. The crowd screamed. Geordie caught the ball near the corner flag, steadied himself and centred. The ball swooped down into the penalty area as Lennie ran in to meet it. He flicked his head down to the left and the ball bounced over the goal line near the post.

'G-O-A-L'

The roar exploded and mushroomed from the ground. Lennie spun round and raised his right arm. Geordie ran in and jumped on his back, and he was smothered under a welter of congratulations. They ran back to their positions as the goalkeeper booted the ball back to the centre, and Lennie trotted past the injured right half who was on the ground receiving treatment from two trainers in tracksuits. He stopped and looked in. 'All right?'

'Piss off! You dirty, fouling bastard.'

He jumped back shielding his face with his hands, as though being overtaken by an avalanche. The crowd laughed out and Mr Hawk stopped blowing his nose and wiping his eyes to look what they were laughing at.

The game restarted and the Town immediately established themselves. Lennie began to dominate play, and his fluid change of pace and direction were continually taking him past his half back. With Chris driving hard from behind, the whole team was functioning better than it had done for months. They threatened to score each time they crossed the half-way line and the crowd shouted for another goal before half-time.

The ball was running out of play. Lennie sprinted and caught it deep in his own half, facing his own goal. The right winger crowded his back and tried to hook it away from his feet. The other Town players were covered. The touchline was a foot away and the crowd over the wall called their advice.

'Hit it out.'

'Over t'stands'

Lennie flicked the ball up, bounced it on his thigh, and fell backwards scissoring his legs. The wingman turned his back instinctively, and the ball bulleted over his head, back over the halfway line to Bobby Prince. He slipped and lost possession. The ball was transferred back into the Town's penalty area. The crowd called a warning but the defence was completely off balance and the centre forward had time to run the ball forward before shooting it along the ground into the net. The players looked at Lennie as they lined up in silence.

In the remaining minutes to half time the Town went to pieces. Their confidence and rhythm flew, and the crowd cheered loudly when the referee blew his whistle and the players began to walk off the field.

They clattered into the dressing-room sweating and looking worried. Eddie was pouring tea into thick white cups. They carried their cups to their places and sat down. Clifford Anderson walked in and closed the door.

'Well played, lads, keep it up!'

He crouched down to speak to Chris. Eddie poured himself a cup of tea and had a sip before replacing the jug on to the tin tray.

'Everybody all right?'

'Have a look at this, Eddie.'

Eddie pulled off a wad of cotton wool and went to have a look at the muddy cut on Geordie's knee. Lennie put his empty cup on the bench and reached to the table for a towel. He leaned back and wiped his face, leaving a greasy stain on the coloured bands. Clifford Anderson pressed down on Chris's knee to push himself up.

'Right lads; we can get six today against this lot, if you'll just relax and play football. You looked like world beaters for twenty minutes and then what happens? You make one mistake and you go to pieces! Now get a grip and stop worrying and let's have them points. Keep it up, Len. Let's have some more. Everybody happy?

'Right then. Get out there and let's have 'em.'

The bell rang high up on the wall and they all stood up. Chris tucked his shirt in and turned to the line.

'Come on then, lads.'

The game restarted with a rush. The Town quickly found their rhythm and began to move forward like waves running before a wind. Lennie and Chris emerged as the dominant figures. Lennie was dominating the attack, Chris the defence. By linking the two in midfield, they were controlling the game. But they could not score. The away team packed their defence and settled down for a siege. The crowd became impatient, and their solid roar of encouragement faded to individual moans.

'Stop mucking about.'

'Give it some boot.'

The Town attacks became frenzied, but they could not score. It was like shooting against a brick wall. They lost spirit, and their opponents began to come away with the ball and look dangerous.

Chris intercepted a pass and dribbled the ball out of the penalty area. Lennie was marked on the halfway line but he still called for it. He received it, and was spinning for goal three yards away before his shadow could check his tackle and turn in pursuit. He covered the open ground swiftly as the full backs started to swing across. The centre half crouched for the tackle. Lennie chipped the ball over his head and sprinted past. The goalkeeper raced out for the ball and the full backs closed in fast. Lennie reached the bouncing ball first and lobbed it over the goalkeeper's head, then ran round him. The full backs converged on the goalkeeper and the three of them turned and watched Lennie dribble the ball over the goal line and leave it in the net.

'G-O-A-L'

Everyone in the stand was on their feet, and men on the terraces tried to lift their arms from the crush, to wave them, and slap each other's backs.

It was easy then for the Town, their confidence returned. Bobby Prince headed in a centre from Lennie five minutes before time, and Lennie hit the bar and the goalkeeper's chest with two long-range wallopers. For the first time since the opening matches of the season there was no movement to the exits until the referee blew his whistle. The crowd gave the Town a big hand as they left the field, and the applause increased when Lennie crossed the red ash to the tunnel. He looked up and saw his dad waving. He smiled and raised his right arm. The crowd thought it was for them and gave him an extra cheer.

They slammed into the dressing-room shouting and laughing. Eddie was pouring tea. Lennie carried a cup to his place and sat down. Chris walked across to him.

'Good game, Len.'

'Ta.'

'I hope it's going to be regular now.'

Lennie sipped his tea.

'Any chance?'

'I don't know yet. I'll have to wait till I get back to school and see what happens.'

'You're wasting your time at school, lad.'

Lennie looked up at him.

'You're wasting your time. I've been in this game for ten years now, and I've played for England and I've seen some good players. But I'll tell you what; you're going to beat 'em all.'

He walked away and peeled off his shirt. It clung tight in damp folds as he pulled, and his body steamed when he got it off. Lennie took his boots off and unwound the mud from round the studs. Clifford Anderson came over and gave him a hug.

'Marvellous, son! I was proud of you today.'

'Thank you.'

'Tired?'

'Buggered.'

'Go and get in that bath then.'

He washed quickly, then climbed out of the crowded bath and felt at the showers.

'What's up, Len, is she waiting for thi?'

'I didn't know Len had got woman trouble.'

'That's no trouble who he's going out with.'

'I wish I was in that kind of trouble.'

'He'll soon be the only player director in football.'

'He'll be able to come from the Board meetings then and tell us what they're saying about us all.'

Lennie stepped from under the shower and swept sprays of water from his arms and legs with his flat hands.

'My dad's waiting for me outside.'

'Hear that! His dad's waiting for him outside.'

'Come and pull this one, Len.'

'It gets pulled enough without asking him.'

'Bollocks, Armstrong! At least I've got summat worth pulling.'

Lennie grinned and walked into the dressing-room. Eddie told him to turn round while he dried his back. He dressed and walked down to the manager's office. Clifford Anderson handed him a sealed brown envelope which he placed in his coat pocket.

'See you Tuesday, then, son.'

'Right.'

'And if anybody else comes to see you tell them it's illegal to approach schoolboys.'

He was surrounded by autograph hunters before the swing door had banged behind him.

'He's here.'

'It's Lennie Hawk.'

Mr Hawk leaned back against the wall. Lennie signed his name across coloured pages, across his name in the programme, and across his face in newspaper cuttings. He took a book from a boy wearing a blue cap with a castle on the badge.

'Hey, up, Tommy lad, couldn't it wait till after t'holidays?'

The boy blushed and backed away with his book. When he had signed them all, Mr Hawk pushed himself off the wall, and they walked away, along the asphalt between the back of the main stand and the line of players' and officials' cars.

'Len!'

They both looked round. Jane was running towards them. Her hair swished across her shoulders in time to the bounce of her breasts; and on every stride her coat split open to the belt, showing her thighs pushing tight inside the skirt. She slowed, and walked the last few paces shaking her hair back into place.

'Wait for me.'

Lennie watched the rise and fall of her breasts under the mingled tweed.

'I thought you'd have gone.'

'We're still waiting for father.'

'Enjoy it?'

'You were marvellous, Len, everybody says so.'

Mr Hawk looked from one to the other smiling.

'Jane, this is my dad.'

'Hello.'

He enclosed her hand in his big white paw. Blue mining scars mottled the hairy back and knuckles.

'Hello, love.'

'Wasn't he super, Mr Hawk?'

'Not bad for a learner.'

'A learner! Daddy says he played like a veteran.'

'But my daddy knows a bit more about football than your daddy.'

He grinned and Mr Hawk chuckled. Jane looked from one to the other.

'Do you know, he's always making fun of me, Mr Hawk.'

'Don't worry, love, he's always making fun of everybody.'

'Len, come and meet mother.'

Lennie looked over her shoulder at the group moving across the asphalt to the cars.

'I can't, we've to go, haven't we, dad?'

'Nay, don't bring me into it.'

'O come on, I said you would.'

She grabbed his sleeve and tried to pull it like a dog with a slipper. Lennie pulled back like the foot inside it. He brushed the sleeve with his flat hand.

'Don't you know this is a forty guinea coat you're molesting? Best Crombie from Austin Reeds.'

'Come on, Len.'

'Go on, and I'll see thi at home.'

'See me nowhere! You're coming as well.'

'It's thee they want to see, not me.'

'We're both going home then.'

'Of course, you as well, Mr Hawk.'

They walked back along the asphalt. The four people standing before the row of cars stopped talking, and fanned out to watch them approach.

'Mother, I'd like you to meet Len.'

Lennie shook her hand.

'Hello.'

'So this is the young man I've heard so much about.'

'And this is Len's father.'

She smiled and shook hands.

'This is Mrs Rowley, and these are my brothers, Edmund and Charles.'

'Howdo.'

'I just had to congratulate you about the game. I thought it was so exciting.'

'He plays almost as well as he dances.'

Lennie looked at Mrs Rowley.

'Did you enjoy it, Mrs Rowley?'

'I wouldn't have missed it for the world.'

'I don't suppose Mr Rowley's come?'

'He's away for the week-end on a Youth Conference. Not that he would have come anyway.'

'I didn't get you that ticket, did I?'

'You remembered then.'

'Not till just now.'

'Still, you can't expect stars to cater for every whim of their fans, can you?'

'Stop it, Claire! You're making the boy blush, isn't she, Mr Hawk?'

'That'll be the day.'

'What do you mean?'

'When anybody makes him blush.'

They all laughed and looked at Lennie.

'What did you think of him today?'

Mr Hawk looked down and shuffled his feet. Then he looked up.

'Well, it's like this, Mrs Leary. I was pleased but I wasn't right surprised. You see, he's always had it in him, our Len, it was just a matter of time before it came out.'

'Well! Now there's an expert's opinion if ever I heard one.'

A door banged at the back of the stand and they all turned. Mr Leary strode quickly across the asphalt. He nodded at Lennie.

84

'Well played, young man. Ready, ladies?'

He walked through the group and unlocked the door of a grey Bentley.

'Well, cheerio, Len.'

'Ta-ra, Mrs Leary. Ta-ra, Mrs Rowley.'

'I say, Gwen, why not invite Jane and Len out for a drink tonight and we'll have a little celebration?'

Mrs Leary was halfway into the car. She backed out again and looked at her husband holding the back door open.

'That's a good idea, Claire. What about it David?'

'I expect they've made other arrangements.'

'I've arranged to see my mates.'

'There; what did I tell you? Come along, ladies.'

Mrs Leary dropped her head and stepped into the car. Mrs Rowley stayed on the asphalt. 'What a pity. Can't you persuade him, Jane?'

'It'll be a change, Len.'

'I'll see you, and we'll decide then.'

'Do your best, Jane.'

Mrs Rowley climbed into the back seat. Mr Leary slammed the door. Jane stooped into the mini with her brothers. The engines revved and the headlights poked out into the dusk. Lennie and his dad walked away along the car park.

'Well?'

'Well what?'

'How did I play?'

They turned into the main road. The two cars nosed out behind them and swept away in the other direction.

'Tha played a blinder.'

Mrs Hawk started talking as soon as they walked through the kitchen door.

'You're late, aren't you? Have you walked it? You won then? You ought to have heard that man on Sports Report. I bet your tea's ruined. Scored two goals, didn't you? I'd forgotten all about it till Mrs Jackson knocked on t'wall. Did you see their Alf at t'match? Mend t'fire, Arthur. Watch that plate, Len, it's red hot. Did you get your money today?'

She stood at the side of the table waiting. Lennie didn't look up from his plate, so she looked at Mr Hawk. He didn't look up either.

'Where you going tonight, Len?'

'Out.'

'He's celebrating wi' t'Leary's and t'party.'

'He's not.'

'He is.'

'How do you know?'

'I met 'em outside t'ground.'

'And you with your pit cap on! What they like?'

'How do I know? I only saw 'em for a minute.'

'What did they have to say?'

'Nowt much. They just congratulated our Len, that's all.'

'Jane there?'

' 'Course she was.'

'Nice lass?'

'Seems to be.'

'What's her mother like, smart?'

'I suppose she is.'

'I say, fancy meeting them. And where you going tonight then, Len?'

'I don't know as I'm going anywhere yet. I'm seeing Frank and Bill first.'

'You want to go if they've invited you.'

'How do you know what I want to do?'

'It's only manners.'

'I'll go if I want to go.'

'And what about Jane?'

'What about her?'

'She'll feel awful.'

'How do you know?'

'O shut up, Len. If you can't talk sense, don't talk at all.'

'I'll bring 'em down t'club to see you.'

'You've no need to bother, embarrassing everybody.'

'Who's on tonight dad?'

'Tommy and Freda Gaunt, lovely singers.'

He put his coat on and looked through the mirror.

'Have you got a clean hanky?'

He felt in his pockets and brought out the brown envelope.

'There's my money here.'

He gave it to his mother.

'How much?'

'Ten pounds, I suppose.'

'Haven't you opened it?'

'I forgot all about it.'

She slit the flap with her fingers and looked inside before taking out ten new notes.

'I say, isn't it grand? How much do you want?'

'Gimme ten bob, I've got a bit of silver in my pocket.'

'Oo, you want to take more than that if you're going out with Jane's mother and dad. We don't want 'em to think we haven't got owt.'

'Oo no, Mam, we don't want 'em thinking that.'

'You can always bring it back if you don't spend it.'

'I can't, you know I always throw it in t'bin if I've owt left.'

'O get out, you clever devil.'

'Let's have some money then.'

She gave him two pounds.

'Is that enough?'

'You'll have to watch her tonight, Dad, now that she's got a bit of money in her pocket.'

'Ar, tha can bet she'll be making that whisky and orange crack.'

'Go on with you. And don't you be showing yourself up.'

He stood in front of the Town Hall watching the approaching cars. He looked up at the clock, but had to cross the road to see the time. Jane drew up and hooted twice. Lennie ran back across the road and whipped into the car.

'Anchor, and don't spare the donkeys.'

'I thought we were going out with mother and father?'

'Do you want to?'

'Well, they did invite us.'

'I know, but do you want to?'

'They're looking forward to it.'

'Your dad wasn't so keen.'

'Daddy's always like that.'

'Where they going, anyway?'

'The Queen's Head.'

'My favourite rendezvous.'

'O shut up.'

She accelerated away from the kerb without looking back. Lennie was pushed back into his seat and a car squealed behind. He looked at her from the sides of his eyes.

'Hey up, we haven't made a suicide pact, you know.'

'You're like a big baby wanting your own way.'

'We can go up after, can't we?'

'You don't know what you want, that's your trouble.'

He put his arm round her and leaned across with his lips pouted and eyes closed.

'Yes I do darling, I want you.'

She jerked her head away and watched the road like somebody wry-necked.

'Are you trying to get us both killed?'

'Anything, darling, as long as it's together.'

'You fool.'

He stood just inside the taproom door and looked round. He spoke to Jane then let the door go and walked to the bar.

'Lads been in, Stan?'

'They're in t'best room.'

'What's up, have you got a dart board in there now?'

'They've got a woman apiece.'

'Who are they?'

'I don't know their names, they've been in here a few times. I hear tha had a good un today.'

'Fair.'

'What you drinking?'

He nodded at Lennie and looked at Jane standing by the door.

'Pint and a glass please. We'll have it through there.'

Lennie pointed over the landlord's shoulder to the big square hatch at the other side of the bar. Two men were looking through, talking and glancing at him.

Lennie opened the door for Jane, and they crossed the draughty hallway to the lounge door directly opposite. The bench round the wall was full and most of the chairs were occupied. Lennie fetched the drinks. As they passed between the tables people stared and leaned across to each other. Frank stood up and blew a fanfare up a rolled newspaper.

'Ta, ta tar!'

The two girls at the table giggled. Jane looked embarrassed. Lennie put the glasses down and found two chairs.

'Can tha remember Irene and Sylvia, Len?'

'You were in t'taproom that night we went up to t'school dance, weren't you?'

'And you were rude to us.'

'Not to both of you – just you.'

'Well, to me then.'

'What you come in here for, Frank?'

Frank looked round as though a blindfold had just been removed from his eyes. 'It's more comfortable, I suppose. We never thought about it, did we, Bill?'

'Taproom's all right for darts, but it's not sort a place tha takes a bird on Saturday night is it, Len?'

Jane looked at Lennie. He bowed his head and placed his hand on his heart, 'Et tu, Bill?'

Sylvia giggled and nudged Irene.

'What's he on about?'

'I'm on about Julius Caesar, love. You know, that story where all his mates creep up and stab him to death. Lovely story. There's blood everywhere.'

'Aren't you funny?'

Jane nudged him with her knee. Frank and Bill had a drink.

'Tha played well today, Len. Didn't he, Bill?'

'Not half. Seen t'Pink?'

He unrolled the newspaper like a scroll. Across the top it said, GREAT TOWN WIN and underneath, HAWK STRIKES TWICE. They all read the headlines and looked at Lennie. He didn't say anything so Bill rolled it up again and dropped it down the side of his chair. Frank flicked his head at Sylvia and Irene.

'Do you know Sylvia and Irene, Jane? They work for your dad.'

'Do you really? No, I can't say I recognize you.'

'We didn't think you would.'

'Mind you, the mill's a big place, isn't it?'

'We'll have to watch what we're saying tonight, Irene, else there'll be us cards waiting for us on Monday morning!'

They giggled and tasted their Babychams.

'What do you do there?'

'We work in t'warehouse, amongst t'bales, don't we, Irene?'

They giggled again.

'Just up your street that, isn't it, working in t'whorehouse?'

Bill coughed. The two girls looked at Lennie and clicked their tongues at each other.

'I say!'

'Do you like it, working at the mill?'

'It's a job, isn't it?'

'They say Father's terrible to work for.'

'We don't see much of him. But everybody's scared stiff when he comes round. Aren't they, Sylvia?'

'I say, Irene, can you remember that time when he caught that lass smoking behind them bales?'

Irene remembered and laughed out.

'She must have been crackers. She was standing there like, watching t'front door and having a quick drag, when he creeps in through t'back with old Thompson.' Irene doubled up and her nose nearly stuck on the stick in her glass. 'It was just like a pantomime, you know, when a wolf or summat's creeping up, and t'audience's trying to warn t'hero. Everybody started whistling and coughing and humming and singing.'

Irene straightened up, laughing and talking: 'And she didn't take a ha'peth a notice, she just stood there watching t'front door. Can you remember her face, Sylvia, when Leary tapped her on t'shoulder?'

Sylvia lifted her face and laughed at the ceiling.

'She went as white as a sheet, then as red as a beetroot.'

'She nearly swallowed that fag!'

Sylvia sat up straight and wagged her head with her chin tucked in.

'"Go and collect your cards," he said.'

'She never moved a muscle, did she?'

'"Go on! This minute."'

'She was petrified.'

'"You know the regulations! You can read, can't you?"'

' "I'm sorry, Mr Leary." '

' "Why do you think these notices are plastered all over the walls, to make the place look pretty?" '

'Then he turned on old Thompson.'

'Poor old sod, he thought he'd had it an' all.'

' "And if this is what happens every time you leave the building, Thompson!" '

' "It's t'first time, Mr Leary." '

' "Yes, and it had better be the last!" Then he stormed out and banged t'door behind him.'

'This lass started crying. What did they call her – Elsie?'

'She works at Bexley's now, you know. I saw her t'other week, she says it's a lot better.'

'Everybody crowded round her. It was a right carry-on, wasn't it?'

'Nobody's smoked in there since though, have they?'

Frank stood up.

'Pint, Len?'

Lennie finished his pint and gave him the glass. Frank asked round and went to the bar.

'Fancy being sacked for a little thing like smoking.'

'I felt ever so sorry for her, didn't you, Sylvia?'

'Smoking isn't a little thing down at the mill.'

'Well, you're bound to be on your dad's side, aren't you?'

'I think a warning'd have been enough, don't thar, Len?'

'No, would it buggery.'

'Trust him to side with her, Irene.'

'There isn't any sides. He runs a paper mill and to stop it being burned down he puts notices up about smoking. This lass don't care a bugger 'cos it's not her mill, so she smokes. What does she expect?'

'I know, but a little thing like . . .'

'You know nothing! You'd have done t'smack same thing in them circumstances.'

Frank returned with a tray of drinks. He waited for Bill to clear the empty glasses from the centre of the table, then he put the tray down in the space.

'It's worse than being on t'kop up there.'

They all went quiet and watched him space the glasses

round the table like someone sharing loot. Then he took the tray back. Lennie leaned across and picked up Sylvia's glass. She grabbed his wrist.

'Hey, that's mine.'

'See what I mean? Hey, that's mine.'

He put it down. When it touched the table she let go of his wrist.

'And what if I'd drunk it?'

'You'd have bought me another.'

'What if I'd no money?'

'I'd have fetched landlord and had you thrown out.'

'You're all t'bloody same, aren't you? Whether it's a paper mill or a rotten glass of Babycham!'

'Hey up, steady on, Len!'

People were turning from other tables. Frank returned from the bar.

'It's t'same at t'pit. There's more safety regulations stuck up and down.'

'That's because you don't take any notice of 'em.'

Lennie started to drink his pint. Frank opened his mouth to say something, but watched Lennie drinking instead. He emptied his glass and banged it down.

'I'm off. Coming?'

'I thought tha wa' coming to t'Mecca?'

'See you.'

He walked away. Jane stood up and played the piano on the back of her chair.

'Good night.'

'What's up with him then, Bill?'

'Nay.'

'What's tha been saying to him?'

'I haven't been saying owt.'

'Good riddance, I say.'

'And me.'

'O shut it, you two.'

'And I thought we were going to have a right time tonight.'

'Little tin god.'

'Be quiet, you don't even know him.'

'I don't want to, either.'

Frank and Bill sat and stared into their pints. Sylvia and Irene talked about Lennie and Jane.

They drove up the hill out of town. Behind them the lights prickled and popped in clusters. At the top of the hill the sky was big and open, and the stars twinkled like holes in a blackout. Lennie looked out of the window.

'What's the matter, Len? – Len?'

'I'm fed up.'

'About what happened back there?'

'I suppose so.'

'I thought Frank and Bill were your best friends?'

'They are.'

'No one would have guessed.'

'We're always on at each other like that.'

'Are you?'

''Course we are, you don't know us.'

'And I suppose it always upsets you like this.'

'Be quiet a minute, Jane.'

The car accelerated down the hill, between detached houses built at the front of fields.

'We'd better not go to the Queen's then if you're feeling like that.'

'Do you know, it never used to be like that at one time.'

'You're growing away from them.'

'We used to have some smashing times, us three, mucking about and chasing birds.'

'Is that what you want now?'

'I envy 'em sometimes, they're satisfied with what they've got.'

'And what about the other times? The times when you don't envy them.'

'I don't know.'

'What do you want to do, Len?'

They drove over the quiet road.

'I'll tell you one thing I'd like to do. I'd like to play in a match with the best footballers of all time. I lay in bed sometimes and think about it. There'd be some old timers playing, like James and Gallagher that I've heard my dad talk about,

93

and Pelé and Law. And me at inside left. And we'd play with a golden ball.'

'What do you mean a golden ball?'

'Like the sun when it's going down in a clear sky, all golden and glowing.'

'I know, but why?'

'I don't know, it'd just have to be gold in a match like that.'

'It's only a dream though, Len.'

'I did dream about it once. I dreamt that I caught this ball a pearler, and when it hit the net it went straight through and out of the ground. It carried straight on up into the sky, and as it rose it grew bigger and bigger till it was just like a second sun in the sky. And when you looked up you couldn't tell which was which, there were just two golden balls, shining side by side.'

'That's strange, Len.'

'And do you know, every time I score I think of that ball when it went straight through the net.'

The road cut through a wood. The trees were like the walls of a corridor. The headlights shone yellow in the black, and above the corridor the sky was navy blue.

'Stop here, Jane.'

'Why?'

'Go on, stop.'

She slowed, and turned into an open gateway leading through the trees. He put one arm down over her shoulder and felt her breasts through the coat. He unfastened a button and slipped the other hand inside. She snuggled down to him.

'You've got lovely breasts. Soft yet firm, as they say in Hank Janson.'

'I can feel your heart beating.'

He kissed her mouth, and his hand felt over her body, lightly and quickly like a blind man, down her back and thigh to the stockings above the knee. She scuffled her legs and the nylon scraped.

'No, Len.'

She clamped down on his hand. He kissed her hard, but she arched her back like someone in a dentist's chair, and shook her face free.

'No!'

He took his hand away and faced the front.

'What's the matter?'

'Nothing. I don't want you to, that's all.'

'Why not? I thought you liked me.'

'I do like you, you know I like you.'

'What's the matter, then?'

'Nothing! I don't want you ... O Len!'

She sobbed his name, and turned to the window crying into her fist.

'What are you crying for? I haven't done anything yet.'

'I know you haven't. Don't think I'm awful. I'm very sorry.'

He put his arm round her and pulled her close, patting and rocking her like a baby. She sobbed on his chest.

'Shsh, don't get upset.'

'It's not that I don't want you to.'

'Let it drop now, it doesn't matter.'

'I want to, Len, I really do, but not in here, not first time. I want it properly, not hunched up in this tin can.'

'I'm sorry, love, you just got me worked up, that's all. You look lovely tonight and what with that couple of pints inside me, and you sat there flashing your legs ...'

'I didn't mean to.'

'Especially legs like yours.'

He slotted his flat hand between her knees and rubbed her thighs. Jane sat up and scrambled in her bag.

'I bet I look a complete wreck.'

'You couldn't look a wreck if you tried.'

She sniffed at her handkerchief and tossed her hair back over her shoulders.

'Do you always talk like that when you're trying to make love to a girl?'

'I've never tried before.'

'Not much you haven't. I've heard about you up the school field.'

'They're a right pair of touts, aren't they, your brothers? You want to watch 'em, you know, they probably creep about your house sniffing at your sheets and watching you through the bathroom keyhole.'

'Don't be vulgar.'

'Not that I blame 'em, mind.'

'Come on, let's go.'

She backed the car out and they left the wood.

Tilted arc lights shone up from the car park on to the ivy at the front of the Queen's Head.

'There are more cars here than there were at the Dale this afternoon. I'll bet there are more folks inside as well.'

'There's Daddy's car.'

'And there's Daddy.'

'If you're going to be sarcastic all night I'm not going in.'

''Course I'm not. I'll just fix my tash on and pop a couple of marbles in my mouth and I'll be as right as rain.'

'Don't be silly.'

'Do you think they'll let me in without a tie on?'

'O shut up.'

She got out and banged the door. Lennie waited for her to come round the bonnet, then they walked across the car park.

'They might not, they don't at the Mecca. I can remember a gang of us going when I was about fifteen and they wouldn't let Frank in because he'd no tie on. We had a right argument, but they wouldn't let him in; so we all trooped out and nipped up Chase Walk and stopped a bloke who was coming down. Frank asked him to sell him his tie, but he wasn't having any so we got him up against a wall and threatened him. He got a bit frightened then and started to shout so Frank clobbered him and whipped his tie and we all ran away and left him lying at the bottom of this wall. Frank put this tie on, I can remember it now, it looked terrible, red and green stripes over a mauve shirt. Anyway, that was it, he'd got a tie on, so they let him in.'

'That's awful, Len!'

'I know it is.'

Heads turned when they walked in, and the loose circles of people went quiet in turn as they worked their way round the rims to the other side of the room.

'They ought to provide snow-shoes to get across this carpet.'

'There they are, look.'

Mrs Rowley and Mrs Leary were sitting behind a copper-topped table. Behind them the wings of a stone fireplace spanned the width of the room. Logs were burning in the square hole in the middle. Mr Leary was leaning on the wooden mantelpiece talking to a man with a tash. He nodded at Lennie, then turned away. Mrs Rowley smiled and leaned back in her chair.

'You made it then?'

'No, it's my ghost you can see.'

Mrs Rowley leaned forward and cocked her head.

'Sorry I didn't ...'

'He says he's glad we came.'

Mr Leary snapped his fingers at a waiter in a white jacket. He veered across and stood at the table with a tray under his arm like a loose-leaf file.

'Hey up, Scotty! I didn't know thar worked here.'

'Tha does now.'

'What would you like to drink, Len?'

'Pint, please.'

'What about a short? Mind you, the club chairman shouldn't be encouraging his players to drink at all.'

'No, I'll have a pint.'

'Fruit juice, Jane? Are you all right, ladies?'

Mr Leary turned back to the man with the tash, and Scotty took the order.

'What do you think of our local, now that it's been modernized, Len?'

'Don't ask him, Mother.'

'Why, doesn't he like it?'

Lennie made a hole with his finger and thumb and showed it to Mrs Leary.

'Very chick.'

'Don't take any notice of him, he's just trying to be awkward.'

'I thought you young people liked modern décor.'

Lennie looked round, nodding his head like an expert.

'Very nice.'

'What about the ceiling? It's beautiful wood.'

'Marvellous! It must have cost 'em a fortune in orange boxes to nail that lot together.'

'You won't get any sense out of him, Mother.'

Scotty weaved across the room balancing the tray on the fingers of one hand. He put the glasses on the table, Mr Leary paid him and shook his head at the change.

'Are thar having one, Scotty?'

'I'll have a double scotch.'

'That's what thar thinks.'

'What's up? Tha can afford it now that tha moving wi' t'nobs, can't tha?'

'Does tha want that tray ramming down thi throat?'

Lennie stepped forward and Scotty backed away, sneering into the crowd.

'Who's that, Len?'

'Scotty, he used to live down our street. You know that gang I was telling you about? Well he was one of them.'

He tasted his pint, then held the glass up for inspection.

'Not as good as the Anchor.'

'Even though it is the same brewery.'

'It must not be kept as well then.'

'No, of course not.'

A man and woman stood up and left. Jane moved one of the chairs to the side of her mother and Lennie sat down on the other, facing her. He lifted his glass and caught Mrs Rowley's eye down the side as he tilted it to his mouth. She smiled across at him. He put his glass down and looked down at her legs. They were crossed and showed her knee and thigh. Her hidden knee had pushed her calf round, and the veins under her stockings were like rivers on a map. He looked up and she was still smiling at him. They both had another drink. Lennie took the glass from his mouth, then changed his mind and finished the pint. He stood up.

'Anybody want another?'

Nobody spoke so he pushed his way through to the bar and had his glass refilled. He had a drink then started on the return journey. A man demonstrating how to head a football bumped him with his shoulder. Lennie jumped back on tiptoes holding the glass at arm's length. The beer swilled from side to side so he placed his hand on top like a lid, to save any from spilling.

'I say! I'm dreadfully sorry.'

'It's all right, there's none spilt.'

The man looked at Lennie as though he'd seen him before somewhere.

'Hey! you're Lennie Hawk, aren't you?'

He pulled Lennie into the circle before his audience.

'You'll never believe this, but here is the man himself. I've just been telling them about that header of yours this afternoon, it was a beauty.'

They all smiled at him.

'Celebrating the victory, eh, Len?'

They all laughed.

'Never touch the stuff.'

They all laughed again.

'Come now! It's nothing to be ashamed of. You deserve a drink after the way you played this afternoon.'

'Honest, I never touch the stuff, this is for my dad outside. He can't come in, you see, because he's crippled and he has to stop at the door in his invalid car. This'll warm him up a bit though, it gets cold, you know, sat around in car parks all along.'

They let him through. Mrs Rowley smiled when she saw him approaching with his head down, grinning at his beer.

'What's so funny?'

'Some folks up there.'

'You don't like it here, do you?'

'It's a load of cobblers, all this standing about trying to impress.'

'Do you know what Alfred says about this place? He says the people in here are like industrial diamonds. They glitter, but they scratch.'

'He's not far wrong either.'

'He showed me that essay of yours on Catherine the Great, it was very good.'

'She wasn't a bad old bird, Catherine.'

'He thinks a lot about your work, you know.'

'He doesn't reckon much to me though.'

'You'd be surprised. He thinks you're wasting your talent, that's all. He says you've got too much talent.'

'He's a good bloke, Mr Rowley.'

Mrs Rowley laughed.

'You should know, you probably see more of him than me. Do you know there are some days when I only see him at breakfast? He's so busy that he doesn't come in for tea and I'm often in bed when he arrives home at night. It's work, work, work. There's his drama group, and educational meetings and school committees, he never stops. He may as well be in lodgings.'

'He wants to watch his pockets. I know plenty of blokes who'd jump at the chance of keeping you company for an hour or two.'

'You'll have to tell me their names, it gets terribly lonely at times.'

'Same again, Len?'

'Yes, I'll try another, Mr Leary.'

Jane watched Lennie empty his glass. Mrs Leary whispered into Mrs Rowley's ear and they stood up and excused themselves.

'You're drinking quickly, aren't you, Len?'

'You never know, they might run out.'

'Beer's fattening, you know, it contains a lot of calories.'

'I know it does, two hundred to a pint. It all depends on how much energy you use up though. If your energy output exceeds your calorie input then you lose weight. If your calorie input exceeds your energy output then you get fat. If they are equal your weight remains constant depending on body type and ...'

'You're drunk, Len.'

'I'm dying for a slash as well. You've got to hang on as long as you can though, because once you've been you're never away.'

'I don't want to know about it.'

'I think I'll write a book about it. The Psychology of Pissing by L. Hawk, Doctor of Pissology.'

'You're disgusting.'

'What you laughing for then? I'll have to go now though, or tie a knot in it.'

He left Jane sitting on her own behind the table. He pissed his initials on the wall then splattered a cork tip to shreds in the channel. Mr Leary came in and stood two stalls away, but he couldn't do anything until Lennie had zipped up and turned away. Lennie looked in the mirror and bared his teeth. His eyes looked back at him as though they had been in a sandstorm. Mr Leary finished and they walked back in to the room together.

'I bet you're cursing Jane for dragging you up here, aren't you?'

'Owt for a laugh.'

'Jane seems to be growing very fond of you.'

'Does she?'

'Don't you think you're both rather young, though, to be seeing each other so regularly?'

'What's age got to do with it?'

'What do your parents think about it?'

'I don't know, I've never asked them.'

'And what about the future? What about when you go to university?'

'I've not gone yet.'

Mr Leary lifted his glass by the bowl and the brandy slid up the side in a block.

'Are you serious about anything?'

'Not if I can help it.'

'I should hate to think you were leading Jane on.'

'Where to?'

'Now don't start getting clever with me.'

'I'm not, I just don't like being preached at, that's all.'

'I think I do have the right to know what's going on, you know. After all, I am Jane's father.'

'What's that got to do with it?'

'FOR GOD'S SAKE, TALK SOME SENSE!!'

Everything stopped round them. Mr Leary blushed as people turned and stared. Lennie had a quick drink but his laughter forced the beer through his lips in a foamy hiss. He swallowed the rest with a gulp and opened his mouth wide to laugh properly. Mr Leary's blush ripened to a glow. The people watching started to laugh at Lennie as though they were watching the laughing sailor outside the Fun House at Blackpool. Mrs Leary stood up and Jane shook Lennie's arm.

'Stop it, Len! People are looking.'

'Let 'em look.'

Mr Leary stood by him, seething. Lennie quietened down and everyone stopped laughing, and slowly turned away. He bobbed forward at a woman who was still staring.

'Bu!'

She looked away, embarrassed. Jane pulled Lennie's arm.

'I think we'd better go, Len.'

'Yes, I think he'd better. I've never been so embarrassed in all my life.'

'It was you who shouted, not me.'

'O, be quiet, Len, please.'

'Get your coat on, Jane, we're leaving.'

'I'm running Len home first, Daddy, it won't take me long.'

'You're coming home with us, now. A five mile walk might sober him up a bit.'

'Who's drunk?'

Mrs Rowley stood up and Mr Leary helped her on with her coat.

'I'll take Len in the mini if you like and Jane can go with you. It'll save you a trip into town afterwards.'

'Don't trouble yourself, Claire, he's not worth it.'

'It's no trouble.'

'It's more than he deserves! Ruining your evening like this.'

'I think you've taken the whole thing far too seriously, David. If you'd played as well as Len did this afternoon and then had a few drinks to celebrate, don't you think that you'd feel a little boisterous?'

'Boisterous! He's been downright insulting.'

'You what! I bet you insult folks every day at work, when you're as sober as a week of Sundays.'

'See what I mean? Good night, Claire.'

'But just because you're boss you think you've a right to.'

Mr Leary spun round and marched straight across the room.

Mrs Leary shrugged her mouth and shoulders and followed him. Jane watched them across the room as though they were a train she had to catch.

'You've done it now.'

'I haven't said owt yet.'

'JANE!'

'Coming! 'Bye, Len.'

'What about Christmas then?'

'I'll write. Daddy's furious.'

'O.K. Ta ra, love.'

She pecked his cheek and dashed away. Mrs Rowley tightened the belt of her coat.

'Are you ready, Len?'

'We don't have to go as well, do we?'

'Not if you don't want to.'

'Let's be off then. It's bad beer anyway.

'What time is it?'

'Have a look.'

She took her hand off the wheel and stretched it towards him. Her sleeve shortened and Lennie peered at her watch.

'Quarter to eleven. I'll just miss Sports Special.'

'Come home with me and watch it. I'll run you home afterwards.'

'Can I? We're on, you know.'

'What? Oh yes, I saw the cameras.'

Lennie looked out at the school as they topped the hill. It stood back from the road like a black screen against the clear sky. They passed it and ran down towards Town, then turned up Hillside Avenue. There was no one about, and most of the houses were dark behind the street lamps. Lennie got out and banged the door.

'Jesus! It's cold enough for a walking stick!'

'Quietly, Len.'

Mrs Rowley hurried down the path to the kitchen door at the side of the house. Lennie stood behind her and watched her unlock it. She closed the door quietly behind them and slipped the bolt.

'Central heating, eh?'

'Give me your coat. You can go and turn the television on while I make coffee.'

When she walked into the room Lennie was sitting on the carpet with his back to the settee.

'What's the matter, aren't our chairs good enough for you?'

'I always watch football like this, you feel closer to the game. It's like being in the trainer's box.'

Mrs Rowley sat on the settee beside his head, and put the tray down on the animal rug's back. Lennie glanced sideways at her knees.

'How do you expect me to watch football? Hey up, we're on ... that's what I look like from the stand, is it?'

Bobby Prince rolled the ball to Lennie and ran off down the centre. Lennie waited for the rush of the opposing inside men, then back-heeled the ball and slipped between them like stepping through a swinging door.

'See that?'

'Your coffee'll go cold.'

'I'll save it till half-time, I'll get stomach cramp if I drink it while I'm playing ... there's our first goal here, look ... Beauty! I knew I'd get to it ... Good ball, Chris. Just you watch us two once I've got settled in, we'll work wonders for that team ... this is where they score. Flashy bugger, straight over my head to their man, I watched this goal from off the floor. We were awful then ... It's a good job half-time's not as short as that ... look at me running my cobblers off! We couldn't score, could we? ... It's here, this is it! ...'

'Everybody went mad when you scored that one.'

The game was cut, and a man behind a desk stopped watching his monitor set when his own face flashed on it. He smiled and linked his fingers on the desk top.

'Well, that was the match I covered. Prince added a third goal towards the end to give the Town a convincing three one victory. As you saw on your screens two of the Town goals came from young Lennie Hawk, who on this showing looked a world beater. He had everything, ball control, speed, a good head, and a cannon of a shot, and in this only his second league game he absolutely dominated the proceedings. This boy is the most exciting player I've seen for years, and I'm going to stick my neck out right now and predict that his rise to the international scene will be the most sensational in football history! And now for our next match in today's league programme.'

'Good gracious! there's praise for you, Len.'

'I should think so, tip I gave him.'

'You're a lucky young devil, you know. You've got everything at your feet, haven't you?'

'Luck's nothing to do with it. It's just skill.'

'Do you know, I really envy you, Len.'

'I don't know what you've got to be envious about.'

'Don't you?'

'You want to think yourself lucky, there's plenty would in your shoes.'

'I'm not talking about money, Len. I'm talking about being bored and nothing happening to me, about things just going on and on and on.'

Lennie started to sing to the silver screen.

'Can't buy me lo-ve, no no no N O.'

'Don't make fun of me, Len.'

She put her hand on his shoulder. Lennie stopped singing, and glanced down at it as though it was a bird that had just landed.

'I'm not doing. I'm just singing.'

'You don't know what I'm talking about, do you?'

He watched the match on the screen and didn't answer.

'That's why I envy you because you're the sort who never will.'

She squeezed his shoulder.

'I wish I'd been Jane's age when I met you at the dance.'

'She wouldn't have got a look in.'

'That's a safe compliment. You never had to make the choice, did you?'

'You'll do for me as you are now.'

'Will I?'

She tightened her grip and Lennie looked round. She took her hand away from his shoulder and drew a pair of glasses round his eyes with her finger.

'You've got big eyes, like a bird.'

He climbed up on to her and threw a leg over, forcing it

down between her thighs. The footballers on the screen kicked the ball to each other and shot at the nets.

'Let's go to bed, Len.'

'In a minute.'

'No, now.'

'It's nice and warm here.'

'It's better in bed.'

'I've never been in bed with a woman; except my mother when I was little.'

'Quickly, Len, let's go upstairs.'

She pulled his arms away and pushed him off.

'Do you know, I bet my mother's not much older than you. But what a difference.'

He leaned forward and tried to put his hand up her skirt, but she spun away from it and walked out of the room.

'Turn the television off.'

Lennie crawled across the carpet to the set and watched a goalmouth scramble on all fours. A defender punched the ball from under the bar. Lennie sat back on his heels as the ball was placed on the spot.

'Len!'

The goalkeeper dived the wrong way and the ball passed over his feet into the net. Lennie turned it off and felt his way out of the room, and upstairs in the dark.

'Where are you?'

'In here.'

'I thought the war was over.'

'People can see shadows.'

Mrs Rowley moved in front of the window and pulled her underslip over her head. Lennie unhooked her bra, and put his arms round her and caught her breasts as they fell.

'Not in front of the window, Len, people have owl's eyes round here.'

'I wish I had.'

'Come on, quickly.'

Lennie got undressed and lay beside her on the bed.

'It's just like summer when you don't have to get in.'

He propped himself on one elbow and felt her body in the dark.

'Do you like me, Len? Tell me.'

'You're marvellous.'

She hitched up the bed and pushed hard against him. He fell on to his back and had to put his hand over the side to save himself from falling out. His face was smothered in breasts.

'Kiss them.'

He lifted them up to speak.

'They're big.'

'They're not firm any more.'

'They're lovely.'

'Only when I'm lying on my back.'

He let them flop back all over his face, and breathed in the pocket between.

'Come on Len, love me now.'

'Let me look at you first.'

She fell away and lay still.

'You might not like me.'

'Go on, let me.'

He felt back over his head and found the cord. Click. Mrs Rowley was lying tilted to the wall, with one knee raised. Lennie looked down her then smoothed his hands lightly over her breasts as though they might burst under pressure.

'You've got a body like Marilyn Monroe.'

She lay still and didn't answer. He gathered the flesh of her stomach into his hand and squeezed hard. She turned sharply towards him and straightened her leg.

'Don't! I know I'm fat.'

'You're not fat. There's plenty to go at, that's all.'

Now that she was facing him she looked at him.

'You've no fat at all, have you?'

She felt up his arm, then down the gully between the smooth packs of muscle, to the fern of fair fluff on his belly.

'It's big, Len.'

'I was first in the queue when they gave them out ... Hey! steady on, there's a thread on it if you want to take it off.'

'It makes me want to do that. I want it now, Len, I want it all.'

'I haven't got anything, you know.'

'Come on, never mind that.'

'That's all Mr Rowley's short of, being lumbered with Lennie's lad.'

'Come on, Len!'

She pulled him over and into her, and they closed together. She made a lot of noise and Lennie tried to kiss her quiet, but she fought free of his mouth and shouted as though he was hurting her. He worked hard and reached his climax quickly, then settled down on top of her like a dead weight. But she shook her head and bucked him back to life. He tried to withdraw but she held his arse down . . .

'No, Len, no, not yet.'

He came to her again, snuffling his face into the hot air at the side of her head, gagging himself with the pillow. She forced her head back, under the ridge of the bed head and bit into the wood until her adam's apple bobbed in her tight neck and forced up the shuddering sobs. Then she sagged, and lay still moaning softly like a baby. Lennie rolled off panting.

'Jesus, talk about extra time.'

She snuggled down under the wall of his back.

'You were wonderful Len, oh, I loved it.'

'Two games a day's too much for anybody.'

She giggled and peeped over his side like Chad.

'Tell me something.'

'What?'

'Am I as good as Jane?'

'I don't know, I've never made love to her.'

'Go on, tell me, Len.'

'I've told you, she won't let me.'

'Is that why you came home with me?'

'No, 'course it isn't.'

'Honest?'

'Honest.'

'Will you tell when you do?'

'Why do you want to know?'

'Will you?'

'She's never had it though.'

'Will you, Len?'

'As soon as I've chance.'

'No, tell me, I mean.'

He rolled over on to his stomach.

'I'm buggered.'

'Was I good for you?'

'Marvellous, just like Marilyn Monroe.'

'What do you mean?'

'Well, sometimes when I've been with girls I've imagined that it's Marilyn Monroe I've been loving and not them, and you were just like I used to imagine it.'

'Did you like her, Len?'

'I loved her. Did you see her in that picture when she was bouncing that little rubber ball with a bat, and her legs were all splayed and her arse filled the screen in that spotted frock? Jesus! It fair made you want to grab hold of it, a cheek in each hand like this.'

'Ow! That hurts.'

'I'm worn out.'

When he awoke it was black and warm, and a clock was ticking. Mrs Rowley was snuggled up to his back, fitting round the curves and into the hollows. He lifted her arm carefully as though trying to pinch it, then rolled out from underneath, and crawled to the clock. Ten past two. He got dressed and folded the top sheet over her. She moaned and stirred. He slid his hand all the way down the banister and found his coat thrown over the knob at the bottom. Click, Bang. Out into the cold silver silence and up the path. He vaulted the gate, then collected all his loose change into one hand and ran all the way home.

When Lennie arrived the first morning after the holidays, the school was singing in assembly. The corridors were quiet and bare, and smelt of scrubbing. Leary was on late duty.

'Happy New Year, Hawk.'

'Arseholes, Leary.'

'So nice to hear those cultured tones again.'

'How's your Jane going on?'

'Very well, thank you. She had a very pleasant evening at the Young Farmers' New Year Dance on Saturday.'

'Young farmers! Young twats.'

'You've had it, Hawk, Father's determined.'

'He's a stupid bastard an' all.'

'What do you expect after that fiasco up at the Queen's, Welcome Home flags?'

'Fiasco my arse. I had a bit too much to drink, that's all.'

'And then you started insulting him.'

'He's no sense of humour, that's his trouble.'

'He was furious.'

'I suppose thar put a good word in for me.'

Leary grinned and turned to a clean page in the late book.

'Well, it's not a thought one relishes, is it, one's sister going out with you?'

'Well, one will have to get used to it, won't one.'

'I don't think so, Father's seen to that.'

'Has he? Just wait and see then.'

The hall doors flew open like saloon doors, and were fastened to the walls by the pressure of the packed mass disgorging into the corridor. Boys shouted 'up the Town' as they passed Lennie, then turned round and grinned at him as they walked along. Harry Andrews greeted him by jumping on his back.

'Hey, up, Len! Have a good Christmas?'

'Could have been better.'

'How could things be any better for you?'

'Tha'd better ask his delightful father.'

'Oh, I see. You're still courting then, are you?'

'Well, there's just been a temporary breakdown, that's all, Harry, but do not adjust your sets, normal service will be resumed as soon as possible.'

'I thought it'd have been a one a night job now. I've heard that's how you do your training, running away from your fans.'

'Nay, Harry, that wouldn't keep me very fit, they can't run very fast with their knickers down, you know.'

Leary walked away.

'Coming, Len?'

'I'm going to see t'old man first.'

'What about?'

'See if he'll let me off playing for t'school.'

'What if he don't let you? Will you leave?'

'I'll see what he says first. But I can't go back to school football now.'

'You've made a world of difference to the Town; in fact you looked international class on Saturday.'

'I should be showing summat now, that was my sixth game.'

'Six! You talk as though it's sixty.'

'It's enough.'

'That first goal was a beaut. How many's that now?'

'Nine.'

'Bloody hell, nine goals in six First Division games, and I bet Leary still put your name down in the late book.'

'Come in! – Hello, Hawk.'

'Can I have a word with you please?'

'Certainly, sit down.'

Doctor Bennet was sitting behind his desk with his back to the window. Lennie sat down facing him, in one of the armchairs by the fire.

'I thought perhaps we'd seen the last of you. Or is the Rolls outside and you've just come to pay us a farewell visit?'

'What do you mean?'

'You haven't turned professional then?'

'No.'

Doctor Bennet leaned forward over his arms.

'Why, Hawk?'

Lennie laughed out. Doctor Bennet sat up and straightened his glasses.

'That wasn't meant as a joke.'

'You sound as though you want to get rid of me.'

'Not at all, but you puzzle me, that's all.'

'Why do I?'

'I came to see you play on Saturday.'

'Did you? You ought to have let me know, I could have got you a complimentary ticket.'

'I only decided on the spur of the moment. I met Mr Brook in town and he persuaded me to go along.'

'I didn't think you were interested in football.'

'I'm not, but I'd heard and read so much about you over Christmas that I just had to go and see for myself.'

'Did you enjoy it?'

'The experience, yes. The game, I can't say as I don't know enough about it. But it was quite obvious even to my ignorant eyes that you are an outstanding performer.'

'Thank you.'

'And I must admit that I felt a certain pride at seeing a boy from this school playing so well amongst all those men.'

Lennie smiled and inspected his hands.

'But then I thought, if the boy is so good, why doesn't he sign professional forms and make a living from the game? For surely that is one of the aims of life, to be able to earn money by doing what one enjoys.' Lennie made diamonds between his fingertips and lined them up straight. 'And judging by the energy you put into the game I would say that you certainly enjoy it.'

'I love it.'

'That's what I thought, but tell me something, Hawk.' He didn't speak again until Lennie looked up into his face. 'When you're playing at such great speed and under such continual pressure don't you tend to lose something? Isn't it comparable to spoiling a delicious dinner by having to bolt it down too quickly.'

'You're talking about luxuries, I'm talking about necessities.'

'You mean football's compulsive to you?'

'That's right.'

'Which amounts to the same as loving it I suppose. Now tell me something else. How long will it be before the young Saturday tiger stops returning to its cage on Monday mornings?'

'That's what I've come to see you about.'

'About leaving.'

'No, I want to be excused from playing for the school.'

'I see.'

Doctor Bennet leaned back and Lennie leaned forward, as though they were attached by a lead.

'And what if I say no?'

'I don't know, but I couldn't go back to playing school football now.'

'You're keen, aren't you, Hawk? Yes, that's the word for you, keen.'

Lennie looked up at him, then over his shoulder to the window. Snow was falling like slow rain, colourless against the grey sky. Flakes came to the panes, crisp, then melted and streamed down the glass in tears. The fire was an orange and black shell. The cup on the mantelpiece was polished shiny.

'Yes, I'll excuse you, Hawk.'

Lennie smiled and stood up.

'Thank you.'

'Did you think I would?'

'Yes.'

'Well, you'd no grounds for such optimism because I'm a firm believer in the principle of school first.'

'I know, but you're a fair man, you'll listen to folks.'

'This decision won't be very popular, it will cause controversy.'

'Decisions usually do.'

'There'll be the usual cries about precedents, etc., and I don't like to create dissension amongst the staff.'

'I'll be off then.'

'Right, Hawk, but take care, try not to let this football inter-fere with your studies too much.'

As soon as the door clicked shut behind him, the secretary bobbed round the half open door of her office.

'Phone, Len.'

'Hello ... yes ... Hello, Mr Anderson ... Yes, it's all right ... He's a good bloke ... What rumours? ... Oh that! It's nothing, we just had a few words that's all ... New Town Star in Drunken Brawl with Chairman – Daughter sent to convent.' He laughed down the phone.

'I'll be all right ... Yes, I'll remember ... What kind of experiment? ... O.K. ... See you tomorrow night then, ta ra.'

Lennie walked into the classroom. Everyone was lolling about, talking, waiting for Mr Rowley to arrive.

Leary looked up from his file and waited for Lennie to sit down.

'Will you be available on Saturday, Hawk?'

'I'll be available at Manchester, if tha wants to come and watch us.'

'You're not playing for the school any more, then?'

'Sorry, Leary, old love.'

'You don't think I'm disappointed, do you?'

'Not much, tha'll be down on thi knees at half-time chanting "Hawk! Hawk! Where art thou Hawk?"'

He knelt on his desk top, and prayed with his face raised to the celluloid shades. The girls giggled. Jennie smiled up at him from the desk in front. Lennie stood up then jumped down on her, screaming.

'He grabbed her by the throat! She screamed. He squeezed tighter and tighter and forced her down to the ground.'

'Len!'

'His face was a mask of desire, his eyes were blind with lust as he ripped the blouse from her throat and her breasts drooped bare to the knee caps. "Stop it I like it," she whispered. "I'll give you twenty-four hours to give over."'

'Stop it, Len! you fool.'

Lennie sat down, next to Harry and Jenny ruffled herself back to normal.

'Didn't you like that, then?'

'Charming! I love being raped.'

'They all do, if they can pick their own man. Have a nice Christmas?'

'Yes thanks.'

'Been working hard?'

'Not as hard as you. You've been receiving extra tuition, haven't you, at Rowley's?'

'Bloody hell! You can't move a muscle, can you?'

'Fancy you going for extra work.'

'If you must know, I've been shagging his wife.'

'O Len, you always finish up by being vulgar.'

'There's nowt vulgar about it, is there, Jenny?'

Tears softened her eyes, and she turned away and started to read her history book as though it was the most interesting book in the world.

'What have you been going to Rowley's for?'

'I've told thi.'

'I bet he's pleased, isn't he?'

'He reads to me while I'm on t'job.'

'Nowt like having jam on it, is there?'

'I don't know, I never bother when it's that week. Hey up, he's here, slim Jim!'

Mr Rowley appeared in the corridor. The top half of his body rocked from side to side, and he scowled in through the windows all the way to the door. The class scraped their chairs round and opened their books. He swung his briefcase on to the desk while he was still walking, then stepped down the aisle and turned on Lennie.

'Happy New Year, Hawk! It hasn't taken you long to make the fur fly on this fine January morning.'

'You've heard then.'

'Yes, I've been told.'

'You'll have no more bother now when you're reffing.'

'If I'd have had any say in the matter you'd have played for the school or nobody!'

'You didn't though, did you?'

'It's too much, Hawk! What about your work? When is that going to get done?'

'I'll do it.'

'You were bad enough before.'

'I've never been bad.'

'I'm talking about the frequency of its appearance, not the content! It's too much, the pressure of the professional game and your studies.' He was approaching Lennie's desk unconsciously, as though he was being hypnotized.

'Hawk, you've got some very important examinations coming up in a few weeks' time.'

'I know I have.'

'And brilliant as you are, you will have to work very hard if you are to do well.'

'I know I will.'

'But how can you, if you continue to play with the Town? You'll be training two or three evenings a week, you'll be roving the country at week-ends, there'll be the cup coming up shortly. It's impossible, Hawk!'

'How do you know?'

'Of course I know! I can tell you now what will happen, you'll fall between two stools.'

'Or land with a cheek on each one.'

'And less of that kind of talk.'

Mr Rowley was standing at the side of Lennie's desk, looming over him. He was red-faced, and his breathing lifted his chest and shoulders as though the five yards down the aisle had been five miles.

'And you just don't care, do you, Hawk?'

Lennie looked from Mr Rowley's belly up to his face.

'Course I care.'

'It's your attitude, it's all wrong.'

'My attitude! My attitude! It's always my attitude!'

Lennie jumped up, and knocked his chair back with the backs of his knees. Mr Rowley staggered away as though a boxing glove had sprung out of a box at him. He steadied himself on a desk lid, then stood up straight and stepped forward.

'Hawk, sit down! Just who do you think you are, adopting that attitude?'

Lennie stood away from his desk, leaning forward like a bulldog, squaring up to Rowley across the aisle.

'What if my essays are always late, they're good, aren't they?

That's all you're bothered about, my essays, you don't care a damn about me, any of you. I bet you can't wait to wave me ta ta with my "A" levels notched on your gun belts.'

He dropped down on to his chair without looking back, then screwed it round to the front and stuck his legs straight out under the desk. Mr Rowley looked down on him, then turned and walked slowly back up the aisle. He sat down behind his briefcase and used it as a pillow for his arms.

'Hawk, I'm telling you this for your own benefit, you're taking on too much.' Lennie stared down at his shoes as though he was trying to stare them out. 'Why couldn't you have waited until after the exams, until next season? You've plenty of time.'

'I might have cocked my clogs by then.'

'You might have what?'

Lennie looked up at Rowley's puzzled face, then he burst out laughing, and the atmosphere was broken. Others in the class started to titter, and laugh, and their noise ripped open the hole made by Lennie, and filled the room. Rowley shot up and smashed his flat hands on to the desk top at either side of his briefcase. The noise stopped dead.

'Get out, Hawk! Get out of my sight before you drive me crazy!'

Lennie straightened the papers in his file before closing it, then he walked out of the room looking hurt. The corridor was empty. As he turned the corner by the gym he nearly collided with a boy coming round the other way. He grabbed him by the lapels and stood him up against the wall, then sang into his face.

'You! You're driving me crazy.

What'll I do, O what'll I do.'

The boy stood back, on his toes, with his palms pressed to the tiles.

'Give up then, Len, give up now.'

Lennie let go and walked down the side of the gym singing. The boy hurried away in the other direction straightening the knot of his tie, and twitching his neck.

'There's a letter there for you.'

Mrs Hawk held the drooping stack of cups safe in both hands, and nodded towards the fireplace. Lennie walked across the room and lifted the letter from behind the clock. He held it still near the wallpaper, then lifted it to the light and ripped the top off the envelope.

Dear Len,

I may be able to see you tomorrow evening (Monday) 7.30 usual place. Must rush now, missing you; Daddy's been awful.

Love Jane xxxx

He screwed it into a ball and lobbed it on to the fire. It bounced back into the hearth. He crouched down and pushed it between two burning cokes, and held it with the tip of the poker until it disintegrated to black ash.

'Is it from Jane?'

'My clog makers.'

'You haven't seen much of her lately, have you?'

He waited at the top of the Town Hall steps dancing rhythmically from foot to foot with his back to the studded wood. People passed below, bowed and silent against the freezing wind, and the cars on the road were determined and swift. The snow was slanting down in shudders as though being shaken from the sky, and it blew along the pavements in sheets like sand. Lennie ran down to the bottom of the steps then back up again.

'Come on, love.'

He banged a drum solo on the bottom of the door with his heels, then bent down and had a look through the letter box. The clock began to strike. He stood up quickly, and the flap snapped back into place. When the clock had struck eight times, he walked down to the pavement, and chalked GONE HOME. LEN. on the bottom step.

He looked in at the curtains as he passed the house. His mother and dad were arguing loudly. Their voices faded, and he ducked his head and ran down the bitter entry on to the flags. Behind the blackness of the yard the night sky was smudged with the lights of the pit, and whistles and grunts travelled out of the darkness, across the allotments on the back of the wind. He approached the back door and the argument rose again, but this time more distant through two doors. The door was locked so he knocked, but the voices continued after the bang had settled. He turned round and kicked the door like a mule until the wood shook under the hammer. The voices stopped and the bolt was scrambled loose on the inside by his mother.

'Are you trying to break it down, you dozy devil?'

''Course I am!'

'Why didn't you knock?'

'I did, but you were too busy shouting to hear owt.'

'I don't care, there's no need for ...'

'O get out a t'road and let me come in.'

'Hey, don't talk to me like ...'

He walked straight at her, and she had to step behind the door in front of the sink. She waited with her arms folded while he hung his coat over the washer, then followed him into the living-room. Mr Hawk was standing straddle-legged in front of the fire, with his hands in his trouser pockets, ruckling up the pockets of his jacket.

'And you can get that jacket off, Arthur, 'cos you're not going out!'

'Aren't I?'

'I don't know how you can think of it night after night, when you're on t'dole.'

'What the bloody hell do you expect me to do, sit on my arse in here all day?'

'I wouldn't care, but it's our Len's money you're drinking away.'

'Our Len's money! And whose bloody money is it that's kept him going all these years?'

'I wish you'd both stop shouting.'

'I'll go bloody mad if I stop in here any longer!'

'Your dad's driving me crazy, Len! ... God, what a life!' She turned to Lennie and burst into tears.

Mr Hawk smashed his cap on to his head and pulled it straight with the back and peak.

'I'm off!'

'You do! And I'll be straight down to that ground in t'morning, and I'll tell 'em not to give our Len another penny!'

'Do you think I'm bothered?'

He crossed the rug to the door, and Mrs Hawk grabbed hold of his jacket sleeve as he passed her.

'You're not going!'

Mr Hawk held his arm away from his body, and looked down at her hand as though he meant to bite it off.

'Get off, before I knock you off.'

'Let him go, Mam.'

'That's right, you stick up for him.'

While she was looking at Lennie, Mr Hawk raised his free hand and lashed her across the face. She fell backwards on to the arm of the easy chair, then bounced off, to the floor in a heavy pile. She sat flat, with her legs splayed like a Guy Fawkes and her pink knicker legs showing just over the knees. Mr Hawk swiftly bent to pick her up. She knocked his hand away and continued striking the air after he had stood up.

'Get off! Don't dare touch me!'

She coughed and shuddered and started to sob, each sob swelling from the beat of her heart to the burst of her breath. She was heart sluffed. Mr Hawk stood astride her legs looking down, then he whipped round white-faced with his teeth bared.

'What thar staring at?'

'You.'

Lennie stooped to help his mother, but she just sat sobbing in a loose heap. Mr Hawk slammed out of the house. Mrs Hawk stopped crying and lifted her head. When the footsteps had passed the window she scrambled up like a baby learning to walk, and ran upstairs. Lennie sat on a stool and poked the fire into shapes and lights. One flame flickered golden. He stirred the coke to keep it burning but the flame shortened, and turned to blue. His mother stopped rumbling around above his head, and she came down set and determined, as though she had just witnessed the death of a relative. She assembled the ironing board and fetched the creaking cane clothes basket from the kitchen. Lennie moved to the table and began to work. They did not speak, and the only sounds were the scratch of the pen and the bump of the iron on the padded board.

Mr Hawk returned an hour later covered in cold, and reeking of beer and cigs. Lennie and his mother didn't look up. They were still working and they hadn't spoken a word. Mr Hawk skulked about for a bit, looking at the paper and smoking, then he stood up and stood in the middle of the rug.

'What's for t'supper?'

Mrs Hawk concentrated on her ironing; Lennie on his essay.

'What's up, have you both gone deaf or summat?'

They didn't look at him.

'Right! I'll get my own bloody supper then!'

He shuttled noisily from the kitchen to the table, banging a barricade of food round Lennie's books.

'Let's finish this first, Dad.'

'Tha should have started earlier instead of hanging around t'Town Hall steps all night!'

'I didn't hang around long enough!'

'Let him alone, you're not starving.'

'It's time he was in bed anyway, he's got to go training to-morrow.'

'He's got to go to school an all.'

Lennie packed his books away. His mother started to lift the supper pots from the dark polished wood.

'You can put them back for a start!'

'We usually eat off a cloth at this house. Or are you too drunk to notice that there isn't one on?'

She flicked the white cloth into the air. It unfolded and para-chuted down on to the table, creased in four with a diamond at the intersection of the two lines.

'You'll have to finish it after supper, love.'

'Drunk, you've never seen me drunk.'

'I'll do it tomorrow.'

'I thought you said it'd to be finished for tomorrow.'

'Tomorrow afternoon. I've got a couple of free periods in t'morning.'

'He's a selfish devil, your dad.'

'Just shut up, will you! I've just about had enough from you tonight.'

'It's just about your barrow, hitting women.'

'Are you going to shut up?'

'And you reek a booze!'

Lennie opened the stairs door.

'Aren't you having any supper, love?'

'No.'

'What's up wi' thi?'

'What do you think?'

They were still at it through the floor boards when he went to sleep.

'Len! Len!'

Mrs Hawk shook the hump under the blankets.

'Len.'

'What?'

'Wake up.'

He reared up and looked into the dark through Chinese eyes.

'What's up with you? It's still dark outside.'

'It's your dad, he's gone to sleep in t'chair.'

'So what?'

He shrugged her off and turned over.

'Len! He can't stop down there all night, he'll catch his death a cold.'

'Wake him up then.'

'I can't, he's hopeless.'

'Oh, leave him.'

She clicked the light on. Lennie tried to make a hood of the blankets but she held them down over his shoulders. He whipped the blankets off and swivelled his legs over the edge of the bed.

'Go fill a bucket of water, that'll shift him!'

'Don't talk so ridiculous!'

He followed his mother downstairs in his pyjama bottoms. The fire had died and crumbled to a layer of grey ash. The electric light was stale without the glow from the grate, and cast nothing but chill shadows. The dirty supper pots were still on the table, and the clock ticked loudly in the stillness of the room. Half past two.

'Look at t'time.'

'I know, I must have dozed off. When I woke up t'light was still on and your dad hadn't come up.'

Mr Hawk was asleep in the armchair. His head was balanced on his chest, ready to roll down the slope of his body and out-stretched legs.

'Come on, Dad, get up.'

Mr Hawk didn't move.

'Dad, get up!'

His head jerked back and his mouth sagged open.

'Wha! Who is it? Who is it?'

'Come on, let's have you.'

Lennie grinned and pulled his dad on to his feet, but he collapsed and sat astride the chair arm like a cowboy, his eyes blank like a fish's.

'Wha's a matter, Len? Are tha a'right?'

'I'm champion, come on.'

Lennie supported him under the armpits to the stairs bottom. Mrs Hawk fluttered behind them like an old angel in her nightgown.

'Ger off now, Len, I can walk ... Anybody think I can't look after mishen ... All these years looked after us ... all these years ... our Len's money ... Who's looked after us all these years? ... Our Len's money ... Is it my fault, is it my fault on dole?'

Lennie tried to push him upstairs, but he just lay sprawled out on the steps.

'Ger off, ger off, Len.'

'Get at t'front of him, Mother.'

'Can't we carry him?'

'Carry him! Wha' you mean, carry? I don' wa' nob'y carry me.'

He hoisted himself up in mechanical stages like a puppet and stood swaying on the second step. Then he timbered backwards slowly. Mrs Hawk stared, and screamed through her hands.

'Le-e-en!'

Lennie caught him and pushed him straight. But their base was too small, and the stairs were to steep for safe progress.

'Mam, go and fetch a brush.'

'What sort a brush?'

'A sweeping brush.'

'What do you want a sweeping brush for?'

She walked into the kitchen for a brush.

'I don' need nob'y carry me.'

Lennie steadied him with one hand and shoved the brush head into the middle of his back.

'Right, go on.'

Mr Hawk lifted his foot and mounted a step, leaning back on the brush. Lennie played it out step by step until his hands were spaced near the end of the handle. Then he followed, pushing and supporting. Mr Hawk climbed the stairs at right angles, like a mountaineer being pulled up a steep slope.

'What's up with him, Mam? He wasn't like this when he came in.'

'He's been at that whisky that we had left over from Christmas. He's nearly emptied t'bottle.'

'He never hardly touches it, does he?'

'I know. He's gone to pieces since he was thrown off work. He can't stand it, you know, Len, when he's not working.'

Mr Hawk reached the landing and his weight shifted forward. The brush head dropped from his back.

'Steady on, Dad!'

He had to run, to stop himself falling flat on his face. He shambled across the landing and into the bedroom finishing with a dive on to the bed. Lennie's laughter filled the house. He stood in the doorway pointing at his dad and looking back at his mother.

'See that?'

'Shut up, Len! Are you trying to waken everybody in t' district?'

He turned and shambled past his mother into the back bedroom, finishing with a dive on to the bed. He lay still on the cold slippery eiderdown. The bulb shone through the shade like a frosty orange, and the wind knocked on the window and tried to get in.

The traffic lights switched to red. Lennie got off the bus and crossed the road into the car-park. The floodlights were blazing down from their steel pylons at the four corners of the ground. It was noisy in the corridor, like the mornings, when the full-timers were training. When he walked into the dressing-room the first team were getting stripped and the noise of the second teamers came through the showers, from the other changing-room. There were no part-timers or juniors present. He stood in the doorway looking round, and the players turned on him like a pack of wolves.

'Here he comes! King bleeding football himself!'

'Didn't he send a taxi for you then?'

Lennie walked to his peg and hung his coat up. Nobody spoke to him while he got undressed. He turned to Chris who was stripping at the side of him.

'What you all training tonight for, Chris?'

'Boss's orders. When we got here this morning he got us round the board and explained this 4–2–4 that he's going to try out. Then we went out for half an hour, but he said that it wasn't much use unless you were here, so he told us to report back at six.'

'There's no wonder I'm popular.'

'We had a right pantomime, Pete Fowler said he wasn't coming back for anybody.'

'I see he's come though.'

'He said we'd be here every night till we'd got it worked out.'

Clifford Anderson came in followed by Eddie and Max, the second team trainer. They were all dressed in red track suits.

'Come on, lads, chop, chop.'

He bounced a ball on the floor and caught it in spanned hands. The players continued to change as though he wasn't there. He shuffled his feet and bounced the ball hard.

'For Christ's sake get a move on and stop acting like big kids! If Len's not here full time what else can we do at this stage?'

They punched their heads and fists into their jerseys, and made the zips whiz on their tracksuit legs.

'Is everybody ready then?'

Nobody answered.

'Right, Len. The other lads know what I'm after, I want you to act as midfield link with Chris, with Bobby and Roy up the field striking. O.K.?'

'I can go up as well though, can't I?'

'Yes, 'course you can.'

'That's all right then, 'cos I've got to be amongst them goals.'

The other players sat with their heads down between their legs as though waiting to be sick.

'It won't make much difference to your game, you'll have more graft but if it comes off you and Chris should find yourselves with much more space to work in.'

'You want Chris to concentrate more on attack.'

'That's it. I want midfield domination, and if I can't get it with you two buggers then I'd like to know who can.'

'I want to be upfield an all though.'

'Don't worry son, I want you to be. Right, let's go and have a look at it then.'

When they ran out the cold made them gasp, as though they were diving into a pond in turn. There wasn't even the darkness to muffle in, just a freezing light leaving them gaunt and exposed to the icy gusts. The ground was solid under their rubber studs, and the ball bounced high and awkward off the frozen ridges. They sprinted and danced about with the cuffs of their sleeves clenched tight in their hands.

'It's not fit to play!'

'All bleeding day, and we finish up on night shift.'

'Lennie wants shagging.'

'I'll kick his balls in if he comes near me.'

'Come on, lads, let's get cracking.'

The game started and the players kicked the ball about as though it was Lennie. Balance and ball control were difficult, and speed was a positive hazard. They were playing like men cold and fed up and the ball was in the air too much for the plan even to start functioning. When the ball was passed down the centre the two strikers either went for it together or stood back and left it. All the centre half had to do was step between them and keep booting it clear. Every time this happened they snarled at each other, Roy Hann reverted to his former position, and started to impede Lennie. Clifford Anderson blew his whistle.

'Roy, you must stay up that middle.'

'Bollocks to this, it's useless!'

'Don't talk so bloody stupid, man, we've only been playing it half an hour.'

'I can't play centre forward.'

Bobby Prince looked at him hard, with his hands on his hips.

'You're not kidding either!'

The other players laughed. Roy walked up to him with his fists swinging at his sides.

'You shut your bleeding trap! It's you that's causing the balls up and you reckon to be a centre forward.'

The reserve team grinned round at each other.

Clifford Anderson silenced them both in a second.

'You'll both be lapping in a minute! Now call to each other, and the man off the ball get away so that you're in position to one two the centre half. Lennie, give them plenty of it.'

The game restarted. Lennie fed them with every ball he received, then the wingmen started complaining.

'Hey up! Aren't we playing then, or what?'

'There's only one ball, you know.'

'Well, let's see some of it then.'

'You heard what the boss said.'

'Bugger that, let's see this ball. I've got frostbite in my left knacker standing out here.'

'As long as you don't get it in your prick you'll be all right.'

'Bollocks! Let's see this ball.'

There was so much hesitancy and confusion amongst the first team that the reserves scored three times without any hint of reply. Laurie Key was unsure of his new job as cover man, and the full backs didn't know whether to go for their wingmen or lay off. The defence came under heavy pressure and Chris dropped back to help. The midfield link broke down, and Lennie dropped back to see where the ball was. The two strikers and the wingmen were left isolated and freezing up the field. Clifford Anderson blew his whistle.

'Chris, come away from that goalmouth!'

'I know, but they're struggling back here.'

'They're bound to be at first, they'll get used to it.'

Laurie Key was marching about the penalty box kicking at the pitch with his head down.

'What's up, Laurie?'

'I don't know whether I want a shit, shave or haircut at this game. Who am I supposed to be marking?'

'Nobody, if they all fall back and mark up properly. That should leave you free to cover behind, O.K.?'

'I'll say so.'

'Right then, let's have you.'

Clifford Anderson ended the game at half past nine. The reserves had won 5-0. They formed an avenue at the tunnel mouth and clapped the first team through. The first team players passed between them, snarling and cursing. Laurie Key was the last man off the pitch. Pete Fowler whistled and gave him the slow handclap.

'Here he comes, the cover man! Cover, Laurie, while I go for a shit!'

Laurie grabbed him by the chest of his tracksuit, pulling and gathering the material in his hand.

'I'll cover your face with my fist if you don't shut your teeth!'

Fowler jerked free, and straightened the collar of his tracksuit as though he had a tie round it.

'What's up! Can't you stand being beaten?'

'Being beaten! We'd have murdered you in a normal game.'

Clifford Anderson followed them up the tunnel into the corridor.

'That is your normal game from now on, Laurie.'

'Bloody hell, boss! Why start buggering around now, just when we're picking up.'

'That is the time to bugger around, Laurie, when you're picking up.'

The players bathed and dressed quickly. When they were ready they prowled around the massage table in their overcoats uncertain whether to go or stay.

'Go and see the boss, Chris, and ask him what we're doing tomorrow.'

Eddie came in smiling.

'Usual time in the morning, lads.'

They all cheered. Eddie grinned.

'Then back at six – till further notice.'

They groaned and cursed. Bobby Prince ran at a football and lashed it straight through the showers into the other changing-room.

'I hope he catches two cancers!'

Pete Fowler rushed back with the ball rubbing his leg.

'Which stupid bastard kicked this?'

Bobby Prince ran at him pointing back into his own tweed overcoat.

'Me, I kicked it! It was me, why?'

Fowler stepped back and eyed him up with his face averted, then he looked round at the others, who were watching the scene in silence.

'What's the matter with you lot?'

Bobby Prince pushed up to him and stood eye to eye, chest to chest.

'What do you think's the matter with us?'

'How do I know what's the matter with you?'

'That's because you're thick, you're as thick as pigshit!'

Fowler shoved the football under one arm and turned to Eddie.

'What's up with everybody, Eddie?'

'Haven't you heard?'

'Does it bleeding sound like it?'

Eddie grinned and kept him waiting.

'For Christ's sake tell me then!'

'New training orders, usual morning stint then back at six till further notice.'

Fowler spun on his heels and half volleyed the ball through the showers. It flew straight back and hit him up the arse as he turned round. The other players had to laugh. Fowler glared at them as though he was going to ask them out in turn. He picked on Lennie.

'Would you credit it? Twenty-odd full-time professionals carted back at night just because of a school kid.'

Lennie stood up from tying his shoelaces and lifted his coat from the peg. 'Piss off, Pete.'

'I'll come and give you some fist in a minute. You'll be the boss's black-eyed boy then instead of blue-eyed.'

Lennie walked towards him and faced him across the table.

'Come on then, I've just about had enough tonight. Anybody'd think all this was my idea.'

'It's for your benefit.'

'It's for everybody's benefit, you stupid-looking twat!'

'Some benefit, five nil.'

Some of the first teamers nodded and muttered in agreement.

'What do you expect first time? You want to give it a chance before you start moaning.'

'It's bloody ridiculous.'

'All he's trying to do is utilize his resources.'

'Utilize his resources! And what's that supposed to mean?'

'In simple, everyday English, he's trying to make the best of what he's got. Make, M-A-K-E the, T-H-E Best . . .'

'All right! All right, brain box! You want to stick to school if you're that bleeding clever!'

'I'd sooner come down here and torment you.'

'Look at him! He's even got books in his pockets.'

They all looked at Lennie's coat pockets, squared off and solid on each hip.

'They're to put down my socks when I'm playing against filthy sods like you.'

'Oh go and balls!'

They left in gangs, grumbling to each other over the backs of their cars in the car-park. The doors slammed and they shot out of the line and raced for the gate Le Mans style. A queue formed and the cars cleared their throats while they waited. Lennie walked along the line and the drivers looked up at him in turn. Chris slid his window down.

'Get in, Len, I'm going past the top of your street.'

The car in front curved left into the main road, and the hooters behind began to blurt. Fowler's car whipped round into the space as Lennie opened the door and ducked in.

'Do me a favour before I come down tomorrow night, Chris. Get somebody to check all their guns and knives before we start.'

'You don't want to bother about them.'

'I'm not.'

They followed Fowler on to the main road. He accelerated, and quickly left them behind.

'What do you reckon to this 4–2–4, Len?'

'It'll be all right.'

'That's what I think.'

'Nobody else does.'

'Except boss, he's dead keen to have it working for the cup.'

'We could go a long way this year, Chris, we're just coming good at the right time.'

'Got a bet on?'

'My dad's get ten on, at eight to one. My mother'd kill him if she knew.'

'He's on t'dole, isn't he?'

'They've just thrown a lot of men off at the pit.'

'You'll be struggling a bit then?'

'We're managing, they're not used to it, that's all. It makes my dad feel ashamed when he's not working, and my mother doesn't help him any.'

Chris stopped outside the Anchor and sat back in his seat. Lennie squeezed the handle down and the door opened.

'Are they giving you owt?'

Chris jerked his head back in the direction of the Dale.

'Expenses.'

'Is that all?'

'I'm only an amateur, you know.'

Chris looked across at him, but the light from the street lamps was cut off at Lennie's shoulders, and his face was in the shade of the car.

'When we win the cup, they'll shake my hand and give me a canteen of cutlery.'

'You've got a slate off, Len.'

Chris shook his head. Lennie got out, then leaned back in through the space of the open door.

'See you tomorrow night, then.'

'Right. And if you're ever short, Len, let me know, I can always lend you a bit.'

Lennie blushed and Chris revved up loudly.

'Ta, see you then.'

He banged the door and walked down the quiet street. Most of the lighted windows were upstairs. His mother and dad were waiting for him when he got in. Mrs Hawk was standing in front of the fire in her nightgown and curlers, clutching her clothes and a hotwater bottle to her breast. Mr Hawk was slumped in the armchair, and his eyes looked strained and red-rimmed when he looked up over his shoulder.

'I thought tha'd got injured.'

'Look at time! Where you been?'

'What you waiting up for? You know where I've been.'

'It was getting late though, we wondered where you were.'

'Well, you can go to bed now then, can't you?'

Mrs Hawk took the clock off the mantelpiece, and steadied the wad of football coupons that had been wedged behind it.

'Are you coming, Arthur?'

'In a minute.'

'Go on, Dad, I've some work to do.'

'They were arguing in t'club tonight, Len, that Town'll not be able to keep thi if tha keeps on playing as tha are doing.'

Lennie fetched his books out of the kitchen, then sat at the table facing the wall.

'They were saying that tha bound to sign for a richer club.'

Mr Hawk sat still waiting.

'It'd break your heart if I did, wouldn't it?'

'Nay, lad, it's up to thee.'

'It would though, wouldn't it?'

'Tha'd earn a lot more money if tha went away. Bloody hell, Len, some of them offers tha's had!'

Mrs Hawk walked to the stairs bottom and opened the door.

'I'm off then.'

'I'll be up in a minute.'

'And don't you be long, Len. I'll put t'alarm on a bit earlier 'cos you're getting terrible in a morning.'

She moved the alarm finger, but it turned too far and she had to spin it all the way round the clock face. The bell rang briefly when it passed eleven.

'Don't be long, Arthur.'

Her footsteps upstairs were solid and slow, radiating from the core of the house. Then they were overhead making the boards creak.

'I'd just like to see t'Town good again, that's all, and I think wi' thee and Hanson in t'team they could be.'

'Like they were when you were a lad?'

'Nay, they'll never be as good as that again. For five seasons they were t'best team this country's ever seen. Cup winners twice and league champions three times. Tha should have seen 'em, Len.'

Lennie put his pen down quietly, and settled his face into his cupped hands.

'Good half back line, hadn't they?'

'Good half back line, Buller, Blackshaw and Bloomer! It was the finest half back line that ever strode a football pitch. I once saw Blackshaw head a goal from forty yards. I've never seen owt like it since.'

'And what about Mickey Cunliffe, he'd got a good shot, hadn't he?'

'Mickey the Mule! Goalkeepers used to run behind t'nets when they saw him coming. And does tha know, Len, he was that bloody cheeky with it, he never used to stop smiling. He'd beat his centre half with this grin on his face and then he'd give a funny little laugh just before he shot. He once broke a goalkeeper's arm from just inside t'box.'

'Bobby Prince's not bad with his right foot.'

'Bobby Prince! Mickey'd more strength in t'muck under his toenails than he's got in all his body. Two hundred goals in five seasons, there's never been a centre forward like him.'

'Lennie Silver was your favourite though, wasn't he, Dad!'

Mr Hawk swallowed, but there was still the break in his voice when he spoke.

'Lennie Silver was the daddy of them all.' Lennie picked up his pen and started to doodle on the inside of his file. 'Ar, there'll never be another Silver shadow. Tha should have seen him, Len.'

'Was he better than me?'

'He was capped for England when he was seventeen.'

'Did he play like me?'

'No, he wasn't as aggressive, he wasn't as fast either.'

'Had he got a good shot?'

'Not as good as thine; he wasn't as good with his head either. In fact it's hard to say what he'd got when you break it down like that.'

'He must have had something, Dad. He only played four seasons and he got a hundred an odd goals. And Cunliffe never got as many after he'd been killed.'

'I don't know what it was. He just used to drift about wi' t'ball at his feet, just like a white ghost, just like a shadow.'

'I wish I could have seen him.'

'They used to try all sorts to stop him, following him about, pushing, tripping, pulling his shirt, but it made no difference, he just used to drift past 'em with his shirt sleeves flapping.'

'He must have had a good body swerve.'

'Never noticed it. You'd see a player crouching for his tackle, and Shadow would just go up to him and walk past. Sometimes he'd leave him still crouching, still waiting as though he hadn't come yet. Crowd used to go mad, and you'd get that feeling inside you that you'd just seen a miracle. It was bloody marvellous.'

'How did he get his goals then?'

'He just used to place 'em. He never made t'net bulge or owt like that.'

'Not like me then?'

'And he never missed a penalty in four seasons, and every one was smack same. Just one step and a push into t'corner a t'net. More like a golfing putt than a shot.'

'I wish I could have seen him.'

'When he got killed that summer, it wa' t'end a t'Town, they just faded away after that.'

'And they never found out who did it, did they?'

'No, they never found out. It happened all them years since, and they still don't know who did it to this day.'

'You've been a good supporter a t'Town, haven't you, Dad?'

'There's been none better for nigh on forty years.'

'Forty years . . . It's a long time.'

'When I was a lad it was allus my ambition to play for t'Town, but, when I realized I wasn't good enough, I thought next best thing'd be to go and give 'em a shout.'

'You've not had a lot to shout about since Shadow's days though, have you?'

'They've had one or two good seasons, but nowt's happened for years, not till thar came into t'team. Tha's made a hell of a difference, Len, it's not same team any more. There's a different atmosphere altogether now at t'Dale, you can feel it, crowd's getting interested again. Does tha know, I've heard more talk about t'Town in t'club this past few weeks, than I've heard in ten years?'

'Everybody's hoping for a good cup run, aren't they?'

'Ar, but nobody's saying much, they daren't.'

'They shouldn't build their hopes up at this stage. It's too early yet.'

'They've got to build their hopes on summat, and it's too late for t'league.'

'Do you think we've got a chance then?'

'If thar stops, I think you have.'

'Where do you think I'm going when I've got my exams in June?'

'What's exams matter when they're offering thi forty and fifty pounds a week?'

'Well, you've no need to bother, 'cos I'm not going anywhere.'

'That's all right then.'

The only sound then was Mr Hawk's slow, heavy breathing.

'When I used to watch Lennie Silver I used to think, there'll never be anybody as good ever wear a Town shirt again. But now I've seen thee, especially this last couple a games, I'm not sure. And I don't want thi to go anywhere else till I find out. 'Cos if I thought I'd reared a lad who was a better player than Shadow it'll more than make up for not being good enough myself.'

Lennie looked round. His dad was low in the chair, staring straight ahead at the blank television screen. He continued to stare even though Lennie was watching him.

'You've no need to bother, I'm all right at t'Town.'

'They're not a rich club, but they're fair. I think tha'll get a fair deal if tha stops.'

He stood up, yawning and stretching tall.

'Thar wants to get to bed now, it must be nearly twelve.'

'I'll just finish this first.'

Two bumps on the ceiling rattled the hanging chains, and swung the bowl holding the light bulb.

'I'll be off then, else thi mother'll be awake all night.'

He went upstairs, and the hum of voices came through the boards until the light clicked and the bed creaked. The fire was slowly dying under a collapsed crust of coal. Outside the wind had dropped, and no pit sounds carried across the allotments. Lennie read his last paragraph and began to write.

The pitch was bone dry and as bumpy as a beach as they lined up under the lights. Clifford Anderson stood on the half-way line turning his head to both teams as he gave his instructions.

'I know this pitch isn't fit to play on but I'm risking it, because I want this new formation working for the cup. Now use your common sense, and let's have no needle as we did last night. Right then, off we go.'

In the first minute the ball hit a ridge and bounced over Laurie Key's foot, leaving Fowler with an open goal. The second team were all smiles as they trotted back for the centre. The first team were silent and taut as though they were all shackled together. Clifford Anderson blew his whistle and Bobby Prince played the ball to Lennie. He turned and pushed it back to Chris. As the opposing inside forwards rushed past each other Fowler hit Lennie from behind. His knee caps drove hard into the hinges behind Lennie's knee and his shoulder tilted forward into his back. Lennie went down like a skittle and Fowler trod on his hand as he jumped over him. The foul had been missed in the hurly burly of the kick off, and Eddie trotted across, watching the play all the time.

'All right, son?'

'Champion.'

He rolled his sleeves up and looked down the whites of his forearms. They were grazed pink, and his left elbow was bleeding. He sucked the fingers of his trodden hand then went to look for the ball.

The second team scored again when the ball shot up and hit George Armstrong's hand in the penalty box. But slowly the flow of the game shifted as the first team acknowledged and understood their new roles on the field. Lennie and Chris began to dominate the middle of the pitch, and for the first time in two nights Billy Boscombe and Geordie Paling were allowed to use their fast powerful legs on the wings. The reserve full backs had to leave the centre of the field to attend to their wingmen, leaving gaps for the two centre forwards to spurt through. Roy Hann scored when he one-two'd the centre half with Bobby Prince. The centre half complained to his defence that he couldn't mark two of the bastards. They didn't like this double thrust, and they didn't like Lennie who was rein-forcing them. His shooting was vicious, and there was always the chance that they might get hit up the arse or in the balls. And it was too cold for this.

Geordie Paling centred, and the ball was headed out to Lennie on the edge of the penalty area. He drew his foot back and Fowler turned his back instinctively. He hit the big number 10 from two yards and the ball bounced straight back to him. Fowler staggered forward pulling his shoulder blades together as though he had an arrow in his back. Lennie moved swiftly forward into the penalty area and threatened to shoot again. Two defenders ducked, and he ran past them and side-footed the ball into the corner of the net. Fowler was still flexing his shoulder blades when Clifford Anderson whistled time. He fol-lowed them into the changing-rooms and sat on the table with his legs swinging while they got undressed. 'A lot better to-night, lads, it's coming on well. If it's off at Manchester on Saturday we'll have another go Saturday afternoon.'

There were moans all round. Clifford Anderson smiled.

'Now, I will give you something to moan about. You'll be wanted Sunday morning, and every morning and evening next week.' He raised his hands to silence any complaints. 'I mean to have this system working like clockwork before the cup, and I'll drag you out of your beds at the dead of night if necessary.'

He looked round at the players, but they shuffled about and looked away from him.

'I know it's a lot to ask, but you won't be complaining when you're striding out at Wembley.'

He pushed himself up off the table, and landed with both feet together. There was a silence as he walked across the room and out of the door.

Chris dropped Lennie outside the Town Hall and he caught a bus up the hill towards school. He leaned backwards and dropped off as it dragged past the bottom of Hillside Avenue. There was a light on in the Rowleys' front room. Lennie pushed the gate wide open, on to the privet hedge between the two blocks of semis, then he opened the gate at the other side. He walked quietly down the Rowleys' path and pressed the bell on the side door. Before the vibrations had faded he was back up the path and round the hedge. He crouched low, and watched through the spaced stalks. The door opened and a woman's legs stood behind the trestle. Lennie stood up as they stepped forward and turned towards the road.

'Pss! It's me.'

'Oh!'

'Is he in?'

'Come on, quickly.'

He ran round the hedge and down the path into the kitchen. Mrs Rowley followed him in and locked the door.

'I almost screamed out just then.'

'I had to see whether he was in or not.'

'I thought you were coming last night?'

'I couldn't.'

'Why not?'

'We didn't finish training till nearly ten.'

'I was expecting you, I was ever so disappointed.'

She put her arms round his neck and crossed them at the wrists. 'You're neglecting me, Len.'

Lennie squeezed the cheeks of her arse. 'That's why I came tonight.'

'I'd have gone mad if Alfred had been in.'

'We'd have had to go down to the greenhouse. You can't beat it up to your knees in plant pots.'

'You are coarse at times, Len.'

'That's why you like me, isn't it?'

She pulled him close, gripping him tight round the neck. Lennie looked over her shoulder into the hall, then walked away from her into the front room.

'Where is he?'

'He's got a play rehearsal down at the Guild Hall.'

'What time will he be back?'

'It's usually well past eleven. The play opens next week so I should think he'll be pretty busy.'

Lennie took his coat off and crouched down on his heels in front of the fire. He spread his hands to the flames and inspected his trodden fingers. Mrs Rowley sat on the settee and watched him in profile. 'That's how the miners sit, isn't it? I've seen them at the street corners. They say they can sit like that for hours.'

'Do they?'

She reached forward and grasped his shoulder hard. He turned and looked at her.

'I've missed you, Len.'

'You've got lovely legs.'

'Thank you.'

She slid forward on to her knees beside him.

'It's good to have someone to tell you things like that.'

'Did you see Jane at the week-end?'

Mrs Rowley sat back on her heels, and her skirt hitched up over her knees.

'Yes.'

'What did she say?'

'Nothing much.'

'She must have said something.'

'She told me that she's not giving in to her father.'

'That's what I like to hear.'

'And her father's not giving in to her. He says that Jane's not going out alone until she stops seeing you.'

'The rotten dog.'

'Are you really fond of Jane?'

''Course I am, why?'

'You're not just using her to spite Mr Leary, are you?'

'Mr Leary! I don't care a bugger about him.'

'He's not awfully keen on you either.'

'He doesn't know quality when he sees it, that's his trouble.'

'Be careful, Len. Mr Leary's a very influential man.'

'Not with me he's not.'

He overbalanced backwards, and rocked about on his spine in a tight ball. Then he released his hands and opened out flat on the rug. Mrs Rowley looked down at him.

'It's getting late, Len.'

'Come here then.'

He pulled her down on top of him, wrapping her hair round his hand and pressing her mouth to his. She sprawled out full length shoving him down into the coarse hair of the animal rug.

'Have you ever had it like this?'

'What do you mean?'

'You on top.'

'No, I'm not flexible enough.'

' 'Course you are, I bet you've never tried. Come on.'

'Wait a minute Len, this skirt's too tight, I can't move my legs.'

'Let me take it off then.'

He unzipped it and she stood up and got undressed. Lennie rested on one elbow watching her.

'I like to see you like that.'

'You make me feel shy watching me.'

'You know you like it.'

'It still makes me feel shy though.'

She knelt down astride him.

'Like this?'

'That's it. Do you like it?'

'I love you Len, oh, I love you.'

'You can't beat a bit of versatility.'

'Hold my breasts, Len, they hurt with all this movement – That's better, I like you to do that.'

'Your nipples are like little brown bowlers.'

'Do you enjoy loving me, Len?'

' 'Course I do.'

'Am I good? Am I as good as some of the young girls you've loved?'

'There's no comparison.'

'Honest, Len?'

'They weren't in the same street.'

He pulled her down and rolled over. Mrs Rowley moaned and hung on as the balance shifted. Then they lay still with the fire down one side.

'I thought you said you liked it the other way.'

'I do, but you can't beat the old position in the end. It's like Nuttalls mintoes, original and best.'

'Don't talk about it like that, Len, you spoil it.'

'I'm only joking.'

'It can't mean anything if you joke about it, it's making fun of it.'

'Hey! What are you getting all serious about?'

'It is serious to me, Len.'

'Look, I enjoy it and it makes me happy. I'm not making fun of anything, it just makes me happy, that's all.'

'It makes me happy as well, and sad.'

She snuggled up to him and the front door rattled as the handle was turned. They looked at each other, then sprang apart up and looked at each other again. The key scraped in the lock and Lennie looked towards the window. Mrs Rowley heaved the settee back to the wall and grabbed Lennie's arm, pointing and pushing.

'Get behind there, and get out when he goes to bed.'

The door banged.

'Claire!'

Lennie threw his coat and shoes behind the settee and crept after them. Mrs Rowley picked his trousers up and threw them over the top.

'Hello, dear, you're early!'

She scrambled into her underslip and snatched the rest of her scattered clothing off the floor. Mr Rowley came into the room wringing his hands.

'Damned cold outside.'

Mrs Rowley watched him bend stiff-legged to the flames. His body hung down like ripe fruit as he cracked his hands together over the hearth.

'You're early.'

'Blasted heating broke down, it became unbearable. Then the bus was ten minutes late, I'm frozen to the bone. Do you know you left the gate wide open? You'll have every damned dog in the district in if you're not careful.'

'I'm going up to bed, Alfred, I'm tired.'

'Are you all right, dear? You look flushed.'

'I'm all right.'

'You're looking very tempting walking around like that.'

He put his arm round her waist and pulled her close.

'I noticed a funny smell when I walked in here, smelled like kippers or something.'

'Alfred, you're freezing!'

She unwound herself and moved to the door.

'Are you coming?'

'I'll have a drink first.'

'Don't be long dear, I'm tired.'

They both left the room, Lennie lay flat on his back and pulled his trousers on. He'd got them as far as his knees when Mr Rowley returned and dragged one end of the settee round to the fire. Lennie rolled with it, then lay still trying to breathe in time to Mr Rowley's asthmatic wheezes. He finished his drink and the settee creaked and lifted as he stood up. Lennie lifted his head and watched him walk to the lamp in the corner. The light clicked off and Mr Rowley passed out of sight round the stiff stuffed arm of the settee.

The castors squealed as he started to push it back to the wall. Lennie breathed in and rolled away right up to the skirting board. He lay to attention on his side as it rolled towards him. Then it stopped and Mr Rowley left the room. His footsteps were slow and heavy on the stairs. Lennie crawled out and got dressed. He put his coat on and stood in the doorway listening. The toilet flushed. He swiftly crossed the hall and opened the door. The latch clicked loudly in the socket when he closed it from the outside. He ran up the path and vaulted the gate, then walked down the Avenue like someone walking down an Avenue.

'Get up, Len, we've laid too long! It's ten to nine.'

He pulled the blankets over his ears and turned over.

'Go away.'

'Get up and don't talk so blasted silly!'

'We've got a day off today.'

'What you talking about? Get up.'

'It's co-op centenary, we've got a day off.'

He held the blankets tight round his head, and his eyes were squeezed shut like a newly born animal.

'You should come to bed on a night. You'd be able to get up in a morning then!'

She stood over the bed and started to worry the bedclothes.

'Gi'o'er then! I'm not a rattle, you know.'

'Well, get up then!'

'Five minutes.'

'Now! You're late already.'

'Is there a fire made?'

'No.'

'I'll have my breakfast in bed then.'

'Oh, get up now, Len, and stop acting so daft.'

He swivelled on his hip, and threw the clothes back like a heavy cloak. 'SHAZAM!'

He stood up on the cold oilcloth, then jumped back on the bed.

'Jesus! Where's my socks?'

'They're where you put 'em. What time did you come to bed last night.'

'I don't know. We ought to have fitted carpets and central heating up here. It wouldn't be so bad getting up in a morning then.'

'Central heating! What are you talking about? Anybody'd think you were used to such things.'

She left the room and went downstairs. Lennie tucked his shirt in and opened the curtains. The sky looked as heavy as lead, thick frost peppered the allotments, and a ragged white veil had been thrown over the muck-stack at the side of the pit. Everything was grey, except for the row of green lavatory doors at the bottom of the yard.

The postman came while he was having his breakfast. He brought a letter from Jane.

Dear Len,

What are we going to do? I'm going to leave home or something. Father's beastly and I'm thoroughly miserable. I'll just have to see you soon or I'll go mad. Write straight back PLEASE!

Love Jane

xxxxxx

'Where's that writing pad?'

'Have you seen t'clock?'

'Ar, many a time.'

'Never mind t'writing pad, you're half an hour late already.'

'Where is it?'

'Look, get off to school, will you?'

'I'll go when I'm ready.'

'I thought you'd finished with that Jane, anyway.'

'Who says it's from T H A T Jane?'

'Well, isn't it?'

'It's my call-up papers if you want to know.'

Mr Hawk appeared in his shirt from behind the stairs door with his trousers folded over one arm like a waiter's napkin. His legs were white and wiry like a plucked chicken, and his scarred knee caps stuck out like clenched fists.

'I wish they bloody well were! Shouting and bawling at this time in a morning.'

'It makes a change from you at night, when you come home from t'club.'

'Don't be so bloody cheeky.'

'And you're getting as bad as our Len. At one time a t'day you'd have been round t'dyke and back by this time.'

Mr Hawk stood with his back to the cold grate and pushed one foot into the concertina-ed leg of his trousers.

'What the bloody hell have I got to get up early for? Every day seems like a month as it is.'

He snapped his braces over his shoulders and rammed the poker down into the dead ashes. Lennie found the writing pad in the cupboard. He sat at the table and turned over the half torn pages that had been used for betting slips.

Dear Jane,

I'm coming up to see you. We'll have to get this thing sorted out some time so I might as well come to your house and do it. If the game's off on Saturday I'll come up after tea. Don't worry, it'll be all right. Love Len

He folded the sheet and slid it into an envelope.

'Perhaps you'll get off to school now.'

'Perhaps I will.'

He missed the first lesson and Mr Rowley didn't see him until the afternoon registration.

'Were you absent this morning, Hawk?'

'I was late.'

'Does that entitle you to miss the whole of the first period?'

'I didn't get here till after ten.'

'I see. Just popped in for morning coffee, did you?'

'No, I was working so late last night that I laid too long. I knew we'd got history first and I was going to come out without having any breakfast, but my mam wouldn't let me. I said, I've not time for breakfast, we've got Mr Rowley first. Never mind Mr Rowley, she said, you can't go out on a morning like this wi' nowt inside you, you'll be getting run down, especially wi' all that work you're doing. Sit down and I'll make you some toast. I've no time, I said, and I was just rushing out when my dad came in from his allotment. He was nearly in tears, a dog had got into the greenhouse during the night. Come and have a look, Len, he says. He's off work, you know, my dad, they're closing their pit down. Well, I could see he was upset, so I thought I'd better go and have a look. Be quick then, I said, I'm late already. It was a right mess. There were plant pots and seed boxes all over, and there must have been a dozen broken panes. My dad was going mad. You see, with him being off work he has to do odd jobs to pass his time on, and he was going to start painting inside the greenhouse today. Well, he couldn't do a thing, state it was in and with this bad back he's got he can't do much lifting, so I thought I'd better clean up for him. Well, I couldn't very well just leave him standing there, could I? When I'd finished I had to run back home for some paper to stuff in the broken panes, and then I measured up and went round to the plumbers to order some new glass. You've got to get your glass back in sharp, because if a wind gets up and gets inside, it'll have the lot away in no time. I was like a collier when I'd finished, so my mam made me get stripped off and have a good wash before she'd let me out into the street.'

'I see.'

'If I'd have got hold of that dog I'd have murdered it.'

'You father will have to make sure that the door is secure in future, won't he?'

'I know, but you wouldn't think dog's'd be roaming around on such nights, would you?'

'Dogs roam around at all time, Hawk.'

'They must do, but you wouldn't think so, would you?'

'Right, you may go.'

Mr Rowley stayed to complete the register, and the class dismissed.

'We've got Priddle first, haven't we, Harry?'

'I don't know how you can stand there and tell stories like that, Len. I don't know how you keep a straight face.'

'You've just got to believe in what you're saying.'

'How can you though if it's not true?'

'It is true if he believes it.'

'You can't go around lying all along though.'

'Who's lying? I had a lump as big as a boxing glove in my throat. I nearly had to send out for my weeping glass at one point.'

Harry laughed and nudged him with his shoulder.

'It's right.'

'I know it is, Len. How's your revision going?'

'I might try and make a start this week-end.'

'Make a start! Haven't you done any yet?'

'I've had a lot on just lately.'

'Just imagine that you've done it, you'll be all right then.'

Lennie swung out at him and they burst into a sprint down the corridor with Lennie commentating from the back.

'And there's fifty yards to go and it's Andrews still in the lead, but Hawk is closing up fast! The crowd is on its feet as they race for the tape! Who's it going to be for the gold medal?'

Grinning children and frowning teachers looked out of their classrooms on separate segments of the race, and two teachers rushed to their doors. But they were too late, the competitors had skidded and grabbed their way round the corner out of sight.

'And it's a dead heat! They'll have to share the medal between them. Please cut along the dotted line.'

Harry leaned back on the toilet wall then placed his hands on his knees. 'I'm buggered.'

'Well come in here then and have a breather while I have a quick shit.'

'I don't want a shit.'

'Tha can have a sit down, can't tha, while tha waiting?'

They sat in adjacent cubicles shouting over the top to each other.

'There's no wonder t'school team's going to t'dogs. There isn't a fit man amongst you!'

'We're not all professionals you know.'

'We're not either.'

'You might just as well be though.'

'Does tha know, Harry, I feel as fit as a bull just now?'

'There's no wonder, all that training you're doing.'

'I'll tell thi what we'll do when I've finished.'

'What?'

'We'll have a cross-country round t'corridors, ten laps and I'll give thi one start.'

'And do you think the whole school's just going to sit there and watch us keep hurtling past, lap after lap?'

'After school then?'

'Likely.'

'Coming to Manchester to watch us on Saturday?'

'Can't afford the time, exams are too near.'

'Oh shut up about t'exams, will tha.'

'It makes no difference whether I shut up or not, they'll still be here in a couple of weeks' time.'

'It'll be off anyway, unless t'weather changes.'

The sun was dropping dead behind the kop and the big blue sky was already pink round the edges. A sharp wind cut across the pitch into the empty terrace, shaking and breaking the drops of melted frost hanging under the cross-bars of the crush barriers. The pitch was still greasy in the sun, but in the shadow, the frost was already sprinkling and sparkling the grass. Under the turf the earth was gripped tight by the cold.

Eddie and Mac were running the lines, and Clifford Anderson was moving amongst the players, coaching and pulling them out for instruction when the play had shifted. The game was nearly over. The first team were leading 4-o. Lennie had scored twice, and had run around as firm footed as someone playing on soft sand. Clifford Anderson watched him harass the goalkeeper into making a bad clearance, then called him to the touchline.

'Leave that to Bobby or Roy, Len. If you get caught up there it leaves too big a gap in the centre of the field.'

'Right. It's just that I like to be up there, that's all.'

'Did you know that a Selector was due to watch you today?'

'No, I didn't know.'

'It hasn't taken you long to attract attention, has it?'

'Long enough, I've had a few matches now, you know.'

'You what! I bet you've played no more than half a dozen times.'

'Well, that's enough, isn't it?'

Clifford Anderson shook his head and watched the play.

'Would you believe it? Six matches and thinking of international football.'

'Why not, if I think I'm good enough? Do you know, I feel so good sometimes when I'm playing that I'm sure I could perform miracles.'

Clifford Anderson smiled at him, but Lennie was serious.

'Off you go then, son, and let's see you perform some next week.'

The sun had dropped behind the kop and the whole of the field was in shadow. A transparent slice of moon showed in the sky, and the wind was bitter now that the sun had gone.

'Right, lads, that's it!'

Chris flicked the ball up into his hands and the players trotted off the field. Eddie picked a bucket up from in front of the trainer's bench and slung the water over the wall on to the terrace. The splattering echoed all round the ground and up into the dark hollow of the stand. He disappeared up the tunnel leaving the ground deserted in the swishing wind, under the darkening sky.

Lennie pressed his face to the window and curved his hand to his temple. There were no lights by the roadside, just the passage of fields and woods under the pale gleam of the moon. He stood up and walked to the back of the bus. The conductor pressed the bell and the bus slowed down.

'All the best next week, Len.'

'Ta.'

He stepped off and looked round. The conductor watched him through the back window, until distance thickened the darkness and he couldn't see him any more. There was no traffic and no houses, just fields and trees under the moon. Lennie tightened his muffler and crossed the road to a lane branching off between high hedges. The cobbles shone silver and his footsteps cracked and carried as he walked up the centre. There was no sign of the town, not even a fan of light, over the farthest field. He walked hard, and he was sweating by the time he reached the nest of houses built round the narrow crossroads. Leary's house stood behind a long lawn and was approached through an avenue of trees. As he walked up the drive the trunks barred the lighted windows at the front of the house. He pressed the bell. Ding Dong and the immediate muffle of running feet inside. Jane opened the door and ran straight at Lennie. He caught her and lifted her high off the ground.

'Oh Len.'

He put her down and she began to sob into his shoulder.

'Oh, I've missed you, Len.'

'Is your dad in?'

'Yes, but you can't see him.'

'Why can't I?'

'You know what he's like, it'll only make things worse.'

'It can't make 'em much worse.'

'You can't, Len, you'll have to go.'

'Jane! Who's there?'

The band of light across the asphalt thickened as Mrs Leary pushed the door open.

'Hello, Mrs Leary.'

'Good heavens! What are you doing here?'

'I've come to get things sorted out about me and Jane.'

'I'm not certain that there is anything to sort out, is there?'

'There's plenty.'

'Don't you think you're taking this matter a little too seriously?'

'I'm not taking it half as seriously as Mr Leary. That's what I've come for, to have a word with him.'

'Well. I really don't know what to say.'

'Gwen! Who are you speaking to?'

Mrs Leary glanced behind the open door then stepped back into the hall. 'Well, as you've come so far, I suppose you'd better come in.'

Lennie followed Jane inside and closed the door after them.

Mrs Leary waited for him to turn round and then she nodded across the hall.

'Mr Leary's in there. You'd better go in and get it over with.'

Lennie approached adjacent doors at the far side of the central staircase. He grasped the knob of the first door and looked back. Mrs Leary nodded so he opened the door and went in. Mr Leary was working at a big desk in front of the window. A lamp on a flexible stem illuminated the mess of papers on the desk top, and left the rest of the room gloomy. He looked up when the door opened, and light flooded in from the hall. Lennie stood still in the doorway and they faced each other across the room. He waited, then moved to close the door. Mr Leary shot up like a jack-in-the-box and his chair tilted back into the curtains. Glass cracked.

'Hawk! What the hell are you doing here?'

'I'd like to speak to you.'

'Well, I don't wish to speak to you, now will you get out?'

'I just want to –'

'I've nothing to say to you.'

'Are you always so rude with people?'

Mr Leary placed his knuckles flat on the desk and his arms bowed as the weight settled.

'Only with people I dislike. Now will you kindly leave?'

'You're not giving me much of a chance, are you?'

'You've had your chance.'

'Look! If you're still on about that thing at the Queen's –'

'I shall never forget that T H I N G at the Queen's.'

'O. K., so I had a bit too much to drink –'

'And what about this pub in Town where you've been taking Jane?

'It's not the sort of place –'

'O give over! You don't think I'm good enough for her, do you?'

'Unfortunately for you, Hawk, your reputation preceded you into this house, and some of the tales I heard were enough to make any father apprehensive.'

'You don't believe everything you hear, do you?'

'Not everything.'

'No, just what suits your purpose.'

Mr Leary propelled himself round his desk with his hand and strode across the carpet.

'Now listen here, I'm not standing for any of that! As far as you and Jane are concerned it's over! Do you hear?'

Lennie cocked his head as though listening for an aeroplane.

'No, not quite, would you speak a little louder please?'

'Get out this instant, you lout! You may be a brilliant footballer and scholar, Hawk, but basically you're a lout.'

'You're a charming man, Mr Leary. And if you're an example of management, there's no wonder labour relations are going to the dogs.'

'Get out!'

He grabbed Lennie's lapel and tried to turn him to the door. Lennie stiffened and looked at the hand as though it was a lump of shit.

'Take your hand off, or I'll knock it off.'

'You'll what?'

He clutched more of the material into his palm and drew Lennie closer. 'You'll what?'

'I said I'll knock it off. You can't frighten me with the sack, you know.' Mr Leary let go, and gave Lennie a backhander across the face. Lennie whipped his fist up and Mr Leary stepped away and flung his arms up. But he was too slow, the straight right bolted into his mouth and knocked him staggering backwards across the carpet. He crashed into the desk and his flailing arms sent the papers flying like a flock of frightened birds. He regained balance and sat on the desk edge staring across the room at Lennie. Blood began to stream down his chin and dot his white shirt with the urgency of a dripping tap. Knock, knock on the door.

'David! David, is everything all right.'

The knob turned and the door inched open. Lennie stepped back and squeezed it with his heel. It clicked shut.

'Go away, Gwen!'

Lennie stood wide-legged with his fists clenched at his sides. Mr Leary rested on the desk, dabbing his lip with a balled handkerchief. He looked down at it, each time he brought it away from his face.

'I'll have you in court for this, Hawk.'

'Go on then.'

'You can go to jail for criminal assault.'

'I wish you would.'

He stopped dabbing and held the soaked handkerchief still in front of his mouth.

'What do you mean?'

'You wouldn't have a leg to stand on.'

'It would be your word against mine.'

'Just try it then and we'll see.'

'You wouldn't stand a chance.'

'Just try it on then. I should love to tell everybody what a rotten bastard you are, and that it was you that made me leave the Town.'

'Leaving the Town! I didn't know you were thinking of leaving.'

'I'm not, but I would if this went to court, just to spite you.'

'It wouldn't make the slightest difference to me whether you left or not.'

'Wouldn't it?'

'No, why should it?'

'The crowd would lynch you if you went near the Dale.'

'The crowd! What do I care about the crowd?'

'You'd care if they all stopped away, and you had to explain it to the other directors.'

'Hawk. You don't think you're more important to the Town than I am, do you?'

'I'm bloody sure I am.'

'You what? Do you know that I've given thousands out of my own pocket to the Town? Do you know that it was my money that kept the Town in the First Division last season?'

He pointed at himself with his bloody handkerchief leaving smudges on his shirt and tie.

'Where do you think the extra cash came from when Prince and O'Niell were purchased?'

'Don't give me that, you wouldn't give anybody the snot from your nose. The Town's no more than an investment to you. Anything you put in down there you get back tenfold in Board Room contacts and prestige.'

'And you're indispensable then?'

'I am just now, and you know it. If I left the Town and blamed it on you, you could say Ta Ta to the Dale. In fact it might mean Ta Ta to a lot of things in this Town.'

Mr Leary stared at him, then tested his lip with his finger, looking at it to see if the bleeding had stopped. A beard of dried blood smeared his chin.

'You haven't heard the last of this, Hawk.'

'In other words I have.'

'We'll see. Now will you get out?'

'Yes, I'll leave, and you just wait till next Saturday. I'll show you who's more important to the Town.'

He slammed the door behind him and walked into the hall. Mrs Leary and Jane were standing at the bottom of the stairs waiting.

'What's happened, Len?'

'Plenty.'

'Is it all right?'

'Is it hell. It's all wrong.'

Jane flopped down on the stairs and began to cry. Mrs Leary went in to see her husband and returned immediately, white-faced.

'Would you please leave?'

'I'm sorry about that, Mrs Leary, but I'd no choice, he hit me first.'

'I don't care who hit who, the whole incident is disgusting.'

'It's worse than that, it's farcical. It's so serious that it makes you want to laugh.'

'I don't find it in the least amusing, and neither does Jane by the look of her.'

Lennie looked down at her lying sideways with her face on the steps.

'I'm off then, Jane.'

He waited and she stood up and followed him to the door. Mrs Leary tried to stop her but she shrugged her hand away and followed him outside.

'I'll see you then.'

She shuddered with sobs, her hair was wet and straggly round her face.

'I'm sorry, Len, I'm sorry. Everything's hopeless, it's just hopeless.'

She turned and ran back into the house, upstairs. Lennie watched her go and then walked away down the drive. Mrs Leary closed the door leaving the front of the house dark, except for the two lighted windows at either side of the door.

When he reached the main road there was no one waiting at the bus stop. He walked straight past it without looking back and the bus passed him between stops. He walked close to the grass verge with his hands in his coat pockets, unhurriedly, mechanically like a tramp. The moon had disappeared behind a shutter of cloud and the wind had weakened to a whisper in the hedges. Cars passed in a glaring rush, slicing the night with their lights, then leaving the darkness untouched behind them. In the intervals between traffic the only sounds were the whisper of the wind and the steady trek of Lennie's feet on the road. He climbed the hill up to school, and from the top the Town glittered in the valley like a shower of fallen stars. He walked down past Hillside Avenue, then turned back. There was no light at the front of Rowley's house. He walked down the path and had a look round the back. It was dark. He closed the gate behind him and walked down into the town, to the Anchor.

The taproom was warm and noisy. Lennie looked round from the doorway then approached the bar.

'Hello, Len! How you going on then?'

'Steady.'

'We haven't seen much of you lately.'

'No, I've been busy.'

'Pint? Or are you in training?'

'I'm in training, but I'll have a pint.'

'What are your chances next week then?'

'It's a home banker.'

'They say Anderson's been having you back at all hours, new plan or summat.'

'Frank and Bill in t'other room?'

'No.'

'Have they been in?'

'No. I haven't seen much of them lately either.'

Lennie finished his pint in two goes and put the glass down on the bar.

'Same again.'

'What's up, got a thirst on?'

'I've been walking.'

'I wa' going to say, 'cos I knew your match was off today.'

'That stuff'll do you no good, lad.'

Lennie turned his head with his mouth at the glass. His lips brushed the froth and it stuck like a blond moustache. An old man was standing at the corner of the bar, smiling at him from under a big cap. Lennie looked away and tilted the glass.

'You are Lennie Hawk, aren't you?'

'Yes, why?'

'I'm just telling you that'll do you no good, that's all, it never did.'

'It all depends to what extent you drink it, I suppose.'

'I know, but one thing leads to another.'

Lennie looked at the stagnant pool at the bottom of the old man's glass.

'Do you want another?'

'I'm all right, lad.'

'Stan! Give him another glass please.'

The landlord looked at Lennie, then at the old man, and took his glass. He threw the flat drags down the sink and rinsed the glass before filling it.

'All the best. I thought I recognized you in your duffle coat. There's not many players wear duffle coats.'

'I'm just trying to think where I've seen you before.'

'Outside the Dale selling papers.'

'That's it, in front of the main stand.'

'Anyway, just do as I say, lad, and stay off the beer.'

Lennie stood on his toes and looked round the room.

'I know what you're thinking, silly old bugger, why doesn't he mind his own business.'

Lennie lowered himself to flat feet.

'I wasn't thinking anything. I was just looking to see if there was any talent about.'

'That's a lot more sensible than listening to advice from old men, isn't it?'

Lennie smiled at him. The old man remained smiling.

'Old timers are saying you're going to be better than Lennie Silver.'

'Are they? I must be playing well then. Did you ever see Silver?'

'Many a time.'

'He was a good un, wasn't he?'

'Best there's ever been.'

'Do you watch the Town now?'

'I've no time, lad. I've a living to make.'

'You shouldn't be working at your age, you ought to be taking it easy somewhere.'

'I would have been if I'd had any sense. That's why I'm telling you to stay off the beer and save your money, you might need it some day.'

'Why didn't you save yours?'

'Because it went to me head.'

'You did have some then?'

'For a few seasons I did. Nowt like players get today, mind you. But compared with most folks in them days I was classed as well off.'

'You're Mickey Cunliffe, aren't you?'

'How did you know that?'

'My dad's told me about you. He said that you never stopped smiling.'

'I've not much to smile about now though, and to think of the money that's passed through my hands.'

The old man shook his head and had a drink of beer.

'Tell me about Shadow.'

'He made me two hundred goals in five seasons.'

'Was he as good as people say?'

'He was so good that he was a menace to his own side sometimes.'

'What do you mean?'

'Well he was so clever with the ball that we just used to stand back and watch. He could put you into a trance if you weren't careful.'

'More of a menace to the other side though, wasn't he?'

'He used to draw defenders like a magnet. They used to

swarm round him like bees. It was easy for me then, I'd just move away and he'd slip it out. Bang. Anybody could have done the rest ... But that was a long time ago, it's different now, just standing there and listening to them all talking as they go into the ground. I see the players come, and all the kids crowd round them with their autograph books, nothing changes much outside a football ground. I feel it most though when they're all inside and there's nowt to do. I go across to that little café near the car park then to pass a bit of time on. But I always get a funny feeling sitting there, listening to that oo-ing and ar-ing. Every time I hear it I get tears in my eyes for being such a fool. I could be in there, I think, sitting comfortable instead of being in here making my tea last, and having to drink it when it's gone cold. When they open the gates near the end I sometimes go across and have a look in, but it's not the same. I feel dishonest creeping in like that. And anyway I can only stop five minutes because I've to be back at my place when the whistle goes. They all pour out then and walk past me, and nobody knows who I am. It's a funny thing, but when you've been somebody, no matter how long ago it was, you still want to tell folks about it, even though you know that they're not interested.'

'I'm interested.'

'You're just being polite, lad.'

'No, I'm not, if I didn't want to listen I'd go away.'

The old man gave a little laugh.

'Is that how you used to laugh when you scored all your goals?'

The old man laughed again.

'You're a good lad. You've worked wonders for the Town, you know. I've sold papers outside the Dale for ten seasons and the crowd's happier now than they've ever been. They're buying more papers an'all.'

'They're fed up of having nowt to shout about. The Town's done nothing since your day you know.'

'They've done nothing since Shadow died. When he went, the heart went, the rest of us just withered away like limbs. And now they've something to hope for again.'

Lennie turned away and had a quick drink.

157

'What's up, lad, am I upsetting you?'

'I'm all right.'

'I'd better shut up then.'

'I don't like to see old people sad, that's all. My dad gets like that sometimes.'

'It's better to be sad when you're old than when you're young. You don't have as far to carry it then.'

Lennie looked at him smiling over his empty glass.

'Do you want another one?'

'No, I'll get you one this time.'

'I'll get 'em. Stan!'

The landlord and his wife had their backs turned, busy at the other bar. Lennie looked past them through the square into the best room. It was like watching the audience from inside a Punch and Judy show. Stan turned round and walked across. He pressed his belly to the bar and looked at the old man.

'I don't want another, lad.'

'Are you sure?'

'No, I'll have to be off. You don't sell papers standing in a pub.'

'Do you want a ticket for next week?'

'No, I should only sell it if you gave me one.'

'I might see you outside the ground then.'

'I'll be there. And don't forget what I told you. It's not good for the heart too much beer, especially if you're the heart of a football team.'

He bent for a bundle of papers propped up at the bottom of the bar, then settled them under one arm and walked away.

'Pint, Stan.'

'Tha gets some right mates, don't tha, Len?'

'Do you know who that was?'

'Old Mickey Cunliffe, he just comes in to get out a t'cold.'

'He was a good player, wasn't he?'

'He'd talk a dog's hind leg off if he'd t'chance.'

'My dad says he's one of the best centre forwards there's ever been.'

'Why don't tha go round to t'best room, Len? There's some nice stuff in there tonight. Or are tha still knocking about with her ladyship?'

'Who?'

'Tha knows very well who. Her wi' t'long hair, Leary's daughter.'

'She's gone away.'

'Funny time a t'year to be going on holiday, isn't it?'

'She's gone on safari to Africa.'

'She hasn't, has she?'

'It's a working holiday. Her dad's trying to increase toilet roll sales and Jane's gone out at the head of this advertising campaign. You see there's a big potential market out there because the natives all use leaves instead of paper.'

'The dirty buggers! Does tha know, Len, I've heard that they sometimes cover themselves in shit to scare off evil spirits.'

'They'll need some paper to wipe that lot off then, won't they?'

Lennie walked round to the best room and squeezed through the crowd round the bar. Stan passed him his pint.

'It's marvellous what you can do when you've got a bit of money, isn't it?'

'I'll pay for that, Stanley.'

The hand that paid was wearing a red-stoned ring on the little finger. Lennie looked over his shoulder. The man was wearing a checked hat with a feather in the side. The woman with him was clad in a leopard skin fabric coat. She smiled.

'My husband's one of your biggest fans.'

'Cheers, Len.'

'He hadn't been to watch the Town for ages until you started playing.'

'No good wasting your money on a bad team, is it?'

'Well it isn't, is it?'

'I said I'd never go and watch the Town again until they'd got a decent team together.'

'He used to watch television Saturday afternoons, didn't you, dear?'

'Mind you, I blame the Manager as much as anybody, he should have bought some new players years ago.'

'You don't look like I expected.'

'How do you expect people to go and watch unless they keep buying new players?'

'He doesn't look like a footballer, does he, Harold?'

'You wouldn't say that if you saw him playing. He's going to take us to Wembley this year, is our Len.'

'You've always wanted to go to Wembley, haven't you, Harold? I don't know why though when you can watch it in comfort in your own front room.'

'I'd like to go once though. Just to say I've been.'

'Have you ever been, Len?'

'He's been there many a time with the England Youth Team, haven't you, Len?'

'Fancy.'

'And he'll be playing there for England before he's much older, or I don't know my football.'

'That would be nice.'

'And we're all hoping that he'll be there with the Town this year.'

'Will you go, Harold?'

'Listen to her, Len.'

'Have I said anything wrong?'

'Well you don't just G o to the cup final. Tickets are more precious than gold.'

'Well, I didn't know, did I?'

'But I must say, I'd like to get hold of one. I'd be willing to pay well over the odds as well.'

Lennie took a long, slow drink from his pint.

'I bet the Manager doesn't know you're out drinking, does he?'

'Nothing wrong with the odd pint on a Saturday night is there, Len? I always say that a drink of beer builds your strength.'

'That's what they always say on the telly, isn't it?'

'I've been ordered to drink as much beer as I can manage.'

'Really!'

'You see I suffer from a rare digestive disease. I went down to London to see this specialist about it last week.'

'Nothing serious, I hope?'

'Well, it's a bit complicated. You see, the digestive juices in my small intestine are a lot more powerful than in most people, so the food is digested at such a rapid rate that my body doesn't receive the maximum nutritional benefit from the food consumed.'

'I see.'

'It does sound serious.'

'In most people it isn't, but if you're burning calories up at the rate that I do when I'm playing football, it means that you can lose weight so quickly that you can starve to death if you're not careful.'

'This isn't going to put you out of action, is it?'

'That's why the Doctor told me to go on beer, because it's high in calories and alcohol is the only substance which digests in the stomach. So it never reaches my small intestine you see, and its digestion isn't affected.'

'Well, fancy that.'

'All this must be hard on the pocket though, surely?'

'The club pays for it all. It costs them fifteen pounds a week to keep me in beer.'

'Good God! There's no wonder they can't afford new players.'

'A dietician sent my mother a special menu, so that I could have it with every meal.'

'What, breakfast as well?'

'I have milk stout on cornflakes. It doesn't half make 'em pop.'

'No!'

'There's only one trouble though, I have to go for a piss every five minutes. So if you'll excuse me.'

'Certainly.'

Lennie moved away to the edge of the crowd, and watched a singer performing on a small platform in the far corner of the room. All the chairs had been rearranged round the tables into loose horsehoes facing him. He started on Ramona with eyes closed and his mouth too near the microphone. He throttled the stem and remembered the rambling rose she wore in her hair. The pianist was playing in his shirt sleeves. He had his head turned sideways listening to the keys and grinning at the audience like a wry-necked idiot. Four boys were trying their luck with two girls sitting on the upholstered bench round the walls. Four pint pots surrounded two stemmed glasses on the

table between them, but the girls weren't having any. The boys
bent in conference, then two of them picked up their pints and
walked away. Lennie sat down on one of the vacant stools.
When the boys saw who it was they leaned across the table
and told the girls. One of them already knew, it was Sylvia.
She nodded. Lennie smiled and Sylvia's friend nudged her.

'Do you know him then?'

'I've met him a couple of times.'

'Isn't he fab?'

'You don't know him.'

'I wish I did though.'

The two boys got down to business. Sylvia's friend was willing now, but Sylvia sat back and watched the singer. She was
wearing a mauve sweater and a hairstyle five sizes too big for
her head. She crossed her legs and Lennie had a look at her
black underslip.

'Where's your mate tonight? What do they call her, Irene?'

'She's courting strong now, didn't you know?'

'Who, Frank?'

'They're talking about getting engaged at Easter.'

'What about you and Bill? Have you packed up then?'

'We've been finished ages. We packed up that night you
were in here.'

'It was good night all round that.'

'It was arguing about you that started it.'

'I didn't do so well either.'

'Aren't you courting now then, either?'

'She was too expensive for an ordinary working lad like me.'

'She was a right snob.'

'Still working for her dad?'

'Worse luck.'

'It's same as they say.'

'What is?'

'It's allus best to stick to your own sort.'

'You're taking the mickey again, aren't you?'

'Me? Never! Nice sweater you've got on Sylvia, it suits you
that colour.'

'Do you like it? It's new today.'

'You fill it out lovely.'

'Sh sh sh! You're embarrassing me.'

'You do though. Are you going off with these two?'

'She might be, but I'm not.'

'Where are you going?'

'I was going to go to the Mecca, but I don't think I'll bother now. I think I'll go home and play my new records. I'm on my own this weekend so I'll be able to play 'em as loud as I like.'

'Can anybody come?'

'Hello, Len.'

Lennie turned round and looked up at Mr Brook.

'Hello, Mr Brook, what are you doing down here?'

'Is that a spare stool? I'll just sit down for a minute.'

He sat down and put his glass of stout on the table.

'I just happened to be passing and I know that you get in here sometimes so I thought I'd pop in.'

'First time I've been in for ages this.'

'I'm not interrupting anything, am I?'

He looked across to the two girls who were whispering fiercely with their heads turned sideways against the wall.

'No, you're all right, I'm waiting for somebody.'

Lennie slid to the front of his stool, then bent forward and started to unfasten and fasten his shoelaces.

'Are you coming then or what?'

'Can't you wait a bit? There's no rush.'

'Look! I'm not sitting here all night waiting for you to get off with him.'

'I'm not trying to get off with him.'

'Not much, you're not.'

'You're only jealous.'

'You don't stand a chance with his sort.'

'What do you mean his sort? Do you think he's too good for me or summat?'

'And what about me? I'll be left wi' these two if you go with him.'

'You'll be all right.'

'I'll not if they won't split up.'

'You'll just have to risk that, won't you?'

'I know, Sylvia, but you're not sure with him, he might go

off with this other fellow and leave you. At least you'll get into t'Mecca free if you go wi' one of these two. You don't have to stop with him then if you don't want.'

'Just hold on a minute while I go to t'lav.'

Sylvia stood up and wriggled her skirt down. Lennie pushed his chair back towards the next table to make the gangway smaller.

'Will you excuse me.'

She squeezed out sideways, pressing his shoulders down with her hands and wiping her breasts along the back of his head.

'Thank you.'

Lennie smoothed his hair down, and watched her disappear round his crooked elbow.

'You nearly got an eyeful then, Len.'

'Where did you say you were going, Mr Brook?'

'What?'

'When you came in, I thought you said you were on your way somewhere.'

'No, I said that I happened to be passing, so I thought I'd drop in.'

'I didn't think you were a drinking man.'

'I'm not, but I don't like to stay in on Saturday evenings.'

'It's not much fun drinking on your own though, is it?'

'No, but it's better than sitting in a bedroom listening to the radio.'

'I suppose owt's better than that.'

Sylvia returned and ruffled herself back into her seat. She lifted her glass and glanced at Lennie over the rim.

'The school team are struggling without you.'

'Are they?'

'They're playing well enough but Leary's getting the lads' backs up all the time. He can't forget that he's Head Boy even on the field.'

'Can't he?'

'No, he hasn't got that way with them that you had.'

'No.'

'I'm thinking of ordering a new strip for next season.'

'Are you?'

Sylvia lifted her foot and inspected the heel of her shoe. Her legs opened as far as the tight skirt would stretch.

'Do you think we ought to have some colours?'

'What? Yes, they'd be champion.'

'It doesn't look as if your friend's coming.'

'No, but I shall be if I sit here much longer.'

'Sorry, I don't know –'

'It's all right, I was thinking aloud.'

'Look Len, if you're doing nothing why not come out for a meal with me?'

Sylvia leaned across the table and joined her friend in conversation with the two boys. Her sweater sagged like a bag of water under the weight of her breasts.

'I'm not hungry, thanks.'

'I was thinking of trying that new Chinese place, I heard Mr Priddle recommending it the other day.'

'Did you?'

'Are you interested in modern jazz, Len? Because I've got an excellent collection at home, and I thought we would perhaps go back afterwards and play a few records.'

The two boys stood up, to one side, and the girls put their coats on. Sylvia followed her friend round the other side of the table, past them. Lennie watched her wobble away across the carpet.

'Jesus wept!'

'What's the matter?'

'I could weep the spirit from mine eyes.'

'What?'

'Talk about an open goal.'

'I don't follow you at all, Len.'

He snatched his beer off the table and gulped it down. He ground his teeth and glanced at the empty glass, grasping it by the barrel as though he was about to throw it at somebody.

'If you're a bit short don't worry, it's on me.'

'It's too late to worry now, isn't it?'

'I'm flush as it happens, I won the staff buster last week.'

'Look, I'm not hungry! In fact I'm fed up to the teeth.'

'Why not come across to my local for a change then? It's only five minutes in the car.'

'I've had enough tonight.'

'Do you want another one here?'

'No, I'm off.'

'What about your friend? What if he comes?'

'Who said it's a he?'

'Well, I, I just thought it would be, that's all.'

'I'll bet you did.'

'What do you mean by that?'

'If you must know my friend's been and gone.'

'When? I never saw anybody –'

'She went when she saw me sitting here with you.'

'O dear, I'm sorry. I hope I haven't spoiled your evening for you.'

'It doesn't matter now.'

'We can still go for that meal if you like.'

'No, I think I'll go and try my luck at the Mecca.'

He stood up and kicked the stool under the table.

'Why don't you come? You get some fair birds in there.'

'I think I'm a bit old for that sort of thing, I wouldn't have a clue with the dances they do these days.'

'Get away with you. You might finish up with a real darling.'

'No thanks, Len.'

'I'll see you then.'

'Have a nice time.'

It had started to rain. The freezing drizzle made him shudder and hunch his shoulder as he walked down Sloame Street. The house was empty. He took the fireguard from the hearth and broke the black crust to let the flames through. It was warm and quiet. He turned the radio on and twiddled around with foreign stations. Then he turned it off and went to the pantry. The shelves were full of week-end baking. A raw joint on a bloody tin plate stood between an apple pie and an egg custard. He stuffed a currant bun into his mouth and switched the television on. The set hummed into focus and showed a frightened witness being interrogated by an aggressive lawyer. He crawled across the rug and clicked the dial round the notches to the other channel.

A line of chorus girls were grinning and wheeling round the stage in time. He switched them off and searched the rack under the television stand for the paper. A photograph of his head and shoulders looked up from the top of the back page. Underneath the photograph it said LENNIE HAWK. The headlines of the accompanying article read, ENGLAND NEED NEW FACES FOR WORLD CUP. He went to the pantry for another bun and sat down with a history text book. After five minutes he hadn't turned the page so he dropped the book down the side of the chair. It did the splits and stood there covers up. The fire was low in the grate. The street was silent. The newspaper lay flat on the rug at the side of the tent of the text book. Lennie sat with his chin on his chest and his legs straight out, like his dad when he had slept there drunk. The clock tick, ticked on the mantelpiece, and a gust of wind scattered rain against the window. He stood up stretching and yawning. There was a knock at the door. His muscles relaxed, making his back arch and legs flex at the knees. He stood still listening like a cat.

'Come in!'

Silence.

'What's up, are you deaf or paralysed?'

He walked into the kitchen and opened the door.

'Jane!'

She smiled shyly at him then glanced along the flags up the yard. Drizzle had settled like diamond dust on her hair, and the layer of tiny drops twinkled and sparkled in the light from the door.

'Come on in, love. Didn't you hear me shout?'

He took her arm and guided her over the trestle. Jane swept her hand over her head and her hair was immediately saturated.

'I stood there for ages, I didn't know what to do.'

'If only you knew how glad I am to see you. Here, let me take your coat.'

'Thank you.'

'Sit down here and get warm.'

He pushed the armchair closer to the fire and sat her down. Then he ran outside and shovelled a bucket of coal like someone in a silent film. He mended the fire and closed both doors.

'I can't believe it. If anybody ever tells me that there isn't a God I'll flatten 'em.'

'I was scared stiff that you'd be out.'

'Jesus! I'm glad I wasn't.'

He pulled her out of the chair and picked her up like a bride.

'I've never been as happy to see anybody in my life.'

She put her arms round his neck and hitched herself higher, to lighten the load.

'You don't think I'm awful, do you, running after you like this?'

'Don't be silly, love.'

'I never even thought about it, I just put my coat on and came.'

'He didn't let you come, did he?'

'No, they went out. I suppose after what had happened they never dreamt that I'd come here.'

'I made a right muck of things, didn't I?'

'It wasn't your fault. I knew what would happen.'

'He just wouldn't listen. Anyway bugger him, you're here that's all that matters.'

He swung her back on to her feet and pulled her down in front of the fire.

'Are you warm now?'

'I'm smashing.'

'I've missed you, love.'

'I've missed you, it seems like ages.'

She stared into the fire and nursed her legs with her chin on her knees. Lennie reached for the cushion out of the armchair and laid it on the rug.

'It's lovely here, Len, it's ever so cosy.'

'Lie down with me.'

'Where's your mother and father?'

'My dad's at the club, my mother's at my Aunt Mary's.'

'What if they come back?'

'They'll not be back for ages.'

'Are you sure?'

'I'm positive. My dad usually calls for her, and they get talking and playing cards.'

'Put the light out then.'

'What for?'

'It's better with the light out, it seems warmer.'

168

Lennie stood up and walked across to the door. Jane stretched out on her back with her head sideways on the cushion. He looked down on her with his hand over the switch.

'Switch it off, Len.'

He switched it off and lay down beside her. Flames flickered and split the darkness, and the room was gloomy and safe like a cave on a stormy night. He cradled her head with one arm and felt down her back with the other one. Jane snuggled close into his chest. He squeezed the softness of her arse and pushed it forward into him.

'Len.'

'What?'

'You can if you want to now.'

'I do want to.'

'I want you to, I want you to so much.'

She felt for his hand and placed it over her breasts. He unfastened the buttons of her sweater and slid it inside.

'Can you remember that night in the car, Len?'

'Do you mean that night when you wouldn't let me?'

'I could have killed myself for it afterwards. I never thought we'd have another chance.'

'You were right though, it's better like this.'

'I know it is, this is how I wanted it.'

'You look nice enough to eat.'

'Don't look at me, Len.'

She tried to cross her arms over her breasts, but he held them back and looked at her. She lay still with her face turned away from the fire into the shadow. He bent down and kissed her breasts in turn, softly like brushing his lips on a rose. She moaned, and pressed his head tight. He couldn't breathe, so he turned his head sideways and listened to the bump, bump of her heart.

'Be gentle with me, won't you, Len. This is the first time anything like this has happened to me.'

'I'll be careful.'

'Don't hurt me, will you?'

'It might hurt a bit.'

'It won't be too much though, will it?'

'No, it'll be all right.'

'Are you going to wear anything?'
'I haven't got anything.'
'What if something happens?'
'It won't.'
'What if it does?'
'Come on, love.'
'Len, what –?'
'Sh sh sh.'
'Slowly, Len. Don't hurt me!'
'Sh. Shsh.'
'Oh, it's hurting! Oh Len!'

Her spine arched and her fingers gripped into his back. She shook her head but he pressed his mouth to hers and fought her down. Her legs flattened and flexed, and her feet crushed and brushed the woollen chips of the pegged rug. Then she broke and went limp like a rag doll. Lennie lifted his head and looked at her.

'Jane.'
'Oh, it hurt, Len.'
'Are you all right?'
'I didn't know what was happening.'
'I haven't loved you properly.'
'I can't any more.'
'Relax, love, you're fighting me.'
'I had to, Len, I had to.'
'You'll be all right now, just relax.'

She lay breathless like someone on thin ice until he had finished, then she began to cry quietly into his chest. Lennie cuddled her up patting her back and rocking her, until she was quiet.

'Didn't you like it, love? – Jane?'
'Yes.'
'Didn't you like it?'
'It was too much, I didn't know where I was.'
'Did it hurt a lot?'
'A bit.'
'How do you feel now?'
'I just want to lie still, and think about it.'
'Are you disappointed?'

'No Len, of course I'm not, but it all happened in a rush, I wanted to laugh and cry at the same time.'

'You'll like it better next time.'

'It'll never be like tonight though.'

'It'll be easier, you'll enjoy it more.'

She kissed him and held her face at the side of his head.

'I love you, Len.'

'You don't regret it, do you?'

'No, of course I don't, I'm too near it just now, that's all.'

She sat up and looked at herself.

'I feel different.'

'What do you mean?'

'I don't mind you looking at me like this now. I feel much closer to you.'

'You are.'

'Isn't it smashing?'

She dived back on top of him weeping and laughing. Lennie grinned and smacked her arse.

'Ow!'

'Come on, my mam and dad'll be here in a bit.'

'Will they mind?'

'Not if we get dressed.'

They got dressed and Lennie switched the light on. They squinted and turned their flushed faces away from the glare. Jane opened the door and went into the kitchen. She turned the tap on and caught the column of water in her cupped hands.

'It's freezing.'

'You'll have to put the kettle on if you want some hot.'

'No, I like it.'

She bent down and carried the water to her face.

'That's lovely, o-o-o it's lovely.'

Lennie passed her the towel and swilled his face. He put his mouth under the tap and filled his cheeks with water. Jane watched over the towel from the side of the sink. He pointed a finger over his lips and squirted two jets round it. One splashed on to the draining board, the other shot into Jane's face. She squealed and lifted the towel. Lennie dragged it away and rubbed her with his dripping face. She screamed and bent backwards away from him. He straightened her up, and she stood still like a little girl while he dabbed her dry. He dried himself and put the kettle on. Jane opened the pantry door and had a look inside.

The crowd overflowed from the packed pavements into the gutter, and boys running on the outside of the throng brushed the wings of jammed cars, honking and pointing towards the Dale. The flags above the ground flew square in a grey winter's sky, and an odd flurry of snow made the queues glance up and shuffle faster to the turnstiles. Lennie walked along the back of the stand past the relays of programme and paper sellers. He bought a paper from Mickey Cunliffe, then stood to one side and watched him whip them out from under one arm, and hand each one folded like a slice of bread and jam.

'Fit, lad?'

'I feel champion.'

'That's good, 'cos they're expecting a lot today. Just look at their faces.'

The crowd looked happy, like a holiday crowd on the prom, shouting and laughing at each other from half a yard.

'Are you sure you don't want to come in?'

'Can't afford it, lad, I'll sit and listen how you're going on.'

'I'll be off then.'

'Ar, don't be standing here till you're late.'

'Anyway, take this, and if you don't use it, sell it. You should get a good price for it today.'

He pushed a centre stand ticket into the slit pocket of the old man's overcoat and walked away.

'Hey!'

Lennie raised one arm without looking back. He raised his arm in exactly the same way when he scored the first goal in the eighth minute. Swarms of small boys spilled over the walls, and dashed between the guard of policemen who were spaced round the pitch like fence posts. The crowd roared them on as they raced across the pitch and surrounded Lennie and jumped up to slap his back. Then they ran back to their places waving scarves and dodging round the advancing policemen, who tried to catch them with arms spread and clumsy sideways lunges. The Town were on top, moving the crowd to orgasms of expectation with their incisive advances. They were exerting such continuous pressure that goals were inevitable, and as they flicked in and around their opponents' harried defence, the crowd lived in anticipation of that final thrust which would send them jumping and laughing wild-eyed into each other's faces. Bobby Prince scored the second goal when he nipped on to a bad back pass to the goalkeeper, and Lennie scored a beautiful goal a minute before half time. The ball dropped to him from a long defensive punt, and before any defender could close on him he controlled it, pivoted and swept the ball high into the goal in one continuous movement.

At half time the home crowd were happy, and they pounded unmercifully the little bastions of away team followers sporting black and white rosettes. A cheer went round the ground as a barrage of red balloons were released on the terrace. They swirled and bobbed above the upturned faces, and each time one dropped, a bunch of arms strained to knock it up again. The teams straggled out for the second half, and up in the stand coats and rugs were tucked round knees, and gloved hands were banged on thighs. The growl grew to a roar as the referee stared at his watch and the second fingers ticked up to time.

Roy Hann immediately scored the fourth goal when he out-jumped the right back for a full centre from Billy Boscombe. While the teams were lining up for the restart the chimes started on the kop.

TOWN! TOWN! TOWN! TOWN!

The peals spread swiftly round the ground until they boomed out like the striking of Big Ben. Both teams looked sideways at the terraces, and the goalkeepers looked back over their shoulders as the monotone thundered up and on. It disintegrated into a running howl when Lennie scored the fifth goal. There was no time for it to gather force again before he scored the sixth, and group of girls behind the visitors' goal started a new chant.

'LENNIE HAWK! CLAP CLAP CLAP. LENNIE HAWK! CLAP CLAP CLAP. LENNIE HAWK! CLAP CLAP CLAP.'

From this nucleus under the wall of the kop it burst and

soaked round the ground like a blob of ink on a blotter. The crowd was watching Lennie and the game at the same time. Each time he touched the ball the chant quickened to a rapid insistent roar.

LENNIE HAWK! CLAP CLAP CLAP. LENNIE HAWK! CLAP CLAP CLAP. LENNIE HAWK! CLAP CLAP CLAP.'

The clapping banged louder and the calls grew hoarser, until the whole ground shook and throbbed with it. Old men looked happier than they had done for years and Mr Hawk stood behind his barrier shaking his head. Mickey Cunliffe sat in the café sipping cold tea, listening to the chant steam across the car park. The man behind the counter stopped rattling plates to listen, and everyone stopped eating and drinking.

'EHI O! CLAP CLAP CLAP. EHI O! CLAP CLAP CLAP. EHI O! CLAP CLAP CLAP.'

'What is it? What is it they're shouting?'

Mickey Cunliffe looked through the small panes at the broad back of the stand across the car park. The row of doors at the bottom were like mouse holes in a skirting board.

'They're shouting Lennie Hawk.'

The man behind the counter stood still and listened.

''Course they are, you can pick it up if you listen. Bloody hell! I've never heard 'em like that before. He must be playing a blinder.'

The away team goalkeeper began to watch the crowd on the kop behind him, and when a sway started he took two paces forward as though he expected the crowd to spill down the hill and bury him under their massive weight. The wave swept down the kop face like wind on a wheatfield, and a loud groan arose as the people in front braced themselves to repel it. But still the chant continued on the other three sides of the ground and it was picked up again on the kop as soon as equilibrium had been restored.

'LENNIE HAWK! –'

When he scored his fifth goal the chant didn't break for the usual spontaneous roar, but held and strengthened as he turned away with his arm raised. All the players stood still and applauded as he walked back to the centre, waving and smiling amidst the stunning beat, beat, beat.

The referee pipped his whistle for the kick off, then blew two long blasts like an ice cream man and began to walk from the pitch. There was so much noise that some of the players didn't hear him and the game continued until the ball ran out of play, and the linesman picked it up and carried it across the red ash. The teams shook hands and to the mighty applause of the crowd, the Town ran up the tunnel, grinning down at their boots. Clifford Anderson shook their hands in turn as they clattered past him on the concrete. He held his arms wide for Lennie and lifted him clean off the ground in a bear hug.

'Well played, son! Well played!'

'Did it look all right from the side?'

'It was marvellous! It looked marvellous!'

'That's good.'

He put Lennie down and walked him to the dressing-room.

'Oh! There's Charles Crawford in my office, he'd like to interview you for Sports Special when you're changed.'

'I can't, my dad's waiting for me outside.'

'Well, I'll go and tell him not to wait if you like, where will he be?'

'He'll be against the wall just by the players' entrance.'

'Why doesn't he come inside?'

'I don't know, he's funny like that, my dad, he doesn't like to think he's pushing in.'

The asphalt was swarming with people reluctant to go home, and some of them cheered and shouted congratulations when the Manager stepped out of the door. Mr Hawk was leaning against the wall with his hands in his overcoat pockets. He took them out and stood up when he saw Clifford Anderson. They shook hands.

'Well, Mr Hawk, what do you think about him now then?'

'He played well in a good side.'

'Yes, they played exceptionally well today, didn't they?'

'I wish they'd have saved it till later though.'

'What do you mean?'

'Well, they'll never play as well again this season, and it seems a shame to have wasted it on such an ordinary team.'

'I hope you're wrong.'

'I hope I am, but I doubt it.'

'Lennie's being interviewed for Sports Special, so he's sent me out to tell you not to wait.'

'I'll get off then and listen to what he's got to say.'

'Why don't you come inside for a drink?'

'No thanks.'

'Are you sure? There'll be plenty flowing in the Board Room.'

'That's all I'm short of, coming home from a football match smelling a booze, missus's bad enough when I come home from t'club.'

He straightened his cap and looked away into the backs of the thinning crowd.

'Has Lennie said anything about his future lately, Mr Hawk?'

'Don't talk to me about his future, I'm stalled of asking him.'

'He's still going to university then?'

'I don't know where he's going, and if you say owt to him you never get a straight answer.'

'I can believe it, he's a funny lad in some ways.'

'Funny lad! Huh! You're not kidding. I'll be off then.'

'Why don't you wait inside in future? It's much warmer.'

'Nay, it's all right, an extra fifteen minutes doesn't make any difference.'

'Why don't you use the stand?'

'You're too far away from the game. I like to be amongst it all.'

He put his hands back into his pockets and half turned.

'I'll be off then, tell him I've gone.'

'Cheerio, Mr Hawk, I'll see you again some time.'

'Our next report comes from the Dale where Charles Crawford will give us the full story of the Town's sensational seven nil victory. Was this game as one-sided as the score suggests, Charles?'

'This game was MORE one-sided than the score suggests, and the Town played so well that the scoresheet could have read seventeen and not seven. This is by far the most exciting display of attacking football I've seen for years, and in young Lennie Hawk, who scored five of their goals, the Town have discovered a player of world class. He completely pulverized the opposition with a display which I shall never forget as long as I live – I have Len with me now ...

'Congratulations Len, I expect you're a very happy young man at this moment.'

'Yes, I feel all right, thanks.'

'What does it feel like to score five goals in your first cup tie?'

'All right.'

'You're a real goal glutton aren't you?'

'I like to score goals, that's what the nets are at each end for, isn't it?'

'What about the performance of the rest of the team today?'

'Very good.'

'And what about this new plan, do you think it worked?'

'It must have done, we scored seven and they never had a look in.'

'Did the crowd have any effect on you, did it inspire you or anything? I've never heard such a din.'

'I never bother about the crowd, but I'm glad they weren't disappointed.'

'You're not a professional yet, are you?'

'No.'

'In fact you're still at Grammar School, aren't you?'

'That's right.'

'I've heard that you've had offers which would turn most professionals green with envy.'

'Have you?'

'Is it true?'

'I have had some good offers, yes.'

'And why don't you take them?'

'I might be going to university in October.'

'Would you prefer an academic life to the glory and riches of football then?'

'I haven't gone yet, I've got my exams to get through first.'

'It'd be a terrible loss to the game if you did. Many experts are already comparing you with the world's best, and one critic I read in the week says that you should be picked for England immediately.'

'Does he?'

'Do you think you're ready for international football?'

'I'm as ready now as I'll ever be.'

'You sound amazingly confident for an eighteen-year-old who only came into regular league football at Christmas.'

'It's the same as they say, isn't it?'

'What is?'

'If you're good enough you're old enough.'

'Do you think this is true?'

'There's no arguing with a statement like that, is there?'

'No. Well, thank you very much, Len. I've already tipped the Town for the Cup, so don't let me down, will you?'

'I'll see what I can do for you.'

'That's all from Charles Crawford at the Dale, and now back to the studio.'

The desks in private study were arranged in widely spaced rows. Mr Rowley was at the front of the room marking books. Each time he completed one he placed it on top of the marked pile and looked round. Harry Andrews was sitting at the back with his briefcase on the desk. He waited for Rowley to start on another book then lifted the flap of his case and listened inside. Lennie glanced round from the front but Harry shook his head.

'Turn round, Hawk, you'll find no inspiration in Andrews's face.'

Lennie turned round and Rowley lowered his pencil to the next book. Harry lowered his ear into his brief case, his eyes staring across the room at nothing. He listened, then sat up and scribbled something on a sheet of paper. He folded it into a tight wad and threw it at the boy sitting in front. It hit him on the neck. The boy brushed the spot with his hand and looked round. Harry pointed to the paper and lipped 'Pass it on', pointing down the row with a sharp jab of his finger. He picked it up, read it, and was aiming it like a dart when Rowley looked up.

'You boy! Bring me that missile immediately!'

He took it to the front and Rowley unfolded the paper.

'BOURNEMOUTH – AWAY, what do you mean, boy, Bournemouth away?'

'It's a message, sir, I was just passing it on.'

'Were you now? Well I'm afraid I shall have to pass a message on to you, you'll be in detention on Friday evening.'

'Yes sir.'

'R O O M I A T H O M E.'

Lennie grinned back at Harry. Harry gave him a thumb up.

'Hawk! Would you like to join the ranks of the unfortunate as well?'

Lennie faced the front and shook his head.

'Well, stop grinning then! And Andrews! Get that brief-case off the desk and let me see what misdemeanours you're committing behind it.'

Harry lugged his briefcase to the floor, leaving a blank desk in front of him.

'What are you studying, the desk lid?'

'No sir, I've just put my books away, it's time for the bell.'

'Is it really? And what forthcoming event necessitates such a rapid exit?'

'P.E., sir.'

'P.E.! You talk to me about P.E., and your mock "A" levels begin on Friday! Get your books out immediately!'

The bell rang.

'Upper Sixth remain seated, the rest of you may go.'

The in-between lesson traffic had stopped, and the school was quiet again before he released them. As they walked down the corridor Lennie grabbed Harry by the lapels and drew him in.

'What you studying boy, the desk lid?'

'He's a rotten sod, isn't he?'

'You've got to laugh at some of the things he says though.'

'I know, that's why he says them, then if you laugh he puts you in detention for making a noise.'

Mr Brook was standing at the changing-room door throw-ing a football from hand to hand.

'At the seaside next round then, Len.'

'Yes, we shall be beside the sea.'

'You stand a good chance there, I should think.'

'I don't know, they've bad sands at Bournemouth.'

Mr Brook played with a smile and watched Lennie get un-dressed.

'Oh! I forgot to ask you, did you enjoy yourself the other Saturday evening?'

'Marvellous! You should have come.'

'No thanks, I'm afraid that kind of thing's not up my street.'

'Look, I'll have to go now.'

Lennie tried to sit up but Mrs Rowley pulled him down. They were lying full length on the settee.

'It's still early yet, there's plenty of time.'

'I'm worn out, we've had a hard session tonight.'

'Training never made any difference before.'

'I've got some work to do as well, we've got exams in the morning, you know.'

He tried to struggle free again.

'You can't leave me like this, Len, it isn't fair.'

'I've got to, I told you I couldn't stop long.'

'You should have kept your hands off me altogether if you didn't mean to finish it.'

'I like to touch you.'

'It doesn't matter about me then?'

'You like it, don't you?'

'Yes, but not when it's left like this.'

'I'm not a stallion, you know, I've got to think about to-morrow.'

'You weren't thinking about tomorrow when you went train-ing.'

'I've got to go training.'

'But you don't have to come up here, is that it?'

She lay across him trapping his arms at his side. He tried to push himself up with his legs but she swung her legs over and flattened them.

'I'll have to go and do a bit, I've done nowt yet.'

'It's too late now.'

'It'll not have to be.'

'Don't go, Len.'

'It's all right for you, you've got nothing to worry about.'

She scrambled up jabbing her hands and knees into his body. Lennie curled tight, flexing his muscles against the rough pushes. She sat on the edge of the settee and swept her hair back with both hands.

'It shows how much you care when you say a thing like that.'

'What's the matter?'

'Nothing to worry about! Don't you think it's anything to worry about, being lonely? Don't you think it's anything to worry about living day in and day out with nothing to look forward to but an odd visit from you?'

She jumped up and leaned straight-armed on the mantelpiece with her head bowed down to the flames.

'And the times when you don't come, when I sit here so tight that I could scream. Straining for the click of the gate, sick inside with waiting. Don't talk to me about worry, Len.'

'I'm sorry, I didn't know.'

He stood up and slowly edged across the room, watching her all the time.

'I know what's wrong with you, you're tiring of me, aren't you?'

'No, 'course I'm not.'

He felt on the table and quietly lifted his coat up.

'You've found a new girlfriend, haven't you, somebody younger?'

He slipped his coat on and started to fasten it.

'Only girl I've been with lately is Jane, once.'

She whipped round and faced him. Lennie stopped fastening his coat and dropped his hands as though he had been caught stealing.

'Jane! It's all over between you two.'

'Who says it is?'

'Her father stopped it ages ago.'

'That's what he thinks.'

'You never told me you'd seen her.'

'I don't have to tell you everything.'

'Why didn't you tell me you'd seen her?'

'You never asked.'

She turned away from him and slapped her hands down on the mantelpiece.

'You're making a fool of me! You're just having me on!'

'You knew that we hadn't finished.'

'You are finished! You are! Her father stopped it all.'

'Hey! Don't tell me what I am and what I'm not, you're not my mother, you know.'

She spun on him her arms raised and fingers clawed. Lennie dodged behind the settee and faced her with his hands resting on the back and his legs spread wide.

'I didn't mean it like that, honest.'

'You rotter.'

'Honest! I meant that you were telling me off like my mother.'

'You're lying! You're lying! I know what you meant.'

She dropped on the settee and buried her face in the cushions.

Lennie looked down at her from over the back.

'You don't want to believe me, do you?'

She held her fists over her ears and didn't answer. Lennie came from behind the settee and walked across to the door. When he looked back she was sitting up.

'I don't think I'd better come up for a bit.'

'Please yourself.'

'If you think we'd better pack it up altogether, you might as well say so now.'

She ran across to him and threw both arms round his body. Lennie shook her hair out of his eyes and looked round her head at the clock on the mantelpiece.

'I'm frightened, Len, I don't know what I'd do if I didn't see you.'

'I shan't be able to come up for a bit though, I've a lot on with these exams and my football.'

'Try, Lennie, please, I'll go mad if you don't.'

'All right, I'll try then.'

She hugged him tight.

'And the best of luck tomorrow with your exams.'

He stepped off the bus and crossed the road. Harry Andrews was talking to Jenny at the bottom of the drive. They stopped talking and waited for him.

'Hey up, Len. Blimey!'

'What's up?'

'Been out all night?'

'It's all that work he's been doing.'

'I know, he's a crafty sod, is Len.'

'I wish I was an hour behind you two.'

Jenny turned her back on the wind and shuddered.

'Come on, I'd sooner sit and do exams than stand here and freeze to death.'

'I'd sooner stand strapped to a pole in t'nude than face that lot this morning.'

'Listen to him, Jenny.'

'It's right, Harry.'

'We know it is, Len. That's why it's always a straight fight in every subject between you and Leary. Well, speak of the devil.'

The red mini stopped in front of the school gates, and Charles Leary got out. Edmund was driving, and Jane was sitting in the back.

'He's brought your supporters' club as well, Len.'

Lennie walked to the car and opened the door. He stooped inside. Jenny turned away.

'Are you coming, Harry?'

'Might as well. Don't be long, Len. It's too cold for courting this morning!'

'Hello, love – Jesus! What's the matter with you?'

'Nothing, why?'

'You look awful.'

'I'm all right.'

Leary revved up. 'We'll have to go, Jane.'

'Are you ill?'

'No, I'm all right.'

'Where are you going?'

'I'm popping into town.'

'Bit early, isn't it?'

'I'm going to the doctor's.'

'I thought you weren't ill?'

'I'm not. I'm just a little run down, that's all. Mother thinks I need a tonic.'

'Look, Jane. I've got an exam in half an hour.'

'Oh, shut thi trap, you miserable dog! Exams! Exams! Is that all tha thinks about?'

'Jane, either tell him to go, or get out and go down by bus.'

'Don't be so bossy, Edmund.'

'I can't sit here listening to you two all day, I want to be in that room early.'

Jane climbed out and slammed the door. Lennie opened it and bent down: 'You lousy bastard!'

The car accelerated up the drive hooting the crowd out of the way. The swath behind it was quickly filled by children drifting across, and groups re-forming in the centre. Jane leaned back and rested her head on the square stone pillar.

'What's the matter, love? You look as if you haven't been to bed for a week.'

'It's nothing.'

'Has your dad been getting on to you again?'

'No, not yet.'

'What do you mean?'

'I'm a week overdue.'

A gang of little boys walked past, giggling and wolf-whistling.

'Courting again, Len! Give her a kiss then!'

'That's nothing, is it?'

'It is with me, I'm as regular as clockwork.'

'You might have counted wrong.'

'Don't be silly.'

'Perhaps it's because you're worked up. That stops it, doesn't it?'

'Sometimes.'

'You'll have to try and relax then. If you keep worrying it'll never come on.'

'It's all right you talking, Len.'

'Have you told anybody else?'

'Of course I haven't.'

'What about the doctor?'

'It's too early yet.'

'You can't be! Not first time!'

'That's what I keep saying to myself, but I've never been late before.'

'You'll be all right, get a couple of stouts down you or something like that, something to make you relax.'

'And what if nothing happens?'

'It's bound to.'

'What if it doesn't? What will we do then?'

'How the hell do I know?'

Tears brimmed up in her eyes and overflowed down her
cheeks.

Stragglers stared as they hurried past up the drive, between
the sodden flower beds and the bare avenue of trees.

'I'm sorry, love, I don't know what to say that's all.'

'I didn't want to see you, I didn't want to tell you anything
until I was certain.'

'First time though. We can't be that unlucky.'

'I hope not, Len.'

'When will you know for sure?'

'Not for a week or two yet.'

'Jesus! I'll go mad if I've to wait that long.'

'If I don't see you I'll write as soon as anything happens.'

'Write as soon as you know.'

'I will. But what if I am?'

'Don't talk about it.'

'What will we do, Len?'

'God knows. But I don't suppose he'll tell us.'

'I wish I hadn't seen you.'

'Don't be silly. I've as much right to worry as you.'

'I know, but this morning, having to tell you this morning.'

Lennie glanced up at the school. The thick black edges of
the buildings stood firm and strong against the vast boulders
of grey cloud rolling behind.

'Try not to worry too much, Len.'

'It's useless saying that.'

'I know it is, but you've got to say something.'

'I suppose you have, even though you know it's no good.'

'I didn't want to tell you, but now that I have done I feel
a bit better.'

'I'm glad, it might relax you a bit.'

'I couldn't have stood it much longer, having to keep it all
to myself.'

'It might bring it on.'

'You'd better go now or you're going to be late.'

'I wish I was at home with two broken legs.'

'You'll have to go, it's nearly quarter past nine.'

'I can't sit there for three hours this morning.'

'You'll have to.'

'And then this afternoon, and tomorrow, and – I can't do exams now.'

'You'll have to, Len, you'll have to!'

'I can't, it's impossible.'

'Don't make things any worse, Len. Please!'

Lennie watched a bus grow bigger as it crawled up the hill.

'There's your bus here.'

'You won't go home, will you?'

'No, course I won't. Write to me straight away, won't you?'

'As soon as anything happens. Best of luck.'

'It's you that needs that. I'm going to pray every night before I get in bed. Please Mr Postman.'

He saw Jane on to the bus and waved to her through the window when it started. He watched it turn the bend out of sight then turned and walked quickly up the centre of the drive.

SILENCE! EXAMINATION IN PROGRESS.

He pushed the door open and walked in. Harry and Leary were distributing sheets of manuscript paper. Rowley was standing in front of his desk reading a question paper.

'Nice to see you Hawk, I was just about to post your paper on to the Dale.'

Lennie sat down and looked at the span of blank pages angling over each other like a hand of cards. Rowley dealt the question papers personally, turning them face down near the inkwells.

'And let me remind you for the last time to read the questions carefully. It is not the slightest use blinding the examiner with an original thesis on Oliver Hardy if he asks for your knowledge of Oliver Cromwell.' He paused before placing a paper on Lennie's desk. 'What's the matter, Hawk, aren't you staying?'

Lennie took his coat off and hung it on the corner of his chair. It buckled on the floor and fanned out like a thick black wedding gown. He glanced across at Leary who was twisting his neck trying to read the questions upside down through the paper. Rowley walked back to the front and looked at his watch with the deliberation of a referee.

'Right, ladies and gentlemen, you may begin.'

There was a rustle of paper, then silence while they were being read.

'You may begin, Hawk.'

Lennie turned his paper over without moving its position. Leary sat back smiling, and making faces round the room. Then his face straightened as he bent to his writing. Lennie reached round into his coat pocket for his pen and winked at Harry who was sitting at the desk behind. Harry dropped the corners of his mouth, Lennie smiled and turned round. He tapped his papers into a shallow pile, then read the questions and ticked off the ones he was going to answer.

'Bad luck, lads!'

Clifford Anderson stood in the doorway and patted the players on their backs as they filed past him steaming like dray horses. No one replied and they undressed in silence.

'Cheer up then! We had to lose some time. Better now than next week.'

They looked down at their feet as they walked past him to the bath. He waited for Lennie and took him into a corner.

'They had the guards on you today, didn't they, son?'

'Not half. Old man o't'sea had nothing on them two.'

'I know it's asking a lot, Len, but could you get down a couple of mornings next week?'

'Do you mean miss school?'

'Just a couple of mornings if you can. I'd like to do something about this close marking because it's going to happen every match now.'

'I don't know, the old man wasn't so keen about me having next Friday off even.'

'He sounded all right when I spoke to him. He said himself that it would be better if you travelled down with the team.'

'I don't know.'

'I think it would be unwise to bring the lads back in the evening this week the way they're feeling. They'd resent it and I want them a hundred per cent ready next Saturday.'

'It'll have to be on the quiet then.'

'Good lad.'

'I'll come down Tuesday and Wednesday.'

'That's fine, and don't worry about today, even stars have off days.'

There was no rush of autograph hunters when he went out. Only a few boys had remained behind. Mr Hawk pushed himself off the wall with his elbows and started to walk away, past the short line of players' cars. Lennie signed three books then trotted to catch him up.

'Not so good, Lennie lad.'

'I know that.'

'What's up wi' thi?'

'Nowt, except that I'd two men on my back all game.'

'It'd made no difference if there'd have been twenty-two on it last week.'

'I'm not superman, you know! You don't know what it's like being marked like that, they even came t'lav with me at half time.'

'What's tha expect 'em to do, give thi a free run a t'park?'

They walked the rest of the way in silence. Lennie looked behind the clock as soon as he got in.

'Any post this afternoon, Mam?'

'No.'

'What tha allus asking about post for?'

'I'm expecting a letter.'

'Tha wants to get thi mind on thi football and never mind about letters.'

'Who you expecting a letter from, Len?'

'Postman.'

'Don't be so clever.'

'He wasn't so clever this afternoon.'

'Why, didn't he play well?'

'He'll have to play better next week.'

'I played as well as anybody else.'

'I'm not saying tha didn't.'

'Well then!'

'Well then, what? That shows tha had a bad un, doesn't it?'

'I suppose everybody has off days, Arthur.'

'Well I'm glad he's had his today. I don't want to see him play like that at Bournemouth next Saturday.'

Mrs Hawk stopped laying the table, and looked round at him with a fistful of cutlery.

'What do you mean, see him play, you're not going to Bournemouth.'

'Who isn't?'

'You're not.'

' 'Course I'm going.'

'Well! Have you ever heard anything like it? A man who hadn't worked for months, and with no prospects of starting, talking about gallivanting off to Bournemouth.'

'Don't start.'

'You know very well we can't afford it.'

'Why can't we? We've as much money as anybody else, counting our Len's.'

'Our Len's! You've cheek to stand there and consider going to Bournemouth on our Len's money.'

'He's been plenty of places on mine, hasn't he?'

'You're not touching that money! He's going to need that when he goes to university.'

'It's a long way to go at this time a t'year, Dad, you'll have to set off on Friday.'

'I was thinking of going on one of them supporters' trips.'

'I can hear folks talking now, he reckons to be on t'dole, they'll say, yet he can afford to go tripping off to Bournemouth for week-ends.'

'Who the bloody hell's bothered what folks say?'

'Me, I am, I've to live amongst 'em.'

'Well, don't I then?'

'No, not like me you don't – still, I don't know, now that you're not working.'

'You keep getting that in, don't you?'

'Ar, and I have to when you're talking about spending ten pounds to go and watch a football match.'

'Ten pounds!'

'Well how much do you think it'll cost then, a week-end in Bournemouth?' Mr Hawk sat down at the table and slid the cosy off the teapot. 'We've your dole money to live on, Arthur, 'cos our Len's money's stopping where it is. When he goes away he's going to go wi't'same chance as everybody else.'

She walked to the table and poured Mr Hawk a pot of tea. He watched the milk grow darker as the tea splashed into it and rose up the sides of the pot.

'I suppose you're right, lass. I'll have to be satisfied wi' seeing him off on Friday.'

'And I don't like him missing school, cup tie or not.'

'It's the first time, Mam.'

'And let it be t'last, 'cos you're worrying me with your schooling just lately.'

'Why am I? You don't know owt about it.'

'You're not spending enough time at it for one thing.'

'How do you know?'

'You can't be, all this running about you're doing. And you've never said a word about your exams.'

'There's nowt to say until we get t'results.'

Mr Hawk carried his pot to the armchair and lowered it carefully to the hearth.

'Only results I'm bothered about's next Saturday.'

Mr Hawk hurried across the yard from the allotment and opened the kitchen door.

'What time is it?'

'Half past four.'

He pulled his boots off without slackening the laces, and went inside with the heels of his stockings half-way under his feet. He stood with his back to the fire in his jacket and cap. Mrs Hawk was cleaning the cutlery on a newspaper on the table.

'They'll have finished now.'

'And you'd have had all that way to come back in this cold.'

'I'd have known t'results though.'

'You'll know it soon enough.'

'Them at Bournemouth'll know all about it now, and I don't know a thing.'

'O! shut up about it, Arthur, you're enough to drive anybody mad.'

'Our Len'll be getting bathed now, I hope he's played well.'

'I thought you said they were going to win t'cup this year.'

'They are.'

'They'll have won today then, won't they?'

'I wonder if anybody's phoned up.'

'Don't talk wet. Do you think anybody'd waste all that money when they can turn t'wireless on and hear it for nowt.'

'Me. I would if I was well off.'

'Well you're not, so you'll just have to wait, won't you?'

'Look well if our Len's had a bad un again.'

'It's too late to bother now.'

Mr Hawk switched the wireless on and sat down in the armchair. He took his cap off and combed his fingers through his flat hair.

'Why didn't you watch the telly? They give you half time scores and up-to-date information, don't they?'

'I can't stand half times and progress reports, if I'm not there it's torture.'

'And what about that teleprinter? It shows you t'results t'minute after t'games finished.'

'You what! Do you think I could sit here and watch that bloody machine printing a letter at a time? I'd be a nervous wreck before it had finished Bournemouth!'

'Stop shouting then, I'm not in Bournemouth, you know.'

'Shut up now, it's here.'

'I've never known anybody like you for –'

'Shut up!'

'Here are the classified results.'

Mr Hawk leaned forward to the wireless and clasped his hands with his head down. There was a knock on the door.

'First the F.A. Cup fourth round.'

'Go and see who it is, Arthur.'

'Shut up, will you!'

The kitchen door opened, then the middle door and the little girl from next door came in holding a blue hooped milk jug. The draught caught the kitchen door and banged it shut behind her.

'Hello, Corrine love, what do you want?'

'My mam says can she borrow –'

'I'VE MISSED IT! I'VE BLOODY WELL MISSED IT!'

Mr Hawk shot up out of the chair. Corrine stared at him and backed away.

'You young BUGGER! I'll skin you ALIVE.'

She ran at the kitchen door and jumbled with the sneck.

'MAM!'

'I'll give you MAM!'

'Arthur! Have you gone crazy?'

Mrs Hawk grabbed hold of his arm, but he dragged it free and ran after Corrine. She ran screaming and crying along the flags into their house, and banged the door behind her. Mr Hawk kicked it open and ran in. Corrine was trying to burrow between her mother's legs. Mr Jackson stepped in front of them wearing a pair of overalls.

'What's going off? What's she done?'

'How've they gone on?'

'What?'

'How's Town gone on?'

Mrs Hawk ran into the kitchen behind him. Doors were opening in the yard.

'They've won.'

'Have they? How many?'

'One nowt.'

'Are you sure.'

''Course I'm sure. I've just heard it. Now then, what's she done?'

'Nowt now.'

Corrine was still sobbing into her mother's apron. Mrs Jackson patted her on the back.

'I only sent her for a drop of milk.'

'Drop of milk! She can have a herd of bloody cows full now.'

He turned and left the house. Mrs Hawk stood with her hands on her hips shaking her head.

'She banged t'door when she came in, and he missed t'result.'

'I know, but look at her though, she's scared stiff.'

'You know what he's like about our Len's football, it'd have been all t'same if t'Queen had walked in.'

Mr Hawk returned and put a full bottle of milk on the table. He ruffled Corrine's hair and plucked her away from her mother.

'Come on then and let your Uncle Arthur kiss you better.'

She sucked her hands and tried to turn away. He crouched down and rubbed her belly and buzzed on her neck. She started to laugh through her tears.

'That's better, that's a good girl.'

He picked her up and threw her to the ceiling, whooing each time he caught her and threw her up again. He put her down and she danced in front of him for some more. He gave her a new threepenny bit and walked out. People were halfway out of their kitchen doors looking.

'Get in, you nosy buggers!'

Mrs Hawk ran out and slapped him on the back.

'Arthur! Arthur! There's no need for that.'

'I wonder what they'll have to say about it in t'paper tonight.'

BOURNEMOUTH UNLUCKY TO LOSE
HAWK SHOT DOWN

'Bloody hell fire!'

'What's a matter?'

He ran his thumb down the side of the column as he scanned the report, then he squeezed his nail into the page and looked up.

'Listen to this – Bournemouth realized too late that Hawk was badly out of touch, and by the time they had taken the extra man off him it was too late, Prince had run through unmarked and cracked in the winner.'

'Isn't it a shame?'

'I wonder what's up with him?'

'They'll not drop him, will they?'

' 'Course they won't! Town's nowt without our Len.'

'It doesn't look as if they're much with him just now.'

'He ought to be going full time training, that's what it is.'

'He's doing too much training if you ask me owt.'

'He can't expect to keep it up just going at nights.'

'And don't be getting on to him about it when he gets home, he'll feel bad enough as it is.'

'Don't worry, I shan't say a word. You only get a mouthful back if you do.'

'I think he's got summat on his mind, you know.'

Clifford Anderson called the players to the touchline and started to hand out the coloured bibs. Lennie looked up at the clock on the roof of the stand and refused to take one.

'Don't pick me in, I'll have to go now.'

'Twenty minutes, that's all, Len.'

'I can't, afternoon school starts at quarter past one.'

'You could do with it, son.'

'I can't help that, I'll have to go.'

'Can't you give it a miss today?'

'I've missed enough as it is. They'd have a fit if they knew I was down here.'

'Well, what are you going to do about it then?'

'Do about what?'

'Yourself – the team?'

'What do you want me to do? Do you think I'm playing badly on purpose?'

He turned on to the red ash and ran up the tunnel. Clifford Anderson watched him go, then snatched a ball out of the trainer's box and lashed it high on to the pitch. He threw Lennie's bib at Fowler and nodded towards the kop. 'Here Pete, put that on. First team that end.'

Fowler pulled the blue bib off and slipped Lennie's red one on. The teams lined up and the game started. Clifford Anderson ran along the touchline keeping up with the play.

'For Christ's sake put a bit of life into it! George! George! Come on, man, are you a bloody cripple or what?'

Lennie bathed and dressed quickly. The other players came running into the changing-room just as he was putting his coat on. He picked his books up from the table and walked straight out past Clifford Anderson.

'See you tomorrow then, son?'

He didn't answer. Clifford Anderson walked quickly to the door and stepped into the corridor.

'Len!'

The players looked round at each other in silence. Lennie

stopped and waited for Clifford Anderson to walk up to him.

'Who the hell do you think you are walking away like that?'

'Lennie Hawk, same as I always am.'

'And I suppose you think that's clever, don't you?'

'I don't think it's anything. I just answered your question, that's all. '

'When are you coming down again? If it isn't too much trouble to answer.'

'Tomorrow night, I suppose.'

'You suppose, do you! It's got to that, has it?'

'Look, I know my game's gone off, but don't worry, it'll be all right.'

'Don't worry! What do you expect me to do after these last two games, sit down and write you a¹¹ a letter of thanks?'

'I know –'

'You suddenly hit rock bottom, the team goes to pieces round you, and you say don't worry!'

'I know, I know, it was a daft thing to say that.'

'All I can say, son, is that I hope you snap out of it before we go back any further.'

Lennie caught a bus outside the ground which took him through the town centre and up to school. He met Harry in the foyer just coming out of the hall from second dinners.

'Hey up, Len.'

'That's all I'm short of, no dinner.'

'Go to the kitchen. They're big fans of yours in there, aren't they?'

'Bugger it now.'

'Where you been?'

'I didn't feel so good this morning.'

'There's no wonder the slating you got in the papers.'

'Bugger t'papers.'

'Whats' up Len? What's gone wrong?'

'HOW THE BLOODY HELL DO I KNOW?'

Children in the corridors stopped dead and stared at him. He glared round at them with his teeth clenched.

'WHAT YOU LOT STARING AT?'

They hurried on looking back.

'Stop shouting then, you'll be having the old man out in a minute.'

'I'm stalled of folks asking me what's gone wrong.'

'All right, I'll not mention it again then.'

He followed Lennie down the corridor to the cloakroom.

'We got the results on Friday.'

'How did tha get on?'

'Two forties and a fifty.'

'What about me?'

'I don't know, they wouldn't say.'

'I suppose I'll get to know this afternoon.'

'Rowley's been asking about you all morning.'

'What have I done now?'

'He wanted to know why you were away, and if you'd got back from Bournemouth, things like that.'

'It'll be my exam result, when do we have him?'

'Last lesson. I've got my transistor for the draw.'

'I bet he can't wait to get me round t'throat.'

'I shan't be able to take it into Rowley's though, I'll have to give it somebody with a free period.'

'Give it to Rowley, he'll cancel t'lesson to let us listen.'

'He wouldn't let us listen to the end of the world. Who are you hoping for next round?'

'Blind school at home.'

'You'll look well if you get the United.'

'We can do without them, t'way we're playing just now.'

'I reckon they've a chance for the double this year.'

'They should win the league.'

'My dad goes across to every home game. He says they're playing really well.'

'They're a strong side, they never stop running. They ran the Town to death at their place in September.'

'You could have gone there, couldn't you?'

'I nearly did at one time.'

'Do you wish you had done now?'

'No, I'm all right where I am. Anyway, I don't like that style of play, there's too much long ball.'

'Just imagine, you'd be up against Stamper.'

'That crazy bleeder, he'll be killing somebody one of these days.'

The bell rang. Mr Rowley closed his file and placed a text book on top of it. Lennie folded his examination papers and stuffed them into his pocket.

'I would like to see you for a moment, Hawk.'

Lennie waited until the rest of the class were out of the room, then he stood up and walked to the front.

'Have you looked through your papers?'

'Yes.'

'Any complaints about the marking?'

'No, I knew it was a bad paper when I handed it in.'

'I couldn't believe it. I kept looking back to make sure that it was your name at the top of the sheets.'

'I know, it was a load of rubbish.'

'What went wrong? It should have been child's play to you.'

'I didn't feel like it that morning.'

'And look at your other marks, look at that forty for English! Mr Priddle was nearly in tears when he told me!'

He sat up and folded his arms on the desk.

'How much work did you do for these exams, Hawk?'

'Not much.'

'Why not? You realize their importance, don't you?'

'Well, I decided to see how good I really was, so I didn't bother doing any revision.'

'Don't talk ridiculous! You're spending too much time at football, that's your trouble. I forecast this all along, I knew it! You're heart's not in your work any more.'

'I'll be all right, these exams just came at a bad time for me, that's all.'

'In what way?'

'Oh, just one thing or another.'

'You're not in trouble of any kind, are you?'

'No, 'course I'm not.'

'Is there something wrong at home? I hear your father's out of work, is that worrying you?'

'No, I'm just going through a bad patch all round, that's all.'

Mr Rowley leaned forward and stared at him like a fat toad. 'Hawk, what's gone wrong, lad? The spark's gone out of you.'

Lennie looked down at his shoes and shuffled forward until both toes were touching Rowley's desk. Rowley sat back and looked up at the top of his head.

'As you know you've never been my favourite student, for reasons which we won't discuss just now, and at times I may have seemed unfair to you. I know this, but I can assure you that half of my antagonism has been deliberate, and designed to help you. Yes, you may look, but it's true. I've seen you grinding your teeth and clenching your fists when I've been railing you, and this is what I wanted, because I knew that you'd get the last word in with your work. And you did! Those essays written solely to spite me have been a pleasure to mark. But this exam, oh dear, I could have wept, there was nothing there!'

'There's plenty with lower marks than me though, I did at least pass.'

Mr Rowley banged the side of his fist on the desk.

'That shows there's something wrong with you!'

'What does?'

'The fact that you're comparing yourself with other people. You've never done that before, you've always been in a different class to most of them!'

'O.K., so I did bad! But the way I was feeling when I did them papers I'm chuffed to death that I got any marks at all.'

'Why didn't you say you felt ill?'

'I didn't say I felt ill – Oh, I can't explain it to you.'

Mr Rowley leaned forward.

'Listen, you may think this sounds ridiculous coming from me, but if you're in trouble and you think a chat might help then you're welcome to come to my home any time.'

Lennie smiled. Mr Rowley shook his finger at him.

'Don't worry, hostilities will be resumed as soon as you're fighting fit again.'

'I'll think about it.'

'You know where I live, don't you?'

'I think so.'

'Let me know beforehand if you decide to come, otherwise I may not be in. I'm out quite a lot in the evenings.'

'I will, thank you.'

'Doctor Bennet would like a word with you before you go.'

'What about?'

'What the dickens is going on in the corridor? Those boys should be home by this time.'

Lennie turned round and Mr Rowley moved his head to one side to look past his body. Harry was standing with a gang of boys, grinning and miming through the glass.

'Tell them that if they're still there when I come out, they'll all be in detention on Friday.'

Lennie walked away and opened the door. The crowd rushed at him like autograph hunters.

'UNITED LEN!'

'What?'

'UNITED AT HOME.'

'Honest, Harry?'

'Honest!'

'Well, would you believe it?'

'What a draw, Len! There'll be a civil war on round here.'

The gang of boys were wrestling and pushing forward trying to speak to Lennie.

'Rowley says that if you haven't buggered off when he comes out you'll all be in the shit on Friday.'

They stopped shoving and looked through the window. Mr Rowley stood up and fastened the two buckles on his old brief-case, then walked across the room and opened the door. He stood in the doorway and looked right, then left, then right again. When he saw that the corridor was clear he smiled tight-lipped.

'The Headmaster is expecting you, Hawk.'

'Just going.'

Harry and Lennie watched him roll away down the deserted corridor, his steel-tipped shoes ringing and echoing like horse-shoes on the marble slabs.

'What's the old man want you for?'

'I don't know yet.'

They followed Mr Rowley down the corridor round to the main entrance. Lennie knocked on the Headmaster's door and pressed his ear to the wood.

'See you tomorrow, Len.'

Lennie nodded and Harry went out through the front door. He glanced down the steps and ran back in again. The foyer was deserted. He watched the Headmaster's door, then went out again, slowly.

Doctor Bennet was sitting by the fire reading a book. He snapped it shut and leaned back to place it on the desk, but he couldn't reach, so he held it still, and lobbed it the extra distance, like pitching a quoit.

'You're in trouble, Hawk. In the first place your work has deteriorated. Secondly you have been missing school to attend football training, and thirdly you are playing football badly. Are these statements correct?'

Lennie stood behind the door and nodded.

'Right, what are you going to do about it all?'

Lennie stared at him across the room.

'Well?'

'I don't know yet. I'll have to see how things turn out.'

'What things?'

'It's too complicated to tell you. You see, everything's inter-related and it's all one big muddle just now.'

'I see.'

'I can't say anything about it just yet.'

'Well, it sounds like something personal that you will have to solve on your own.'

'These days I've had off –'

'Say no more about it, just work it out, work it out. Right, you may go.'

'And what if I can't?'

'I shall be very surprised and disappointed in you.'

'Folk always seem to expect too much of me.'

'They only expect what you have led them to believe. You can't blame them for that, can you?'

'I suppose not.'

'I have faith in you, Hawk, that's why I'm leaving you alone. I believe your strength and intelligence will see you through.'

'I suppose I'll get over it.'

'I've no doubt you will. Reports of your progress will be

filtering through, I suppose. I shall look forward to them eagerly. Good night, Hawk.'

'Good night.'

The cleaners were working in the corridors, clanking their buckets and shouting over the echoes. Lennie fetched his coat and walked back to the main door. He pushed it open and Jane and Mrs Leary looked up from the mini at the bottom of the steps. Jane got out and started to climb the steps. Lennie walked down to meet her. Mrs Leary looked up through the car window and Doctor Bennet watched from his study.

'Hello, love.'

'Hello.'

'What are you doing here?'

'I've come to see you.'

'What about?'

'What do you think?'

'Well?'

'I'm pregnant.'

'How do you know?'

'I went to the doctor's today. He gave me a test.'

'What did he say?'

'I've to go for another, but it's almost certain.'

Lennie nodded down the steps to the car.

'Does your mother know?'

'I've told them both.'

'Jesus! What did your dad say?'

'What are we going to do, Len?'

'I don't know. What do you want to do?'

'Mummy says we should get married immediately.'

'And what do you say?'

'I don't want to have it.'

'What did your dad say?'

'Nothing. He's going to see your parents tonight.'

'Bloody hell. They don't know owt about it yet.'

'Do you want to get married, Len?'

He shook his head.

'No.'

'I thought you'd say that.'

'Do you want to?'

'Yes, I would have done. You see I love you.'

He bit his lip and looked down, shaking his head slowly.

'I can't, Jane. I know it sounds terrible but I can't get married.'

'I wouldn't want you to if you didn't love me.'

'I couldn't be married, in a house with a kid, I just couldn't!'

'I know you couldn't, Len.'

'What about the child though?'

He looked up and stared at Jane's stomach.

'I'm not going to have it, I'll get rid of it.'

'What do you mean?'

'Father will find me a doctor. He's hoping you'll say no. He'd rather see me dead then married to you.'

'He's a rotten bastard, your dad.'

'Don't say you'll marry me now, Len, just to spite him.'

'I don't know what to say, I just feel terrible.'

'That's settled then.'

She half turned and stepped down with one foot.

'We can't just leave it like this though!'

'What do you want us to do?'

'Shan't I see you again?'

'Len! We can't go on as if nothing has happened. You don't seem to realize.'

'But I like you, Jane, you're the best girl I've ever known.'

'But we can't! It's all changed now.'

'I'll never see you again then?'

'I suppose you will, some time.'

'But we can't finish like this.'

'We shall have to.'

She stepped down with her other foot and turned her back on him.

Lennie reached out and took hold of her sleeve.

'And what if your dad can't get a doctor?'

'Father can get almost anything. He's a very rich man.'

'What about your mother, what will she say about it?'

'She'll be upset, but when she knows that we're not getting married she'll soon accept it.'

'It'll be terrible for you.'

'It won't be as bad as having it. I could have stood it with you, but I'm not having it without you.'

'I'm sorry, Jane, honest I am.'

'I know you are, Len, and I'm glad that you've been honest about it. I should have hated you if you'd married me just for the child.'

'It's selfish though, it's terrible.'

'We'll get over it. It's better to part now than spend a lifetime regretting together.'

Lennie pulled her round and she looked up at him.

'This is it, then?'

She nodded.

'Do you regret it?'

'Of course I don't, I shall always remember it. Look, I'm going to start crying now and I was determined to keep control over myself.'

She placed her hand over her mouth and nose. Her finger ends stretched up into her eye corners.

'Shsh, you'll be having me at it in a minute.'

'I'm going now.'

'Do you think your dad'll still go down to our house?'

'He'll go. He won't let you get away with it as easy as that.'

'Write and tell me how you go on, won't you?'

'Yes, but it'll be all right, don't worry.'

They walked down the steps to the car. Lennie opened the door and looked across at Mrs Leary.

'I'm sorry, Mrs Leary.'

'You're not half as sorry as I am.'

'I'm twice as sorry as you can ever be.'

'And you're not getting married?'

'No.'

'Jane was right then?'

'You can't get married if you don't want to.'

'So you get off scot-free then?'

'What do you mean, scot-free? I'm as upset about it as Jane is.'

'No you're not, or you'd marry her.'

'Look, I've told you!'

'It's your duty to marry her, it's your duty to her and the child.'

'What do you think I am, a bloody soldier?'

'No I think you're a heartless rotter.'

'But can't you see! It'd be hopeless!'

'It's what Jane wants.'

'Not like this she doesn't.'

'She'd take you even now.'

Lennie stood up and turned to Jane who was standing behind him.

'Tell her, Jane.'

Jane cupped her hands to her face and started to sob into them.

'Jane, tell her what we said.'

She blinded her way past him into the car and hid her face on her thighs. Mrs Leary looked over her back at Lennie.

'Now do you see?'

'But she just told me!'

'She hasn't told you anything.'

Mrs Leary reversed the car suddenly and Lennie had to jump back. The door slammed and the car accelerated down the drive. He was still looking after it when Doctor Bennet came out carrying his briefcase and homburg.

'Good gracious, Hawk, haven't you gone home yet?' Lennie stood looking down the empty drive. 'Can I give you a lift anywhere?'

'Yes please, the nearest pond.'

'Rather cold at this time of the year, I should imagine.'

Lennie walked away and Doctor Bennet got into his car and drove past him. He walked all the way home, slowly. Mr Hawk sat back in the armchair waiting for him to come in. He blinked and turned his head to listen to the footsteps coming up the flags. The back door rattled. He jumped up and stood grinning on the rug with his back to the fire. Lennie walked straight in without taking his coat off.

'United, Len! What's tha think about that?'

'Champion.'

'Everybody's going mad in town.'

Lennie sat down at the table and stretched his legs wide in front of him.

'What's up? Tha doesn't look very excited about it.'

Mrs Hawk lifted the iron off the steaming shirt and held it still.

'What's a matter, Len? You look badly.'

He looked up at them in turn.

'Is it your exam results?'

'Jane's pregnant!'

Mrs Hawk stared at him for a moment, then smashed the iron down on to the asbestos square and slumped backwards into the armchair. She closed her eyes and rested her head on the back.

'O Lord! Is it you?'

'Who do you think it is?'

'God!'

Mr Hawk put his hands in his pockets and started to rock forward and back on his toes and heels.

'Well, tha's played a blinder.'

'All that waste! All them years for nothing! You've wasted everything now, your career's ruined.'

'What tha going to do about it, then?'

'Dear, oh dear, all them years for this! He might as well have left at fifteen and got a job then.'

'What tha going to do, get married and sign full time?'

'I'm not going to do owt.'

Mr Hawk stopped rocking and Mrs Hawk opened her eyes and stared at the ceiling.

'We're not getting married.'

'You'll have to.'

'What tha going to do, pay her thirty bob a week?'

'She's not going to have it.'

Mrs Hawk lifted her head and looked across at him.

'What do you mean?'

'What do you think I mean?'

She sat up on the edge of the chair.

'But it's illegal! You'll get into trouble!'

'Who's going to arrange it?'

'Her dad.'

'O Len, it's a terrible thing to do! It's horrible!'

'What else can we do?'

'You could marry her.'

'We don't want to get married.'

'It can be dangerous, tha knows.'

'Her dad'll get her a good doctor.'

'It's terrible! It's terrible!'

She stood up and started to pace about the rug in front of Mr Hawk.

'For Christ's sake, Mam! Stop saying that!'

'Ar, shut up, Mary, we know it's terrible.'

'I know, but –'

'If they don't want to get married and t'lass's willing to go through with it, then it's best thing that can happen.

'I know, but, oh dear!'

'I'm glad somebody's got some sense, anyway.'

Mr Hawk jabbed a finger at him across the room.

'And don't think I'm sticking up for thee 'cos I'm not! Tha wants thi bloody ear'ole thumping for being so daft!'

'O give up, Dad! Didn't you ever do owt wrong when you were young?'

'Ar, but I never got myself into trouble, and we didn't have t'advantages that you've got today!'

'It's no good shouting now.'

'And tha reckons to be educated. Didn't tha realize what might happen?'

'I don't know, I suppose so.'

'I suppose it was t'old tale, it couldn't happen to thee, the great Lennie Hawk. You silly bugger!'

'All right! All right! I know!'

'Tha does now! I thought tha'd have had more bloody sense.'

'Well, you thought wrong, didn't you?'

Mr Hawk took a step forward.

'Don't thee start –'

'Mr Leary's coming to see you tonight.'

'What's he coming for?'

'To torture me, I suppose.'

'What time's he coming, Len?'

'I don't know.'

'I'd better get tidied up then, it's like a pigsty in here.'

Mrs Hawk lifted the clothes-horse from the side of the fire and closed it like a book. She carried it into the kitchen and returned holding a bundle of floppy dusters. Mr Hawk stood still in front of the fire and watched her work. Lennie took his coat off and sat at the table facing the wall.

'Do you want any tea?'

'I could eat a nine-course meal with three pork pies to finish it off.'

'If you think this lot's funny, I don't! You ought to be ashamed of yourself.'

'I think it's hilarious, look at my sides, they're splitting.'

He lifted his shirt and showed her his hip. Mrs Hawk stopped dusting and had a look.

'You clever devil! You're just ten ton, that's your trouble.'

She threw her dusters into the cupboard and sat down. They waited in silence like relations at a funeral.

There were three sharp knocks on the back door. Mrs Hawk sat up and bobbed her hair with her hands.

'That'll be him, let him in Len – Len!'

He edged the door open and poked his head into the space. Mr Leary glared up from the other side of the step. Lennie considered him, then stepped back and walked away.

'Come in.'

Mr Leary closed the door and followed him into the living-room. He looked incongruous in his suit, like the football managers who were always calling to sign Lennie on. Mr Hawk stood in front of the fire with his hands behind his back and nodded his head. Mrs Hawk stood up and rubbed her hands down her dress.

'Sit down here, Mr Leary, would you like –?'

'No, I won't prolong this, I suppose he's told you?'

'Ar, it's a bad job.'

'It's a disgusting affair.'

'He knew all along how I felt about their relationship and then he does a thing like this to her.'

'What do you mean, how you felt about it?'

'I forbade him to see Jane a long time ago.'

'He never told us that.'

'No, I don't suppose he would.'

They all looked at Lennie who was sitting on the edge of the table with his arms folded.

'And what had he done wrong?'

'It's irrelevant at this stage.'

The sneck clicked and the back door began to open. Mrs Hawk ran into the kitchen and bellied Mrs Jackson back into the yard before she could get in. She returned shaking her head.

'Eee, aren't we hampered?'

'I bet she only came to see who we'd got in, the nosy bugger.'

Mr Leary clicked his tongue and jerked a knee straight.

'It almost seems as though he'd done all this to spite me!'

'Hey up, just hold on a minute. He didn't do it all on his own, you know.'

'No, but if they hadn't gone against my wishes it would never have happened!'

'Your wishes! What about their wishes? You can't go ordering young folks about like that.' Mr Hawk jerked his head at Lennie like somebody with a nervous twitch. ''Cos when they get to their age they'll do what they want, whether you like it or not.'

'That may apply to him, but I still retain some influence over my children.'

'Ar, it looks like it! If you ask me owt it's you that's the cause of all this lot.'

'Me! It was I who tried to prevent it in the first place.'

'Don't talk wet!'

'Arthur.'

'Tried to prevent it! It's you that's drove 'em to it! If you'd have just let 'em run a bit and given 'em time to think about what they were doing, they perhaps wouldn't have rushed at it like they did.'

'You're not endorsing his action, are you?'

'No I'm not, 'cos he wants his bloody arse kicking for him. But I'm not going to stand here and listen to him taking t'full blame for summat he only had half shares in.'

Mr Leary looked round the room quickly.

'I can see I'm going to get no satisfaction at all in this house!'

'What did you come for in t'first place?'

Mr Leary stopped turning his head.

'Has he told you about the doctor?'

'Yes.'

There was silence and they all looked down at the floor.

'Well, I came for an assurance that after all this is over he'll never see Jane again.'

'You'd better ask him, that's nowt to do with me.'

'I've already told her.'

'Everything's settled then.'

'But it's for her I'm doing it, not you.'

Mr Leary spun round and marched out, banging both doors behind him. Mrs Hawk fluttered around the rug for a minute then sat down.

'You were awful with him, Arthur.'

'I should think so an' all, bowling in here like that. And I don't know what's tha's got to grin about!'

'You should have seen his face when you were on at him.'

'I can't stand blokes like that. You get some pit managers who are just t'same, you can't weigh 'em.'

'He's not used to being talked to like that, except by me.'

'Don't be so bloody clever, and keep away from him in future.'

'Don't you worry about that.'

''Cos he's let thi off too easy altogether for my liking.'

'He's perhaps glad to get shut of me.'

'Perhaps so, but don't push thi luck too far, he's a nasty piece of work, yond.'

Lennie unzipped his tracksuit top down to the chest and pulled it over his head. His red shirt was stained maroon at the back, as though a pan of water had been thrown on it. He stripped off quickly and stood steaming in his jockstrap. Chris looked up from untying his boot laces.

'What's up, Len, got a date on?'

'No, I want to get home, I've got some work to do.'

'I don't know how you can do it after training. I feel too shagged to read a paper sometimes.'

'I've got to. I've let me work slip a bit lately, and I'm trying to get a grip again.'

'You looked as though you were getting a grip of your game as well.'

'I felt a lot better tonight.'

'I'm glad, 'cos you've looked a sorry sight these last few matches, just like a lion in a cage.'

'Anybody can have a bad spell, Chris.'

'I know they can, but blokes like you look a lot worse when they're going through 'em.'

'I'll be all right now.'

'We could do with a couple of good wins now before the United.'

'Think there'll be any changes for Saturday?'

'They're expecting some, that's what they're all so quiet about.'

The teams were up when he came out of the showers. He stood at the back of the crowd of players and looked between their heads at the board. There were no changes. The crowd broke up smiling. Bobby Prince picked his towel up and tried to flick Roy Harris's balls with the snapping end. He grabbed hold of it, and they tug-of-war'd their way into the showers. The room was hot and damp like a laundry. George Armstrong lay on the table propped up on his elbows, with one leg stretched out under the heat lamp. Clifford Anderson spoke quietly into his ear and then patted his thigh and walked over to Lennie.

'A lot better tonight, son.'

'I felt better.'

'I want you back at your best for the United. I want to win that game almost as much as the cup itself.'

'We'll be all right.'

'I want that Stamper run to death, because if he has a bad game their whole defence will go to pieces.'

'I'll be running, don't you worry, I don't want him anywhere near me.'

'He ought to be playing Rugby League, the big dirty bastard.'

'He's such a crafty sod though. I've seen players carried off when he's tackled them and the ref's had to give a bounce up.'

'He'd have played for England, you know, Len, if he hadn't have been such a lunatic.'

'I know he would, he's a good player.'

'Have you ever spoken to him? He's a real charmer.' Clifford Anderson rolled his eyes and whistled.

'I'll have him.'

'Just make sure that he doesn't have you.'

'I'll blind him.'

'Don't tempt fate, Len, it makes me shudder when you say things like that.'

'Well I will.'

'I hope you do, son, but just keep it quiet.'

He pointed to the ceiling.

'I'm always afraid there's somebody up there listening. I can just see them looking down and saying, "Just wait till you strap your boots on again, lad, we'll see what you're going to do and what you're not going to do." '

'If there's anybody up there he'll know what you're thinking anyway, so it makes no difference whether you say it or not.'

Clifford Anderson stood up smiling and shaking his head. He pushed Lennie on the arm.

'Yes, I think you're coming back to form, son, let's have a good game on Saturday to prove it.'

'I'll see if I can scrounge two points up for you.'

'What do you think to him then, Chris, right?'

Chris looked up from powdering his feet.

'He's a head as big as Birkenhead, and a mouth the size of Tynemouth.'

Lennie knotted his dad's pit scarf and tucked the fringes inside his coat.

'See you Saturday then.'

'Do you want a lift?'

'No thanks, I'm in a hurry.'

'Well, you cheeky sod.'

Lennie backheeled Chris up the arse as he lifted his other foot on to the bench to powder it.

'Bugger off! And don't expect me to stop if I pass you.'

Lennie grinned and walked away. It was misty, and drizzling

outside. A car engine coughed, and parallel bars of light shot into the dark and turned the mist yellow. A car curved out and drew up alongside Lennie as he walked along the back of the main stand towards the main road.

A window wound down.

'Ready for the United, Len?'

Lennie looked down at the shoulder in the front seat.

'Just about.'

'United supporters are saying they'll murder you.'

'Are they?'

'Going into Town?'

'Yes.'

'Jump in then, we'll give you a lift.'

He opened the door and ducked his head inside. A man in the back brought a length of lead pipe down on the back of his skull. He slumped forward between the seats. The driver backed the car round under the high wall at the end of the car park. The two men in front leaned over and pulled Lennie's legs up, while the one in the back knelt on him and pulled his socks off. He began to hit the tops of Lennie's feet with the lead, while the two in front held them firm on the back of the seat. He hit them from the ankles to the toes then took a razor from his pocket and cut lines along the soles. Lennie began to struggle and grunt under the weight. A handkerchief was stuffed into his mouth and he was thumped hard on the jaw. They pushed his shoes back on to his feet and shoved him out on to the asphalt. The car moved slowly out of the car park and turned into the main road. Lennie pulled the handkerchief out of his mouth and tried to stand up, but each time his hands left the ground he overbalanced and fell down again. He began to crawl back towards the line of cars outside the players' entrance, watching the door and trying to keep his feet off the ground. The door swung open and Chris and Geordie came out laughing. The door banged behind them, and the noises were loud in the misty darkness.

'Chris! Chris!'

They stopped and turned. Chris started to run, Geordie followed him.

'Len! What's up? What's happened?'

Lennie looked up into Chris's face as they crouched down beside him.

'Your mouth's bleeding, Len, what's happened?'

'I don't know, some blokes, they've hurt my feet.'

'Let's have a look.'

Lennie sat down and they tried to pull his shoes off. He grabbed hold of their arms and steadied them.

'Be careful, they're hurting! They feel broken to bits.'

Chris crooked Lennie's legs over his thigh and eased his shoes off.

'Christ, Len, they're pouring blood! Get hold of him quick, Geordie.'

They linked arms underneath him and chaired him across the car park, back through the door into the corridor.

'Boss! Boss!'

The shouts cracked like gun-shots through the silence and fetched Clifford Anderson and the rest of the players tumbling out of the dressing-room.

'Lennie! What's happened, son? Billy, phone for Doctor Mark – quick.'

They backed away to let Chris and Geordie through. Max snatched a handful of cotton wool out of a thick roll and soaked Lennie's soles as he was lowered carefully on to the table. He swabbed continuously, inspecting between each dab, then dabbing again as the blood filled the gashes and over-flowed like swollen streams.

'Wriggle your toes.'

Lennie screwed his face up and wriggled his toes, watching them move out of one eye. Max handled each one as though they were bird's eggs.

'I don't think anything's broken.'

'They feel as though I've been kicking cannon balls on broken glass.'

The tops of his feet were already puffing into pink lumps. Three gashes barred one sole. Two more intersected the other one like the X on a hot cross bun. Lennie pressed the hair at the back of his head and winced.

'Have a look at this, Max, it feels as though I've got another head growing.'

Max bound his feet in lint socks and bent his head down like a barber. Doctor Mark hurried in and placed his bag on the table. He lifted Lennie's legs under the knees and unwound the lint.

'Good lord! What happened?'

'I don't know right. Some blokes offered me a lift into town, when I got in they hammered me.'

'Have you phoned the Police?'

Clifford Anderson nodded his head.

'Wriggle your toes.'

Lennie wriggled them while Doctor Mark manipulated them in turn, gazing into Lennie's face as though it was a crystal ball.

'There's nothing broken, thank goodness.'

'What about the cuts?'

'They'll be all right, you must have soles like elephant hide. What do you do, run about barefoot all day?'

'I train in the gym barefoot.'

'Mmm. Do you kick the ball around like that as well?'

'I always have done.'

'I thought so. That's the reason they've stood up to it so well.'

'I've nothing to worry about then.'

'Of course you have! They're in a terrible condition.'

'I know, but if there's nothing broken I'll be all right.'

Doctor Mark applied ointment and lint, and broke open the blue paper round a bandage. The players parted and formed a gangway as Inspector Keegan and a policeman walked into the room. The policeman settled in the doorway with his hands behind his back and feet apart, as though he was guarding the royal route. Keegan stood at the table and watched Doctor Mark winding bandage.

'What happened?'

'I'd just got outside when this car drew up. Somebody wound the window down and asked me if they thought we'd got a chance against t'United. He offered me a lift, then they must have belted me as I got in. Next thing I can remember is the car park tipping up like the back of a coal lorry as I tried to stand up.'

'Did you see any of them?'

'I saw a pair of legs as I got in.'

'Any idea how many?'

'Must have been three.'

'Why must there?'

'The driver, the bloke who wound the window down, and the one in the back whose legs I saw.'

'You didn't see their faces?'

'No.'

'Recognize any voices?'

'No.'

'What about the car, any idea what kind it was?'

'No.'

'The colour.'

'No idea.'

'Where did it come from?'

'Must have been parked waiting for me.'

'What time was this?'

Lennie looked up at the clock on the wall.

'About nine, I should say.'

'You didn't see anything then?'

'I nearly saw the number plate.'

'What do you mean you nearly saw it?'

'Well, when I came round with my head like a banging bucket and my feet on fire, first thing I thought about was the number plate. So I squinted bleary-eyed into the mist and groped forward helplessly. But I was too late, so I fell head first into a puddle and lay there with the dirty water lapping round my battered brow.' He flopped back and his head touched the blanket. He shot up, with his face as sour as a sucked lemon.

'Ooooo!'

Keegan scratched under his chin with the backs of his nails.

'Do you think this is funny then?'

'My head's killing me! Look, it's a waste of time all this, you know as well as I do you haven't got a dog's chance of catching them.'

Keegan looked round the table at the other players.

'Did any of you notice a strange car in the car park?'

They glanced at each other shaking their heads.

'Any idea who could have done this?'

'Could have been some crazy United supporters.'

'Perhaps somebody with a bet on.'

'Could be, but they'd have to be fanatics to do a thing like this.'

'Who's taking me home, then?'

Doctor Mark finished bandaging and stood up straight.

'I'll take you.'

'Shouldn't he be going to hospital?'

'What the hell do I want to be going to the hospital for?'

'I think he'll be all right, Inspector. I'll give him something to make him sleep when we arrive, then I'll keep a close eye on him.'

Clifford Anderson looked at the bandages as though they were a two goal deficit in the cup final.

'Will he be fit for the United?'

' 'Course I will!'

'It's just a matter of time with bruises and cuts, but I would think it highly unlikely.'

'Can we keep this thing quiet, 'cos it'll be murder if it gets in the papers? I don't want to be turning out against t'United with Stamper knowing about it.'

Clifford Anderson nodded and scanned everyone round the table.

'It's true what Lennie says, lads, we'd be better keeping it dark at this stage. Will that be all right, Inspector?'

'Perhaps it would be best. It could cause a lot of trouble with the match coming up.'

'Right lads, not a word then to anyone.'

'We'll be making the usual inquiries of course, but we'll obscure their purpose a bit if you like.'

Lennie felt at the lump standing up like a hairy hard-boiled egg at the back of his head.

'I've got a wicked headache.'

Doctor Mark bent his head forward and greased the swelling with his fingertip.

'You're lucky you've still got a head left to ache. Will someone give him a hand to my car please?'

Inspector Keegan backed out through the crowd and the policeman followed him out of the room. They were waiting at the doctor's car when Eddie and Chris appeared carrying Lennie at the head of the procession of players. The policeman opened the back door and held it while Lennie was being manoeuvred into position with his legs straight out across the seat.

'You can't get up yet, Len!'

'Who says I can't?'

'Doctor said you'd to stop in bed for a week.'

'Doctors always say you've to stop in bed for a week.'

Mrs Hawk ran to the top of the stairs and shouted down.

'Arthur! Our Len says he's getting up!'

'He ought to be!'

Mr Hawk opened the stairs door and ran up the steps. Lennie was sitting on the edge of the bed when he walked in heaving and wheezing.

'Doctor said tha'd to stop in bed for a week.'

Lennie pushed himself off the mattress and stood up. Mr and Mrs Hawk stepped forward ready to catch him as he stood swaying with his eyes shut.

'Hang on a minute, I feel a bit dizzy.'

'What do you expect after three days in bed? I wish you'd get back in, Len.'

'Tha don't want to be opening them cuts again, tha knows.'

'I know I don't, but I've got to be making a move now.'

'Why don't you wait till t'doctor comes tomorrow, love?'

He began to walk across the oilcloth on the outsides of his feet.

'I'll have to have a special pair of boots made with studs in t'sides so I can play like this.'

'Can't tha put thi soles down?'

'I don't know yet.'

He lowered the insides step by step, until he was walking flat in his bandaged boots.

'What do they feel like?'

'They sting a bit underneath.'

'What about t'tops?'

'They feel a bit sore all round.'

'There's no bloody wonder either! Ee, if I knew who'd done this I'd lynch 'em, I would. I'd bloody lynch 'em!'

'Na, don't start getting worked up again, Arthur, he looks as if he's on t'mend now.'

'Getting worked up! I would get worked up if I got hold of 'em. They're bloody crazy, some of 'em over there.'

'I wish you'd stop saying THEY, Dad, it's nowt to do wi' t'United.'

''Course it is! They've always been a load of lunatics at their place. What about that goalie who got his head split open wi' that bottle?'

'I know, but it doesn't mean to say that —'

'And does tha think it's a coincidence that Stamper's been there all them years? They encourage hooliganism.'

'Anyway, it doesn't matter who did it now, I'll be fit.'

'Will tha buggery!'

''Course I will, if I'm walking about at t'week-end I'll be all right. That'll give me a week to get some training in.'

'Tha'll not be able to kick a ball about for ages.'

Lennie walked back to the bed and sat down.

'Is there a report of yesterday's match in t'paper?'

'No.'

'I wonder how they played?'

'They played well.'

'How do you know?'

'Tommy Hughes told me in t'club. He went down to watch 'em in their Jack's car.'

'How did Fowler play?'

'He said he did all right, nowt sparkling, but steady.'

'Another win next Saturday and we'll be well away.'

'You'll look well if you're fit and they don't pick you against t'United, Len.'

'Give up, Mam!'

'Don't thee be so cocky. They're not going to be risking a half fit man in a cup game.'

'Fowler's not in t'same street as me.'

'Nobody said he was, but he might be a safer bet in t'circumstances.'

'Especially as you weren't playing very well before this happened.'

'And if they win again next week tha could be really struggling.'

'Now get back in bed, love, until t'Doctor comes tomorrow.'

He slid carefully under the bedclothes, and turned on his side away from his mother and dad.

Lennie was sitting by the fire with his legs straight out on a stool, when Doctor Mark and Clifford Anderson called next day.

'I thought I told you to stay in bed.'

'I thought I'd be as well here, I'm resting just the same.'

'How's it going, son?'

'Champion, thanks.'

Doctor Mark knelt down and began to unwind the bandages. Mr and Mrs Hawk came over and stood either side of Clifford Anderson.

'I bet you've been walking around, haven't you?'

'You can't keep him still, Doctor.'

'You'd think his bloody arse was on fire.'

'We keep telling him, but you might as well save your breath.'

Doctor Mark peeled the lint off, the tops of Lennie's feet were black and blue and green and purple. He held Lennie's legs up and inspected the soles.

'What they like?'

'They're fine, Len, I'm amazed.'

Clifford Anderson knelt down on one knee like a player on the front row of a team photograph, and touched the bruises.

'Look at these though.'

'That's only to be expected with severe bruising.'

'Tha looks as though tha's got black eyes on both feet.'

Doctor Mark pressed them. Lennie jumped and held on to the chair arms.

'Painful?'

'A bit.'

Clifford Anderson stood up and put his hands into his overcoat pockets.

'Is he going to be fit then?'

They all looked down as though expecting Lennie's feet to provide the answer.

'I don't know.'

'What's his chances?'

'I don't know. They're healing very quickly but it's impossible to say at this stage.'

'When can I go back to school?'

'I wouldn't go before next Monday.'

'I'll have to.'

'Why will you?'

'I'll have to be training by Monday, so I'll have to be knocking about before then.'

Doctor Mark shook his head and fetched two bandages out of his bag.

'What you shaking your head for?'

'Well I don't know what advice to give you, that's all. It's quite true what you say, that if you're going to be fit for the United you'll need a week's training. But it's all too soon, you're not giving them enough time.'

'But you've just said yourself that my cuts are nearly better.'

'I said they were healing quickly, they're not better by a long chalk.'

'They will be though.'

'Listen, Len, I'll have to leave it to you now. You know how your feet feel so you'll just have to treat them accordingly. But you'll have to give those cuts a chance because if they don't close, you've had it.'

'We'll hold the fitness test off until the Saturday morning. What's the matter, what are you grimacing at?'

'Thought of kicking a ball again. Look at my toes, they're curling up in revolt.'

He pointed and they all looked. But all they saw were two clean white bandages covering his feet and disappearing up his trouser leg.

Lennie knocked on the kitchen door and waited. Mrs Rowley opened the door, the light making the privet green behind him. She stepped outside and hugged him. Lennie looked down the path into the gaping mouth of the garage. Mrs Rowley pulled him inside by the sleeve and hugged him again behind the door.

'It's been ages, Len! Are you fit again now? Is your ankle better?'

'My ankle?'

'I must have read about it every day in the papers.'

'O yes, it's a lot better thanks, I started training again on Monday.'

'You'll be fit for Saturday, then?'

'I don't know, it's still sore.'

'It's nice to see you again, I've missed you terribly.'

She held him at arm's length and looked him up and down as though inspecting a dress on a hanger.

'Come on.'

She tried to lead him into the hall but he didn't move.

'Come on, Len, what's the matter?'

'Nothing.'

'Well, take your coat off then, you're standing there like a stranger.'

She started to unbutton it, but he clutched it together with his hands in his pockets.

'I'm not stopping.'

'Don't be silly, Len! You can't go yet.'

'I've got to.'

She grabbed hold of his elbows and held on.

'Len, what's the matter?'

'I've got to go in a minute.'

'Why have you come then?'

'I've come to tell you that I shan't be seeing you any more.'

She released him and walked away, through the hall into the living-room. Lennie waited for a moment then followed. The only light came from the blazing fire. The furniture cast blocks of shadow on to the carpet, and behind the settee the darkness stretched right up to the skirting board. Lennie leaned on the edge of the open door and turned the knob, making the catch shoot in out, in out. He pushed the catch back into the socket with his thumb and turned the knob. His thumb held the pressure. He released it and the catch flicked out like a stubby tongue. Mrs Rowley looked across at him from the settee. She was sitting straight-backed on the edge of a cushion.

'Why, Len?'

'I don't want to any more.'

'What's happened?'

'A lot of things have happened.'

'What?'

'A lot! I've had a bad time just lately with one thing and another.'

'And you're blaming me for it?'

'I'm blaming nobody for it, I'm just telling you, that's all.'

'And what about me?'

'I don't know.'

'Don't you care any more?'

'Of course I care, but it's got to stop now.'

'Why has it?'

'Because affairs like this are no good.'

'It used to be, it used to be some good.'

'It was never any good, there's always been something rotten about it.'

'Good lord! Don't tell me that you're going to start moralizing!'

She jumped up and faced him across the hearth rug.

'I don't mean rotten like that. I mean rotten like a growth, something that rots you inside.'

'It didn't make me feel rotten. It made me feel wonderful.'

'And I've got to get rid of it now, it's got to be cut out before it's too late. You should have seen me play football at Bournemouth! Just like an old man with a sack of coal on his back. You should have seen my exam results. Shit! They were rubbish!'

'And I'm to blame for all that, am I?'

'No, there's been a lot of other things lately besides. I've been in a right mess, but I want to straighten it all out now, I want to be clear again.'

'And I fall by the wayside?'

'You'll find somebody else.'

'Len! How dare you?'

'Well, it's true, if your husband's not doing owt for you, then you'll find somebody who will.'

'Len, don't talk to me like that! Don't say such things.'

222

'Well, I don't suppose I'm the first, am I?'

She ran at him swinging her arms. He caught them by the wrists and held them high above their heads. She pushed her body forward making it arch from heel to hand like a longbow.

'Well, am I?'

'Yes, you are! You are! What do you think I am?'

Lennie relaxed and let go. She overbalanced into his chest and smacked him across the face, driving him backwards into the writing desk. He lifted his knee but she drove on to him, bending him backwards until his head pressed hard against the wall.

'O.K., I'm sorry! I didn't know, I'm sorry!'

'I want you, Len, I want you, don't leave me, I need you! Say you still like me, I'll do anything for you, anything! I'm still young, Len. I'm still good to love, you said I was! You said I was like Marilyn Monroe, can't you remember?'

'Get off me! You're hurting my head!'

She climbed up, shoving his back into the edge of the desk, pressing her thighs against him. She began to jump at him rhythmically so that the front two legs of the desk lifted and fell at each stroke.

'I can feel you want to love me! You know you do, I can feel it against me! You do want to, don't you, Len?'

'My head! You're hurting my head!'

'You do! You do!'

She felt for him. Lennie screwed his eyes up and levered himself off the wall with his neck. He pushed her hard in the shoulders and she fell backwards on to the floor.

'Don't, Len! Please don't!'

She dropped her head backwards on to the carpet and raised her arms and thighs. Her fingers clenched and stretched like a goalkeeper reaching for the ball.

'Len! Len! Come on, please!'

He hooked his fingers into her palms and pulled. She sagged down under him resisting the strain. He bent his knees and lifted her by the armpits but she kept falling away like somebody drunk.

'Get up! For Christ's sake get on to your feet!'

He was sweating. He ground his teeth and looked at the white throat pulled tight by the weight of her head hanging back.

'I'll thump you!'

'I'm as good as any young girls, Len, you said I was, you said I was better!'

He pulled her on to her feet and jerked her shoulders forward so that her head whipped up into line.

'You are, but I've told you, it's nowt to do with it! Can't you see that?'

She stiffened and clenched her fists at her sides.

'You're a selfish pig. You just use people, then throw them away like empty cigarette packets.'

Lennie let go of her and stepped back, she ran at him, thumping. He stopped the punches by clinching his arms round her and holding her tight like a strait jacket.

'Aren't you selfish then? Isn't that why you're going into hysterics, because you're so bloody selfish?'

'Let go of me.'

She looked down at her arms which were held to attention by her sides.

'I didn't know it was going to end like this, I never thought about it ending.'

'Let go! And get out of here, you make me sick.'

She grunted with the exertion of trying to break the clasp.

'You've soon changed your mind, haven't you? I wouldn't make you sick if I pulled you down on the rug, would I?'

'You're vile! You're horrible!'

'Would I?'

He grabbed her swishing hair and wrapped it round his knuckles, using it as a bridle to still her head and push it forward to his face.

'Stop it, Len! I can't stand any more!'

He turned his knuckles and pressed his fist into her scalp, forcing her mouth on to his. He looked straight into her eyes and tried to prise her teeth apart with his tongue. Her eyes stared back, struggling, wide. Then they drooped and closed and her jaw slackened. Lennie jerked her hair and pulled their faces apart.

'That doesn't make you sick, does it?'

She spat into his mouth. He backed away into the doorway, wiping his mouth and looking down at the back of his hand.

'You dirty cow. You dirty filthy cow!'

'Go away. Get out of here!'

'Don't you worry, I'm going! I must have been bloody crazy to waste my time coming up here.'

'You can't hurt me any more. I know why you came here.'

'I came because I wanted to see what it was like with an old bag.'

'You're a liar! You came because you never got anywhere with Jane.'

'Didn't I?'

'No, you didn't!'

He bit his lip and looked out into the hall.

'That's why you came to me, because you were still waiting for her.'

He turned to go out.

'But you'll have to wait a long time now!'

He stopped, and swung round sharply.

'What do you mean?'

'And to think, I actually boasted about it to her, as if you were a trophy that I'd won and she'd lost.'

'You told Jane?'

'Yes, I told her, I told her every detail. I rejoiced in telling her because I thought I'd have you all to myself then.'

'When did you tell her?'

'I thought it would finish it —'

'When did you tell her?'

'And I loved it when she cried. And the more hysterical she became the more I persisted.'

Lennie strode into the room and grabbed her arm.

'I've asked you a question, when did you tell her?'

'At the week-end, if you must know. She was getting ready to go away. So I thought it would be a marvellous chance to finish it once and for all. Now will you get —'

'You lousy cow. You stupid rotten lousy cow!'

'What's the matter with you? Stop it, you're hurting me!'

'I will hurt you, I'll bloody well kill you!'

'My arms! You're hurting them!'

'Didn't you know that she's pregnant?'

She stopped plucking at his fingers and stared at him. He was

225

breathing heavily as though he had been sprinting, and his nostrils were working with his mouth to draw air down. She tried to step back.

'I didn't know. How was I to know?'

'SHE'S HAVING A BABY!'

He raised his arm as though answering a question in class, and swept his flat hand down on to her cheek. She spun back across the carpet and fell under the wall of the settee.

'And you had to tell her when she's going away. You've RUINED IT! You've ruined everything that ever happened between us two.'

'She can't be, she never said anything, she just packed her clothes –'

'She'll look back on it and hate it now, she'll be bitter for the rest of her life.'

Mrs Rowley lay face down and thumped the carpet in slow motion.

'It should have been me. It should have been mine. That's what I wanted. It should have been mine.'

'You! You're not capable of having one.'

She stopped thumping and moaned like a machine running down. Then she started to shudder and sob, and disintegrated into a shaking heap on the rug.

Lennie swung the front door shut behind him. The window rattled as though a banger had exploded in the flowerbed underneath it. As he turned out of the gate a man crossed the road diagonally behind him and began to follow him, down the pavement.

'Are you Lennie Hawk?'

Lennie spun round, his hands flying out of his pockets like streamers round a maypole. The man stopped in the pocket of gloom between two lamps.

'What do you want?'

'I've got an offer to make you.'

'What?'

'It's not the sort of thing you shout across the street.'

Lennie glanced round and moved under a lamp, away from a privet hedge bulging over a garden wall.

'There's nowt to look for, I'm on my own.'

'What do you want?'

The man walked into the light on swishy crêpe suèdes. Each time he breathed in, a cigarette end glowed red under the peak of his cap.

'I'll give you two hundred pounds to fail that fitness test on Saturday morning.'

As he spoke the cigarette bobbed in his lips, and a branch of sagging ash fell off and sprayed down the lapel of his jacket.

'It's not worth it.'

'What, two hundred quid for doing nowt?'

'I'll make a fortune if we get to Wembley.'

'You're miles off Wembley.'

'You must think we've a chance, anyway.'

'It's Saturday's match we're interested in, there's a lot of money been laid.'

Lennie shook his head.

'It's not worth it.'

'Three hundred.'

'You must have plenty to play with if you can go up in hundreds!'

'A hundred pounds'll be like a penny if this thing comes off.'

'Who else are you offering money to?'

'Nobody yet.'

'Somebody must think I'm a good player if they think I can make that much difference.'

'Town'll lose if you don't play.'

'They've won their last two without me.'

'Against poxy teams, they'll not beat the United without you.'

'I might not be fit anyway, it's a bad sprain.'

'We want to make sure.'

'I want five hundred.'

'Right, half now, half Saturday night!'

'Half now, half Saturday dinner time. I'd never see you again if the Town managed it.'

They stopped talking, and Lennie looked across the road until a woman had passed.

'I'll be in the Odeon Café at half past twelve.'

'Don't look for me, somebody else'll bring it.'

'I don't care who brings it, but if it's not there I'll play against t'United on one leg if I've got to.'

'You'll not be much use like that.'

'Why don't you risk it then and see?'

The man looked at him, then turned and spat the wet tab into the gutter. Lennie moved across and volleyed it into the middle of the road.

'Clever young bugger, aren't you?'

'You must think so.'

The man walked past him down the road.

'Where's the money then?'

'What do you want me to do, stand under this lamp and count it out in ones?'

As they walked between the lamps he reached inside the breast of his jacket and brought out a stack of straight notes.

'Here, that'll help your dad's dole money a bit.'

Lennie took the wad between his fingers and thumb like an ice-cream wafer, and held them up to have a look.

'Get 'em in your pocket quick.'

He put them into his pocket then swivelled on his left foot and volleyed the man in the balls with his right. He winced at the impact, and the man groaned and doubled up feeling between his legs. Lennie linked his hands into one fist and swung it up into his overhanging face. His cap fell off backwards as his head shot up. Lennie grabbed his hair and rammed him back into a concrete lamp standard. He held his head at arm's length to stop the blood from dripping on to him.

'Now then, you lousy bastard, who was it?'

'My knackers. My nose's broke.'

He tried to reach up to his face, but Lennie knocked his arms down and pushed his hair, making his head crack on the concrete.

'Who was it?'

'I don't know.'

'I'll bloody well kill thi if tha don't tell me.'

'I don't know.'

His eyes were closed and the blood was streaming down both nostrils. His brow was shiny with sweat and Lennie's hand was slippery with grease from his hair.

'Does tha want some more?'

'I don't know who it was.'

He tried to collapse. Lennie yanked him up by the coat front, and blood splattered his wrist like water from a broken fall pipe.

'Liar! I'll bloody well murder thi.'

'They just gave me fifty, that's all.'

'Who did?'

'I don't know.'

'It was you lot who did my feet, wasn't it?'

Lennie smacked him across the cheek, jerking his face to the side and making the blood whip off.

'My balls, I'm going to be sick.'

'You did my feet, didn't you? It's nowt to do with betting, has it? Has it?'

'For Christ's sake let go, I'm going to be sick.'

'You lousy bastards.'

Lennie let go and punched him in the stomach as he crumpled down the lamp standard. He raised his foot, then stepped back on to it and ran down the hill to the main road, where he slowed to a walk.

'Do a lap to warm up, Len.'

Lennie jogged away on the red ash past the empty terracing.

Chris kicked two balls on to the field and formed a triangle in the centre circle with Mac and Eddie. All three were dressed in red tracksuits. Clifford Anderson stood in the tunnel mouth with Mr Hawk watching Lennie warm up round the pitch. He sprinted from the corner to the edge of the penalty area then coasted up to the halfway line. Eddie prodded one of the balls to him.

'Get the feel of that.'

Lennie flicked it up just inside the touchline, and kept it off the ground with his feet, thighs and head. His control was immaculate. Chris threw him the other ball, then walked off and sat on the terrace wall.

'Both feet, Len.'

Lennie sidestepped the balls to the trainers in turn. Mac returned his hard along the ground.

'First time!'

Lennie sidestepped it away and moved across to return the other one to Eddie.

'Laces, son! Come on kick it with your laces!'

Both trainers backed away towards the far touchline so that he would have to swing at the balls. Right leg, more of a chip than a kick, left leg, the ball climbed steeply, then bombed down like a shot bird, biting into the turf and spinning back. Lennie trotted forward and pushed it to Eddie along the ground.

'Len! Kick the damned thing!'

He looked round. Clifford Anderson had moved forward to the edge of the pitch, and was standing with Chris who had come off the wall. Doctor Mark was in the tunnel mouth with Wilson O'Niell and Geordie Paling, and Mr Hawk was patrolling five yards of red ash. Lennie turned back to the balls, sweating. Mac served. He ran at it and half volleyed it straight over his head on to the terrace. He lifted Eddie's into the Old Stand then turned round to the tunnel.

'They're all right!'

'Go and have some shots! – From outside the box!'

Chris walked to the goal in front of the kop. Bobby Prince and Roy Hann followed him in their overcoats to act as ballboys, while Stan Leadbeater kept Mr Hawk company on his walk. The trainers stood out on the touchlines and pushed a quick succession of passes for Lennie to shoot at goal. His first few efforts were carefully accurate and Chris caught them easily. Then he began to move to the ball, controlling and shooting quickly, as though hampered by a defender. Most of his shots were high and wide, but the ones that did go between the posts were stopped by the net. Roy Hann stood behind the goal grinning while Bobby Prince vaulted the kop to retrieve the balls.

'Why don't you get your hands to 'em, Chris?'

'You what! Why don't you come and get yours to 'em?'

Billy Boscombe kicked another ball on to the pitch. Laurie Key dribbled it towards the goalmouth and joined the ranks of ball boys. Les Adams turned on Mr Hawk and Stan Leadbetter who were still patrolling the front of the trainers' box.

'Are you two trying to make everybody nervous wrecks?'

They stopped walking and stood beside George Armstrong at the edge of the grass.

'That'll do! Right, tackle him, Chris, and no messing!'

Clifford Anderson stepped on to the pitch and started to walk towards the goalmouth. Lennie ran the ball at Chris and their bodies banged together pushing for possession.

'Again!'

They repeated and repeated the movement, until they were both sweating and panting.

'That's enough.'

Clifford Anderson walked up to Lennie and nodded down at his feet.

'Well?'

'They're champion.'

'Are you sure?'

'I'm positive.'

'They must be hurting after that lot.'

'Anybody's would.'

'You look pale.'

'Nervous, I suppose.'

'Are you fit then?'

'Yes.'

'Come and let the Doc' have a look.'

He sat on the wall and untied his laces. Doctor Mark pulled his boots and socks off. The pads of cotton wool round his feet were flat and damp like wet rabbit fur. The tops of his feet were pink, as though they had been in hot water. The cuts on the bottom were knitted together in dry crusty ridges like furrows in a field. The doctor lowered them to the red ash.

'It's up to you, Len.'

'I'm playing then.'

The whole group behind Doctor Mark straightened up, smiling. Clifford Anderson strode off towards the tunnel and the players followed him. Mr Hawk waited for Lennie to put his socks on, and they walked in together. A minor roar exploded from behind the stand, and they both looked up as though they expected to see the sound rise above the roof like smoke.

It was a sunny afternoon. The small white clouds were far

apart, flecking the sky like blotches on fingernails. The Dale was full, the gates had been closed, but there were still thousands milling round outside trying to get in. Mounted police waded through the crowd like cowboys through a river, and tried to disperse them. Lennie bought a paper from Mickey Cunliffe and stepped back to read his headline board.

BIG MATCH
BRIBERY RUMOURS
– FULL STORY

'What's this then?'

'Summat about players being bribed for today's match.'

'What's it say?'

'Nowt much. It's just an article to give t'crowd summat to talk about.'

'Any names mentioned?'

'There's nothing mentioned. It's doing its job though, it's selling papers.'

'They'll write owt.'

'Only because there's somebody to read it.'

Lennie stepped back against the wall and looked around.

'There's some folks about, isn't there? There's nearly an hour to go yet.'

'They've shut t'gates. I reckon there'll be some bother today with this lot.'

'What do you mean, trying to get in?'

'Look? What did I tell you?'

He pointed his papers along the back of the stand to where a crush had formed at one of the exit gates. They were pushing in rhythm against the two big doors, leaning away, then swaying in to the chant of Heave! Heave! Heave! The noise attracted attention, and more people joined the back of the throng to add their bulk to the shove.

HEAVE! HEAVE! HEAVE!

A scream broke out above the chant.

'He's fainted!'

But the chant continued unabated, more urgently, and in quicker time. A gang of boys joined in, grinning and taking a run to add momentum to their shove. But the doors held, flexing

232

slightly down the centre from each blow. A policeman blew his whistle and tried to hurry his horse to the scene, but his progress was hampered by the criss-crossing throng in between.

HEAVE! HEAVE! HEAVE!

The doors were being forced back into a deeper V with each push, and the policeman could make no impression at all from the edge of the mob. They were as tight as a clenched fist.

'Stop it, you're crushing us! For God's sake. Stop it!'

'Help! Help! Heave! Heave!'

A constant scream rose from near the doors, along with a heavy moan like the death wheeze of a monster. The people at the front were turning frightened faces to the people behind, who turned frightened faces to the people behind them. Four mounted policemen were now attacking the crush from both sides, flailing with their whips, trying to break the main flow of power down the centre. Then the doors cracked and flung open. Cheers and screams mixed in the cacophony of surging bodies which oozed through the bottle neck in a solid lump, like the core of a boil. The bulk disappeared and the policemen converged in front of the hole and lashed out at anyone who made a break to get in. Bodies were scattered around the concrete in front of the gate. Some were still, others moved and groaned, and a crowd gathered in an arc to have a look before the ambulance men arrived and carted them away.

'Bloody hell!'

'I knew it! I knew summat like that'd happen today!'

'They'll be like sardines inside.'

'They'll be worse than that if any more get in.'

'They'll have to get t'white horse like they did at t'first Wembley final.'

Mickey smiled and Lennie moved away.

'I'm off then.'

'All the best, Len lad, and watch that Stamper.'

'He'll want to hang his boots up when I've finished with him today.'

'Ar, but don't try to be too clever. They say there's nowt worse than a wounded bull.'

The roar for the United was almost as loud as the one

received by the Town. As the cheers faded a voice spoke clearly from the Tannoy system all round the ground.

'Good afternoon, ladies and gentlemen. The United team is as printed on the official programme.'

The voice waited for the fresh outbreak of cheers and boos to die down.

'There is one change in the Town team, Hawk will be at inside left in place –'

The roar was deep, like a thousand lines, and obliterated the end of the announcement. Lennie held his arms up and smiled. The referee blew his whistle and the captains jogged to the centre to toss up. The teams changed ends, and as the goalkeepers ran past each other they shook hands like opposites in a square dance. Stamper veered across towards Lennie.

'Got bruised feet, lad?'

Lennie looked at the broken teeth in the grinning stubbled head and walked past. The first time he received the ball Stamper ran at him and took off with both feet forward like a long jumper. He landed on the ball, trapping Lennie's feet beneath it. The ball rolled away, but Stamper maintained his tackle and knocked Lennie backwards on to the grass. The referee whistled and Eddie sprinted across the pitch with water flying out of the old football bladder in his hand. Lennie stood up white-faced and sweating.

'All right, son?'

'I'll do.'

'The big dirty bleeder!'

Eddie half turned as though he meant to run after Stamper.

'I'll be all right.'

'You're as white as a sheet.'

'It was t'sight of his face coming in, he looked just like Frankenstein.'

Eddie sponged Lennie's face, then dried it from the brow down his cheeks to his neck.

The early play was even and there were no definite chances for either side. Stamper was following Lennie around the pitch talking to him, trying to make him lose his concentration with an incessant string of insults. Lennie took no notice and distributed the ball first time before his tormentor had time to tackle. But Stamper was restricting his game. Every time he received the ball the home crowd whistled and booed and as soon as he had passed it he ran back to shadow Lennie. Lennie ran off the pitch and sat on the terrace wall with his arms folded. The crowd was delighted. Stamper stood on the touch-line with his arms folded, watching him. Lennie turned round and placed one hand and foot on the wall top as though threatening to vault into the crowd. The referee ran across blowing his whistle like a train and motioned him back on to the pitch. He lectured him, then resumed play with a bounce up. Stamper fell in behind Lennie.

'I thought tha reckoned to be a world-beater then ... Easiest game I've had all season this ... Bad ball! Why don't tha try to beat me – what's up, scared? ... I'll not hurt you, love ... Come on, let's see thi do summat then. They'd have been better off playing Fowler, at least he was fit ... Feet hurting? They'll be red hot when I've finished wi' thi.'

At half time there was no score. Clifford Anderson clapped his hands as they trooped into the changing-room.

'Sit down, quickly, lads!'

They took their tea and sat down, leaning away from the trouser legs and overcoats hanging behind them.

'You're playing well, lads. Lennie, the game lies with you, son. You're going to have to get away from him.'

Lennie sat up and opened his mouth but Clifford Anderson raised his hand like a policeman on point duty and stopped the words.

'I know! I know! You're playing better than anybody else in England could under the circumstances, but it's still not enough. I want him run into the ground, I want him mur-dered! If he goes, the United will go, it's as simple as that. Now, come on, son, give me some of that old magic, because we need it if we're going to win this game.'

As he spoke he squeezed the air with his fingertips as though he was catching the words and extracting the last drops of meaning from them.

'And all of you, for the next forty-five minutes I want you to play harder than you've ever played before.'

He showed them five of the minutes on the spread fingers of one hand.

'Forty-five minutes, that's all it is. Just three-quarters of an hour of hard graft, so come on now, lads, let's have this game!'

He implored them like Al Jolson, then straightened up sweating, and left the room. The players drank their tea and spoke quietly until the bell rang.

The roar for the restart was still in the air when Laurie Key miscued the ball to the United centre forward who had drifted optimistically up the field in the customary manner of centre forwards. He tapped the ball forward and gleefully whacked it into the net as hard as he could. Laurie Key stamped his foot and limped a few paces. The centre forward ran leaping back to the centre, flinging his arms with every jump, and the United supporters, giddy with the goal, set up a constant roar. The United responded and Lennie and Chris were forced back on defence. Stamper assumed control of midfield, and cursing and threatening he drove his team with the ruthlessness of a galley overseer. The United built their attacks with long swift running movements, which seemed to set their whole team rolling towards goal, and the climax of these advances resulted in a series of multiple crashes as they ran full blast into the massed Town defence. The Town packed their goalmouth and braced themselves against the assault as one man, like a sailor leaning into a gale. Every attack was agony, every stoppage temporary relief. George Armstrong kicked the ball behind for a corner and leaned back on the goalpost, wiping his brow with his sleeve.

Stamper started running as the winger swung his leg, and he was in full flight when the ball dipped into the goal area. His jump was a continuation of his run, more of a take off than a leap, and Laurie Key and Wilson O'Niell were smashed aside in mid air as his head rammed the ball against Les Adams's fists. The goalkeeper was knocked backwards as Stamper's knees bunched into his stomach, and the ball flew into the net with the force of a shot. He fell on top of three defenders, then stood up trampling them down like someone stamping grapes.

'G-O-A-L!'

The referee pointed to the centre and tried to run away from the confusion. He was immediately surrounded by most of the Town players who pulled his clothing and pointed back to the incident like men in a medieval illustration, pointing back in awe to a Town stricken by plague. All three defenders injured in the collision had to be treated by Eddie before the game could be resumed.

Two nil down, the Town supporters went quiet. The United eased off and began to play negative exhibition football, passing the ball around at the back, then pushing it to the goal-keeper when challenged. Lennie ran over the half-way line towards Stamper, who invited him by grinning and standing with one foot on the ball. Lennie slowed his approach to a cautious crouch and prepared to tackle. As Stamper drew his foot back to kick, Lennie glanced up at his face and pushed his arms down between his knees to protect his balls. Stamper kicked the ball at him as hard as he could. It smacked the insides of his elbows and bounced back, and he was running for goal before Stamper had recovered balance and could turn in pursuit. The goalkeeper ran out to narrow the angle, but without changing pace or direction Lennie drove the ball straight along the ground into the net. He raised his arm, and walked back past Stamper into the gathering hysteria of his own team.

As the teams lined up Lennie turned to the Town from the rim of the centre circle.

'Let me have the ball now, lads! Just give it to me, and we'll be all right!'

Stamper reintroduced his former tactics, but Lennie began to go past him every time he received the ball. He beat him with a flourish which made the crowd roar, and left Stamper in angry frustration, like a pedestrian splashed filthy by a motorist. As Stamper had dominated the game at the earlier stage with bullying brutality, Lennie was now dominating it with a cultured arrogance that made Stamper's rule seem like a black lapse in history. He was playing at such a high pitch that every time he touched the ball the Town supporters screamed. It was as though the contact between the two sparked a charge through the density of the ground.

'LENNIE HAWK! CLAP CLAP CLAP. LENNIE HAWK!
CLAP CLAP CLAP. LENNIE HAWK! CLAP CLAP CLAP.'

The chant swelled from the walls behind the United goal to
the wealth in the directors' box, and silenced the already sicken-
ing United supporters, who stood paralysed watching the clock
in the roof of the main stand.

Lennie controlled the ball facing his own goal and swept
round Stamper's tackle in a smooth arc like a windscreen wiper.

'Waaah!'

Instead of closing on to the goal in his usual fashion he
turned and waited for Stamper to stand up. The crowd
quietened, and the other players stood off. He crossed the ball
from foot to foot, waiting. Stamper crouched, watching. He
jerked a shoulder forward and feinted a rush, but Lennie made
no move, and held the ball safe between his boots.

'In! In! In! In!'

The crowd chanted for the tackle. Stamper crouched lower
and lower until he was bent double like a man with stomach
ache. Then he snaked in with one leg thrust forward. Lennie
pulled the ball back out of range, tipped it to one side and
dribbled past.

'Waaaah!'

They both turned and faced each other again.

'WAAAAHHH!'

The other players circled at a distance, marking each other.
The crowd quietened and Stamper prepared himself for the
third time. Lennie took the ball slowly up to him, pushed it
between his legs and ran past into the penalty area. Stamper
whipped round and scythed at his legs from behind. He connected at the ankles and Lennie fell like cut corn.

'P-E-N-A-L-T-Y!'

Chris walked forward out of the gathering of players around
the white lines of the penalty box.

'Have I to take this, Len?'

'No, I'll take it.'

'What about your feet? He deliberately went for 'em then.'

'They're all right.'

'Are you sure?'

'I'll take it, it's mine this.'

Chris walked away and Lennie settled the ball firmly on the penalty spot. He stepped back and the crowd hushed. Les Adams pulled his cap over his eyes at the far end and turned his back. The sun sat low over the kop, directly behind the United goal. Lennie took two swift steps and struck the ball. The goalkeeper was still watching the spot when the ball broke the net behind him. It rose above the heads on the kop and was lost in the glaring blur of the sun. There was silence, then a moan from the far end, they couldn't see the ball in the net. The kop exploded, and the whole crowd broke into bedlam. All the players except Lennie and Stamper ran to inspect the hole in the net. Lennie walked back up the centre and Stamper trotted up behind him.

'They say she's a good shag, this daughter of Leary's, is it right?'

Lennie swung his arm without looking and his fist connected with the broken teeth. Stamper fell backwards on to the turf, and the referee raced out of the goalmouth, fumbling at his top pocket for his book.

'I saw that, Hawk! Off! Get off the field.'

Stamper sat up spitting blood and teeth on to the grass.

'Hawk, I'm ordering you off for striking a player.'

Both teams turned at the death shudder which rattled round the ground, and when the Town players saw Lennie walking they sprinted up the pitch to the referee. Stamper stood up and grinned behind the trainer's sponge splashing on to his face. There was absolute silence as Lennie reached the touch-line and crossed the red ash. Eddie was standing in front of the trainer's box waiting for him.

'Lennie, son, what happened?'

Lennie walked past him into the tunnel. Eddie followed and Clifford Anderson met them before they reached the end.

'What happened, Len, what did he say?'

Lennie walked past him, along the corridor into the changing-room. Clifford Anderson and Eddie followed him in.

'Tell us what he said, Len, and we'll report him!'

Lennie undressed and walked past them to the bath, which was still and clear, and steaming.

'You were making him look foolish. We had the game won!'

He soaped himself, rinsed off and stepped out. Eddie left. Clifford Anderson waited for him to say something, but he just walked to his clothes and started to get dressed.

'Twenty minutes left and we had them over a barrel. We were really back in business and then you go and do a thing like that.'

He pointed at Lennie like Kitchener in the war posters.

'If we lose this game, son –!'

He stormed out and slammed the door. Lennie took a wad of notes from his pocket and broke the brown paper seal. He stuffed them into a loose heap in his pocket, then walked out of the room and up the stairs to the directors' box at the front of the centre stand. The people sitting at the back saw him first and the information spread quickly downwards to the front. Mr Leary turned and stood up. Lennie stepped down past the ends of two rows and threw a crushed handful of money at him. The ball broke and scattered like confetti. He threw a second ball, squeezed tighter so that more would carry. A roar filled the stand and everyone's head whipped round, freezing the scene like a photograph. Grey, and tweed, and fur caught sitting and standing and crouching, all with their bodies turned to Lennie, their faces to the pitch. Les Adams was stooping into the back of the net to retrieve the ball. The United team were rejoicing in a heap. Lennie turned away and walked down the steps out of the ground.